PRAISE FOR *USA TODAY* BESTSELLING AUTHOR DIANE BENEFIEL

Solitary Man

NATIONAL READERS' CHOICE AWARD WINNING NOVEL

"I am in love with this story. I devoured this book and didn't want it to end. The chemistry between the characters and the plot kept me wanting to read late into the night. This is my first read from Diane Benefiel but definitely not my last. I can't wait to read more from this amazing author. Thank you Diane Benefiel for getting me hooked on your books!" ~ CJ's Book Corner

"Ryder was exactly who Brenna needed in her life, and trust me when I say you will love him because yeah he really is that good of a guy. Solitary Man is my first book by this author and it will not be the last. I really think you all will enjoy this one as much as I did it is one I do recommend." ~ I'm A Sweet And Sassy Book Whore

"I really enjoyed this book and there were a few twists and turns that kept me completely involved in the story. This is the first time I have read this author and it definitely won't be my last!" ~ Sassy Southern Book Blog

THE JAMESONS US MARSHALS SERIES

Hidden Betrayal

*"As someone who never pre-orders ANYTHING, I put my order in a WEEK before it came out. Know why? Because I just didn't want to wait! And this was definitely the right move. I loved the dialogue between her and Linc--with her saying, "I didn't stay back because *I* was handling it." Yes, he's a hottie with a protective streak, but*

she's certainly no little woman. It really WORKS. In the end, 10/10. Can't wait to pre-order the next one too!" ~ Amelia

"An exciting, romantic read with a sexy hero and a determined heroine who is hell-bent on doing things her own way. The romance heats up as the plot thickens. Link and Mikayla need to work together to survive, but along the way, the sparks start flying. You need to read this!" ~ Danube Eichinger

Hidden Judgment

"Don't buy this book if you want to get anything done!! I couldn't put it down! I laughed, I cried, I felt all the emotions that a brilliantly written romance novel brings. I am anxiously awaiting the third novel in the series!" ~Sandy Morris

"I couldn't put this book down. I thoroughly enjoyed the story line and the characters. Diane Benefiel does a great job bringing her characters to life, and weaves a compelling story. Looking forward to the next installment of this series!" ~Becca E H

HIGH SIERRAS SERIES

Flash Point

"Diane Benefiel takes us on a story filled with mystery, suspense, and action as we try to solve what is going on in the small town of Hangman's Loss. Flash Point is a story that will have you flipping the pages and wondering who is the behind the attacks against Hangman's newest resident and why." ~ Sarah Reads

*"**Flash Point** really surprised me. It's not what I was expecting but I really enjoyed reading it. It's a fun easy read that captured me from the start."* ~ Coffee Chat

Dead Giveaway

"Diane has written yet another winner in her High Sierra series. Murder witness and 'person of interest' Gwen flees with her godson to Cameron's uncle Eli. Gwen and Eli have no use for one another but come together for Cameron's sake and to find the true murderer...and in the process find their way to one another. My evening with Gwen and Eli couldn't have been more delightful, and I look forward to the next installment of the High Sierras." ~seniorphotog

"I loved this second book in the High Sierras series. This is a story of two people who are attracted to each other, but reconnecting under the worst of circumstances. I discovered Ms. Benefiel's books and have loved the careful way she draws you in to the story with characters that make you feel as if you are reading about friends. I am really looking forward to the next High Sierras book, ***Already Gone****."* ~paytonpuppy

Already Gone

"This series has only gotten better and better! Seriously, there's something that really speaks to my heart about Maddy and Logan, and Hangman's Loss FEELS like a small California town tucked away in the Sierras. They're such a power couple! I read this book in just a couple of days--totally sucked me in. It's that perfect blend of fun, sizzle, and suspense! I just want to live in Maddy's life forever but since I can't--I can't wait for the next book!" ~Katharine Montgomery

"A wonderful story about second chances. The minute you start reading, you will be instantly hooked. The author weaves a tale of drama and romance that keeps you enthralled and turning the pages. Maddie is feisty and Logan is her brooding and over protective suffering hero. The sparks fly every time they see each other. Eventually they give in and realize that they are perfect for each other and have always been. This is a great story right up to the last word." ~Simatsu

Burnover in Rescued Anthology

"Sweet, Sexy stories featuring furbabies and helping to save lives, it's a win win for all." ~Kara's Books

"8 stories by 8 outstanding authors. In these stories, there is a tattoo artist, two firefighters, two sheriff deputies, a famous furniture maker, a veterinarian, and a country music singer, and I loved them all. Then add in that each story has a dog or puppy that is rescued, along with a story of love and romance, it is a winning combination." ~Susan D

Deadly Purpose

I loved everything about this book, and it made me want to check out the other books in the series! The immediate suspense drew me in, and the High Sierras setting was perfect, as was the mysterious stranger Meg finds in her cabin. This novel had a well-written, exciting, and descriptive narrative that kept me glued from start to finish. Without giving away spoilers, the author has crafted one exciting, romantic ride, full of twists and turns. I highly recommend this book and can't wait to see what the author comes up with next. ~Sebastian Moran

This book took me by surprise. I didn't expect to get so caught up in this book that my whole day was spent captured in its pages. It has been a long time since I couldn't put a book down but Deadly Purpose did this to me. I loved every page. ~WildfireJane

Clear Intent

"I'd been waiting on this one awhile!! I truly loved the story! I laughed, cried and got so frustrated I couldn't see straight! I'm now hoping there will be more from Hangman's Loss, I don't want to see this series end! Thank you for a very wonderful getaway!! I highly

recommend this complete series!!!! Wow! Just Wow!!" ~Linda Helms

"I've looked forward to every book in this series and have enjoyed each one, loving the characters as it feels you walk with them through exciting, scary situations and sigh as relationships become beautiful. This was an exciting story with almost nonstop action and heart stopping dangers. All of my favorite people in Hangman's Loss are together to help Jack, Dory, Adrian and the town through crisis." ~JLocke

Break Away

"Oh man did I love this book. It was well written and has a great storyline. It's emotional and has a nice amount of suspense. I really need to go back and read the first six books in the series. Now saying that, this book definitely reads as a standalone. I haven't read the first six books, but I never felt lost or like I am missing anything with this story. You will obviously have some small spoilers since the books are all connected. ~CrazyBookLover

"Break Away is Diane Benefiel's seventh book in the High Sierra series and is definitely a second chance at romance. Zoey had a high school crush on Levi, and when he returns home after many years, she realises her feelings have not diminished. I'm a sucker for the sexy, broody bad boy vibe, and Levi has it in spades! But the storyline also has emotion, danger and a powerful attraction that is not only undeniable, but totally unavoidable too. These characters have great chemistry and the romantic suspense plot is well written and a real page-turner." ~Arch_Angel

HIDDEN LOYALTY

The Jamesons, US Marshals – Book Three

Diane Benefiel

www.BOROUGHSPUBLISHINGGROUP.com

PUBLISHER'S NOTE: This is a work of fiction. Names, characters, places and incidents either are the product of the author's imagination or are used fictitiously. Any resemblance to actual events, locales, business establishments or persons, living or dead, is coincidental. Boroughs Publishing Group does not have any control over and does not assume responsibility for author or third-party websites, blogs or critiques or their content.

HIDDEN LOYALTY

Copyright © 2021 Diane Benefiel

All rights reserved. Unless specifically noted, no part of this publication may be reproduced, scanned, stored in a retrieval system or transmitted in any form or by any means, electronic, mechanical, photocopying, recording, or otherwise, known or hereinafter invented, without the express written permission of Boroughs Publishing Group. The scanning, uploading and distribution of this book via the Internet or by any other means without the permission of Boroughs Publishing Group is illegal and punishable by law. Participation in the piracy of copyrighted materials violates the author's rights.

ISBN 978-1-953810-33-5

To the brightest lights in my life, Grace and Sam

ACKNOWLEDGMENTS

Researching material for a book sometimes sends me down rabbit holes where I find it hard to sort useful information from the fluff. That's why it's nice to be able to call on someone who is a true authority. I know nothing about military weapons, but my niece's fiancé does. I want to give special thanks to US Marine Mike for his informative answers to my questions. I asked him how military ammunition is stored and transported, and Mike sent pictures and told me about stripper clips, bandoliers, and ammo cans. One question led to others, and while I was able to include only a small portion of what I learned in *Hidden Loyalty,* I was educated about what I did include. Of course, any mistakes are mine alone.

I also wish to acknowledge Michelle Klayman of Boroughs Publishing Group for being such a wonderful mentor/editor/publisher. In a year fraught with so many challenges from Covid, to teaching a college-level course to high school students, to having a new grandbaby, she's given me unflagging support and the room I needed to make Seth and Bella's story the best I could. Thank you, Michelle. I appreciate you.

HIDDEN LOYALTY

Chapter One

Bella was a pro at hiding her emotions, which was absolutely crucial given her current assignment. Her job this weekend? Be the knockout arm candy to the man sitting in the driver's seat of the car they were riding in. A man who wore sexy and remote as smoothly as James Bond.

Chief Deputy US Marshal Seth Jameson, her boss, her current partner, the man who equally intrigued and infuriated her, had his gaze focused on the road winding ahead of them. Which she knew was misleading. While he *appeared* to be thinking only of mastering the two-tone red and black Bugatti Chiron, she was one hundred percent positive his brain was reviewing and re-reviewing their plan to take into custody the elusive and dangerous fugitive they were after.

Keeping her emotions hidden from Seth was as essential as breathing. Her job depended on it. Her mental health depended on it. And actually, her life depended on it. That block that allowed nothing to show on her face? It formed the foundation of the solid wall she and Seth had erected between them.

Solid, impenetrable, bulletproof.

She allowed few people to get emotionally close to her, to *see* her. Seth Jameson wasn't one of them. She caught herself worrying her bottom lip and pressed her lips together and mentally recited a Russian children's poem. She'd learned the trick to distract herself when she felt the urge to fidget or do some other silly physical action that would give away her tension. Added bonus? The poems reinforced memories from her childhood. Good memories that sometimes she feared would fade to nothingness under the smothering weight of the horrible memories, which burned stronger in her mind.

Seth crossed into the opposing lane to pass two cars, one of them a Tesla Model X. The Bugatti roared as it ripped past the cars like they were the staid Soviet vehicles she remembered from her youth.

Expensive and exotic cars seemed to be the norm in this section of California's central coast, and the Bugatti had been chosen to add to the aura of wealth that would help make their ruse believable.

Bella stared out the window at the incredible view. Far below the highway, waves broke on the rocky coastline and sea lions lolled on the sand like giant slugs. Fascinated, she watched as a huge bull sparred with a smaller sea lion. She battled back the urge to share with Seth what she'd seen.

Keeping her thoughts and emotions to herself had become second nature. It seemed her entire life had been spent trying not to show what she was feeling. She'd learned that lesson as a young child—never let anyone know you wanted or cared about something. A doll you slept with when you were afraid, a bowl of porridge when you were hungry, a book of poetry given to you by your dead father. Caring about such things only made you vulnerable when they were taken away. Show happiness? Not a chance. That too could be stolen from you. Don't show surprise, feign interest if necessary, separate yourself from the present so as not to be affected.

All good training for the task that lay ahead of her.

She closed her eyes briefly, her face turned from Seth. A phone call that morning from her brother had brought unwelcome memories to the surface, and along with them, emotions she struggled to suppress. No one could destroy barriers and rip open the past like her brother.

She brought her attention back to her assignment. The mission was dangerous, maybe the most dangerous of her career, and she needed to emulate Seth's monumental focus to make sure she acted exactly as she'd been coached.

Their task was to gain access to and arrest the incredibly wealthy, eccentric, and heavily guarded fugitive Hugo Montenegro. The first step had been achieved. Seth had constructed a fictitious background as a fabulously wealthy antiquities trader, one who didn't mind skirting the boundaries of what was legal to commandeer items particularly desired by his clients.

Montenegro's interest was in instruments of death, especially those used in ceremonial deaths or notorious killings. Seth had learned of Montenegro's obsession with one item and had been able to use that as leverage to obtain an invitation to the fugitive's home.

Bella's job was to appear decorative. Normally when working, she maintained a professional demeanor as dictated by the policy directives of her employer. That meant wearing clothing that projected a positive image of the Marshals Service to the public and didn't draw attention to herself.

Conservative women's suits, minimal makeup, and her hair pulled back in a bun all served that function well. If sometimes the look felt uninspiring, she reminded herself it was an honor to serve in one of the finest law enforcement agencies in the United States, and there was no room for complaining about the dress code.

For this assignment, however, lowkey and staid had been thrown out the window. She'd prepared carefully, using the stipend allotted to her to purchase attire that would highlight her assets. She had the makeup and accessories to help create the look she'd wear for their overnight stay.

The kickoff was a formal dinner party, and she thought she'd hit the mark for that event. Her hair was pinned at the back of her head in a sophisticated upsweep that showed off her neck. She'd left a few stray curls artfully arranged for interest. She'd used copious amounts of mascara and eye shadow to accentuate the shape and the color of her eyes, making them appear more exotic and a deeper blue. She'd selected crimson red lipstick to draw attention to her mouth.

Her long dress gleamed an iridescent blue that reminded her of peacock feathers and showcased her curves, emphasizing the narrowness of her waist before flaring up, and with the help of an amazing bra, lifting her breasts like a sacrificial offering.

When she'd opened the door of her hotel room to Seth's knock, lust had zapped her with a white-hot jolt. He stood tall and impossibly handsome in black tie. The formal wear should've tamed him, made him look refined, polished, but somehow the smooth black jacket and the stiff white cuffs only served to provide a thin veneer of civilization.

There'd been a moment when she thought he'd been caught off guard. For mere seconds, his slate gray eyes had flashed generating a blistering heat as they'd swept her body from head to toe. By the time that gaze met hers, any reaction to her appearance had been walled off.

The ice man was back.

Looking out the passenger window, she clenched her fist when she realized she'd been rubbing her thumb across the platinum ring heavy with diamonds she wore on her left ring finger. A prop to strengthen their cover.

The car crested a hill and exposed a staggering view. Their destination lay ahead at the end of a long valley on a rise above a gleaming lake, the estate situated in a way that screamed dominance over man and nature.

The gleaming structure of stone and glass could only be described as a palace, but not in the often tacky way Americans had of trying to re-create the homes of European aristocracy. The beautiful façade appeared carved of granite, and glinted silver, its windows reflecting the sun setting beyond the ocean gleaming to the west.

Focusing on the imposing building wasn't enough to keep her thoughts off the man sitting beside her. He may have given her that once-over, but his appearance had hit her equally as hard.

Surreptitiously, she studied his profile which looked to've been carved of the same granite as the structure they were nearing. If she was a pro at hiding her emotions, Seth Jameson was a master. Which made her wonder if she was the only one to sense their strong emotions kept locked behind a fortress wall.

She gave an involuntary start when he reached out to grip her hand. He raised a cool brow. "You're messing with the ring. It looks like you're not used to it. Montenegro will notice that. He'll notice everything about you."

"That's the point, isn't it? He's a sexual predator, and we're counting on him noticing me. I can distract him, and he might say things to me that he wouldn't say to you."

"Right." He returned his hand to the steering wheel. A muscle worked his jaw. "You nervous?"

"A little, but you'll be there." His gaze flicked over her and she shrugged. "I'll do my job."

"No doubt."

They followed the curve of the driveway to the front of the house. Big men in dark blazers and sunglasses with mirrored lenses stood at strategic spots—an upstairs balcony, the front entrance, a walkway that rounded the corner of the house. Hugo Montenegro was taking no chances with his safety. He was a high-value fugitive shining a spotlight on himself this evening.

Seth pulled to a stop behind a Mercedes-Benz. A valet elbowed another to the side for the chance to drive the Bugatti. The young man stepped forward but Seth held him off with a raised hand. Instead of reaching for the door handle, he turned to face her. "We'll be sharing a bedroom."

"We've talked about this, sir. I know what to expect."

"Call me Stephen, even if you think we can't be overheard. You never know where there might be listening devices. We're Stephen Bullock and Anna Novak." Dark brows lowered over his stone-gray eyes. "It's more than the bedroom. We have to display a believable level of intimacy. As you said, Montenegro is a sexual predator and he'll be aware of a beautiful woman. You're supposed to distract him, but that's as far as it goes. The best way to keep him from attempting anything more is for you to stay close to me and make sure he knows you're mine. The story of our recent engagement will support that."

"I'll play my part, *Stephen*. You play yours. If you can convince him you have what he wants, we'll be able to complete this assignment and go home."

He glanced out the window. "The valet is watching. We start now." He leaned forward and pressed his mouth to hers. The shock kept her rigid, then heat flashed and her lips moved under his. The hair at the back of his head, the deliciously thick hair she'd had secret fantasies about, slid through her fingers.

He broke the kiss and moved back, a look crossing his face that was gone in a heartbeat. If she didn't know better, she'd say it was stark hunger. But, as he'd said, acting their parts was critical, and he'd already started.

She gathered her composure, nonchalantly rubbing her thumb across the skin at the corner of his mouth. "Can't have you going to a dinner party with lipstick smeared on your mouth, darling."

"Right. Let's go."

***

Seth rose from the car and took a carefully controlled breath. He hated feeling distracted. God knew Bella was distracting. That was a given and something he'd learned to deal with. Then there was the letter he'd received and had placed in his home safe the day before. A letter from his father designed to jerk his chain and make him feel like a loser. It wasn't going to work. The minute he let Richard Jameson undermine his confidence was when the fucker would win. Seth wouldn't let that happen, but it was still damn disruptive to receive a communication from the man for the first time in two decades.

He rounded the hood of the car and tossed the key to the valet. "The luggage in the back goes inside."

"Yes, sir."

Seth opened the passenger door for Bella. He forced himself to keep breathing as she took his outstretched hand and rose fluidly from the low-slung car. She was always beautiful, but the clothing she normally wore for work was, if anything, on the prim side.

She stood before him in the sharp heels that did amazing things to her legs. Prim was a memory he'd try to cling to. He cleared his throat when the dress all but shimmered over her. The slit up the side went nearly to her hip and had him biting back an oath. Her shoulders were bare, the smooth, flawless skin there another temptation.

The glitter of the diamond pendant nestled between her breasts was sinful, and brought to mind a recurring dream involving his lips being right where the pendant rested. That image always grew more erotic and too many mornings he woke hard, sweaty, and alone. He'd forced hiding his response to her to become routine, but he had the uneasy feeling that arresting the elusive Hugo Montenegro would be a piece of cake compared to controlling his hunger for Bella Nikolaev.

The Bugatti purred as the valet drove the vehicle past them. Bella draped a lacy wrap around her shoulders and took Seth's arm as they approached the wide stone steps to Montenegro's over-the-top trophy house.

A big bruiser stood at the base of the steps leading to an impressive entryway. The iPad he held looked like a toy in his massive hand. His coat gapped open and revealed a gun holstered under his shoulder. Seth would bet his next promotion that the pistol wasn't Bruiser's only weapon.

"Stephen Bullock, with my fiancée, Anna Novak."

Bruiser studied the iPad, then nodded. He raised his head and his gaze snagged on Bella's exposed cleavage. "I need to search you."

"Eyes over here, pal." Bruiser lifted his gaze as Seth growled, "Search me, but you're not touching her."

"I don't search her, she doesn't get in."

"You're not touching her. Call Montenegro. Make sure he knows you're blocking Stephen Bullock and his fiancée." Seth pulled up his sleeve to glance at his large black watch. "You've got two minutes."

Bruiser turned his back and pulled out his phone. In less than the allotted time, he turned back. "Welcome to Chateau Montenegro, Mr. Bullock." He nodded to Bella. "Ms. Novak. Please proceed through the entry doors to the reception room."

Bella's grip loosened on Seth's elbow and he escorted her to the impressive doors. Once inside, they stood in the foyer where guests milled about, looking at the artifacts Montenegro had staged for display. Seth scanned faces, then allowed Bella to lead him to a glass case where diffused light showcased what he recognized as a *tecpatl*, a ceremonial knife used by Aztec priests to cut open the chests of human sacrifices to extract the beating heart as an offering to feed the gods.

Another case displayed a club he knew for a fact had been looted from Mesa Verde: the ruins left by the Anasazi people a thousand years ago. A discreet card explained that the Anasazi had used the club to kill their enemies, some of whom were then cannibalized and their remains tossed off the cliffs where the Anasazi made their homes.

"I see that Montenegro is consistent in his interests," Bella murmured.

"He is that." The artifacts belonged in museums, not in the possession of an individual with twisted peccadillos who was willing to buy them on the black market.

They crossed the foyer to a wide room where other guests stood talking quietly in small groups. Montenegro wasn't one of them. Bella smiled but didn't engage in conversation. The room was overly decorated with European antiques, most French, which didn't look sturdy enough to sit on. He couldn't imagine relaxing on the gold-threaded couch with his feet up on the ornate coffee table watching a basketball game. Not that there was a TV in sight.

He guided Bella across the room with a hand at the small of her back. The material slid over her skin and enough heat radiated through to singe his fingers. Either she was running a fever, or he was the victim of some strange chemical reaction when he touched her. As much as it bothered him to admit it, the truth was probably the latter.

A small man with wire-rimmed glasses and a goatee spotted them and broke away from the couple he was talking with to approach them. “Mr. Bullock, welcome.”

Seth nodded. “Mr. Needham, this is my fiancée, Anna.” No doubt Needham knew exactly who she was, or at least who she appeared to be.

The little man bowed over Anna’s hand. “Mademoiselle, it is a pleasure. Please call me Gerard.” He straightened and waved over a server carrying a tray of drinks. “Dinner will be served shortly, but please, enjoy an aperitif and conversation with others, if you wish.”

He shook a head at the server. Dulled senses could be dangerous when dealing with a snake like Montenegro. From the offered tray, Bella took a wide-rimmed glass that looked like lead crystal and sipped the bubbly drink, closing her eyes and giving a sexy little hum of pleasure as she swallowed. When those baby blues opened and she smiled up at him, the heat arrowing straight to his groin told him he was in deep shit.

With them playing a newly engaged couple deeply in love, the iron grip he’d managed to keep on his control felt like it had been slicked with oil. Damn. Another image he didn’t need to conjure.

“That champagne? How is it?” Conversation might help focus his attention.

“It is champagne, and it’s divine. Would you like a taste, darling?” Her eyes held a challenge as she stretched on those killer heels and put her mouth on his, parting her lips so the tip of her tongue slid against his.

His head exploded with the silky taste that he was convinced wasn’t entirely alcohol. The effect ratcheted up what was fast becoming a craving to an almost unbearable point. Her hand tightened on his lapel as if she suddenly felt the need to hold on for balance, then she stepped back and gave him a sweet smile.

She was killing him one smile at a time. But if the second kiss in less than twenty minutes had affected her, she was hiding her reaction damned well.

"Do you like it?"

He felt buzzed, like he'd actually consumed a dozen glasses of bubbly, and he hoped to god his dinner jacket hid his response to her. "Yeah, I *like* it."

"Bullock. Wasn't sure you would make it."

Nothing like coming face-to-face with a wanted fugitive to pull Seth's head back in the game. Point for him he'd handled Montenegro well enough he hadn't taken Seth's attendance for granted. That was the idea—keep the guy guessing and on the edge.

Seth shrugged at the comment. "There's another party interested in the same artifact as you. He insisted I listen to his offer."

Something flashed in Montenegro's eyes but disappeared when Bella extended her hand and spoke. "Hello, Mr. Montenegro. I'm Anna Novak."

Seth studied his quarry as the man took Bella's hand as his gaze moved over her. He was a slick bastard with his three-hundred-dollar haircut and personally tailored tux that likely cost more than Seth made in a month.

If Bella found the way Montenegro's gaze lingered on her body distasteful, she hid her reaction well. He brought her hand to his mouth, where his lips lingered over her fingers before releasing her.

"How lovely. Welcome to my home. It's a pleasure to meet you, and you must call me Hugo."

"The pleasure is mine, Hugo."

"Anna is my fiancée." Seth kept his voice smooth as he caught Bella's hand in his, rubbing his thumb over the engagement ring. Montenegro caught the possessive movement, a hint of irritation crossing his face.

He gave a formal bow of acknowledgment. "Congratulations. Your good fortune is my loss." His gaze once again returned to Bella's cleavage. "I don't know how I'll be able to pay attention to my other guests with the delectable Ms. Novak in my home. Since you have accepted my invitation to stay the night, perhaps you'll join me for a nightcap before we retire."

"Oh, that would be lovely." Bella's lips curved in a seductive smile as she laid a hand on Montenegro's arm and leaned forward. A man would have to be a saint not to lock his gaze on the bountiful breasts before him, and Montenegro was no saint.

He cleared his throat and eyed Seth. “I don’t suppose you want separate rooms?”

Seth flashed a humorless smile. “I don’t suppose we do.”

Montenegro turned back to Bella with a gusty sigh. “Tell me, Anna. May I call you Anna?” At her nod he continued. “Tell me, how does a man like Stephen Bullock propose marriage? Somehow, I can’t see him down on his knee in front of you,” he paused and his expression turned sly, “at least to propose.”

Bella ignored the obvious innuendo, instead laughing delightedly, her blue eyes sparkling. “You’re right, he didn’t go down on one knee. That’s too subservient for a man like Stephen, but he made up for it in other ways. He was romantic and sweet, and absolutely turned my heart to mush.” She angled her face up to beam at Seth. “The romance was nice but telling me he loved me was all I needed. I said yes.”

Seth felt her words wrap around his heart and squeeze, and he wrestled back the urge to loosen the bowtie at his throat.

A server stood in the doorway and nodded to Montenegro, who turned to the gathering and raised his hands to give a sharp double clap. “Dinner is served. Gerard is at the door. Follow him and he will lead you to your seats at the dining table.”

Montenegro wasn’t giving up pursuing Bella, and offered her his arm. It was what they wanted, but every instinct Seth possessed told him Montenegro was a threat, which made Seth want to keep Bella close to his side.

Chapter Two

Bella cast a coy look over her shoulder as Seth followed her and Montenegro. Seth'd break the fucker's fingers if they slid any farther down her ass. It was a fine ass, and that shimmery material didn't leave much to the imagination. The desire to see the body under the dress was making him sweat. Seth knew what he'd do if he got his hands on her. He'd back her up against a wall, slide his hand through that sexy-as-hell slit in the skirt, then over the soft skin of her rounded buttock—there was no way she was wearing anything but a thong—and then around to the front where he'd—

His thoughts ground to a screeching halt.

Fuck. He buttoned his jacket and ordered himself to get a grip. No matter how much she might tempt him, Bella was his coworker, a subordinate, and his partner. No way in hell would he break the rules he'd sworn to uphold. If he couldn't control his thoughts in a room full of people, he was doomed.

They stepped into the dining room where the table was set with fancy dinnerware. Montenegro cocked his head to murmur in Bella's ear, and Seth caught the light sound of her laughter. They reached the end of the long table and Montenegro made an elaborate show of holding out a chair next to the host's seat. "Anna, I insist you sit next to me."

With another throaty chuckle, Bella smiled at him. "I'll sit here only if Stephen is on my other side."

Montenegro uttered an elaborate sigh. "As you wish, my darling, but promise me you'll understand if I monopolize you during the meal. I find you enchanting."

Seth didn't roll his eyes, but he wanted to.

Bella sat and Montenegro bent over as he helped push her chair forward, not bothering to hide that he was using his vantage point to ogle her breasts. His finger trailed along her shoulder and Seth clenched his jaw.

Montenegro's head dipped so his lips were against Bella's ear, but he didn't lower his voice, clearly intending to provoke Seth. "You are lovely in every way, Anna. Let us hope that we enjoy each other's company as much as I think we will." The bastard's smarmy voice lowered to murmur words Seth strained to hear. "I had feared that this evening would be dull, but now I find I am anticipating the coming hours quite keenly."

The inflection he gave his words made him sound vaguely European. This was an affectation. Seth knew Hugo Montenegro had been born and raised in a gritty neighborhood in East St. Louis, Illinois. He looked up and caught Seth's gaze on him, flashing a smile that reminded Seth of a ferret's: sly and cunning.

Montenegro took his seat and Seth leaned back and draped an arm across the back of Bella's chair, staking his claim.

Montenegro smirked. "Worried I'll steal your fiancée right from under your nose, Bullock?"

"Not a chance. Anna knows she's mine."

As Bella flirted with Montenegro, the waitstaff served the salad. The only ingredient Seth could identify in the pile of leafy greens in front of him was a sliver of radish. Bella's throaty laugh washed over him as she leaned toward Montenegro and chuckled at a comment he'd made. Seth would've never guessed his partner would be so good at undercover work. Playing up her assets and flattering their mark to the point where Montenegro appeared nearly blinded by lust seemed to be second nature to her.

Seth managed to pull his gaze off her when the man at his left made an attempt to engage him in conversation. As his team had compiled files on each person on the guest list, he knew the man owned a horse farm and olive orchards his current wife had acquired from her first husband in their divorce. Seth chatted easily as he studied the other guests. The men in black tie and the women in glittering jewels were exactly what they appeared—members of the local elite who'd be stunned to learn they were dining with a federal fugitive. Company CEOs, a winery owner, a county supervisor, all had no doubt been thrilled to receive an invitation from the wealthy Hugo Montenegro.

Seth cast an assessing gaze at Montenegro. Bella had him all but salivating, distracting their target, encouraging him to the point where he'd become preoccupied with her. But she kept enough distance to keep him challenged and in pursuit.

The goal was for Bella to bring the additional element of sex to the game. Not that the bastard was getting any closer to her than he already was. Seth's plan was to maneuver Montenegro into a meeting at a place of Seth's choosing, a location where the Marshals Service could detain him and keep the risk low. Two previous efforts to apprehend Montenegro had ended with one marshal wounded by hired guns. After that escape, Montenegro became even better at evading capture.

This time the setup was more elaborate, but it was justified. The Marshals wanted to get more than Montenegro. They wanted the antiquities he'd acquired on the black market. They had been able to procure a particular item, a rare object Montenegro coveted. If Bella managed to dangle the possibility of sex like a fishing lure, then Montenegro would be even more likely to take the bait and latch onto the hook.

Which was a good plan, an excellent plan, except that by doing her job, Bella was driving Seth insane. When she'd opened her door at the hotel, he felt like he'd taken a sucker punch to the face. She was fucking gorgeous, and he was the poor bastard with his tongue hanging out, panting after her.

For the year and a half since she'd been assigned to his office, he'd been fighting a losing battle against an over-the-top insane attraction. He'd thought that ignoring how he felt would cause it to wither and die.

The opposite happened.

They'd been circling around each other since they were first introduced, alternating between arguing and sniping, and being distantly polite. None of their evasive tactics worked because no matter what Bella did or said, he wanted her more than the day before. His problem, one he thought he'd had a handle on. But this weekend might prove him wrong.

Seth swallowed the excellent prime rib, then picked up his wineglass to sip sparingly of the Merlot. He spoke with the people around him at the table, all the while continuing to keep an eye on Montenegro.

At sixty-two, the man enjoyed the benefits of his wealth. The skin of his cheeks and forehead looked tight from a facelift or constant Botox. His teeth gleamed blindingly white, and his fingernails were buffed to a shine. His guests would never guess that until eighteen months ago, his address had been a low-security federal penitentiary. Low security being the problem. With the help of a helicopter and a couple of well-trained hired guns, he'd managed to escape a facility where he'd been serving his sentence for insider trading and securities fraud.

The international agents who'd helped him escape were someone else's headache. Seth's attention was focused solely on nabbing Montenegro.

Seth glanced around the ornately decorated room. He would add the fucking castle they were sitting in to his investigation. He wanted to know how the hell the house, with all its fancy furniture, had been hidden when Montenegro's assets were seized. The Marshals Service was in charge of asset forfeiture and he'd make goddamned sure the bastard forfeited these assets.

***

"Anna, are you enjoying the evening?" Hugo reclined at one end of the loveseat, turning to face Bella when she sat beside him. The rest of the guests had departed, leaving her and Seth with their host. Except her "fiancé" had excused himself and disappeared.

"I am, thank you. Dinner was delectable. You must compliment your chef for me." She let her gaze travel the room. "I love your home, Hugo. It makes me think of the wondrous estates of the country of my birth. This room especially has a definite European flair. It feels civilized. Quite a contrast to the objects you have displayed in the foyer."

He gave an easy laugh while toying with a lock of hair that had escaped from her updo. "I am a great admirer of unusual relics and feel compelled to own them. But tell me, beautiful Anna, from where do you come?"

"I am from Prague in the Czech Republic. Have you ever been to my lovely city?" Giving herself a hint of a Czech accent wasn't a stretch. Russian and Czech have similar grammar structures and vocabulary, and Bella had an ear for languages and accents.

When preparing for the assignment, she'd won the argument that Hugo would find her more interesting if she displayed a European panache.

"The Gothic cathedrals alone would demand my attention, but there is so much more to explore than what commonly lures tourists. I find European women particularly lovely." He leaned forward. His head was inclined so close to hers she was afraid he intended to kiss her. She ignored the instinct to back away from him. "In fact, I would like for you and me to become better friends. Would you join me later tonight? I would take pleasure in your company in the hot tub." He gave the word "pleasure" added emphasis.

His breath smelled of the whiskey he sipped from a crystal tumbler. "I'm sorry, Hugo, I'm afraid I've given you the wrong impression."

"Have you? No need to include Bullock, if that's what's concerning you. Three can be one too many."

Seth strolled in, his casual attitude doing nothing to tame his dangerous edge. She'd gone to their room alone to freshen up after dinner, using an elevator of all things. Of course, Montenegro would have an elevator in his home, the pompous twit. After she'd returned downstairs Seth had excused himself and disappeared. Most likely the move was intentional to give her time to work on their adversary, but that didn't make her any less relieved when he finally rejoined them.

A dark brow winged up and his gaze snagged hers when he caught sight of them on the couch. Raw heat was quickly banked.

Irritation flashed across Hugo's face. "Tell me, Bullock, do you make it a habit to leave your fiancée to fend for herself?"

"Does she need my protection in your home, Montenegro? I wouldn't have thought so. Regardless, Anna can take care of herself."

"I see. Bullock, have you experienced the wonderful culture of Anna's home country?"

Bella considered the mistrustful expression on Hugo's face as his tone shifted and became more aggressive. They couldn't afford to antagonize him.

"Stephen can't wait to meet my family and has promised that we'll visit Prague soon," Bella cut in smoothly. "Isn't that right, darling."

Seth leaned over her and she thought maybe he'd brush a kiss on her cheek before taking a seat of his own, but instead he pressed his mouth to hers. He murmured against her lips, "Whatever pleases you, my love."

She often wondered if her boss experienced the normal range of emotions. More than once she'd heard his brother Linc refer to Seth as a machine because he kept such tight control over what he was feeling. At the moment, his slate gray eyes burned with an inner fire that sparked an answering heat from deep inside her. She suppressed a shiver. She'd have to remember that his response to her was part of a well-acted drama.

He stepped back and his expression turned impassive. When she was sure her cheeks weren't flaming, she cast a quick glance at Hugo. He leaned against the cushioned seatback, the speculative look back.

His smile turned cunning when he asked, "Are you willing to share, Bullock?"

Bella's stomach gave an uncomfortable jolt. Seth sat in a chair next to her side of the couch, crossing an ankle over his knee. "Share what, exactly?"

"Don't be coy. You know exactly what I'm referring to. Your fiancée, of course. Our bargain might be more advantageous to you if you were to allow me a night with the lovely Anna."

Seth's demeanor didn't change, but Bella wondered if Hugo was perceptive enough to notice what she did: the tightening of Seth's body, tensed like a panther before it pounced.

Hugo's gaze traveled over her again and she had the unsettling sensation of spiders crawling over her skin. "Don't worry, darling. I have unusual appetites, but I won't hurt you unless you want me to."

With his arm across the seatback behind her, he ran a thumb along the indentation in the column at the back of her neck. It took all her control not to move away from his touch, and she took comfort from the fact that with a minimum of moves she could have him on the ground and crying in pain. His attention made her wonder how many other women had been in a similar position with him but had no choice, and couldn't refuse his advances.

One at a time, Seth shot his cuffs forward and adjusted his sleeves before replying. "What do you mean by advantageous?"

Hugo sighed. “Americans have no subtlety, don’t you agree, my beautiful Anna? They’re all about the bottom line. Your fiancée is thinking ‘how will this benefit me?’ more than he’s thinking of you. But I too can play that game.” Bella breathed easier when he removed his arm to lean forward to address Seth.

“First, show me proof that you have what you say you have, the blade that sliced off the head of Marie Antoinette. I insist on seeing it. Show it to me with the appropriate provenance, of course, add a night with your delectable fiancée, and I will meet your exorbitantly high asking price. No uncivilized haggling or drawn-out negotiations.” His mouth widened in a humorless smile that made Bella think of a coiled snake waiting to strike. “That is, unless I can convince your fiancée that her future is much more secure with me.” He turned his black eyes on her. “What do you think, Anna? Can I entice you to leave your fiancé?” With a long, thin finger, he dipped between her breasts and lifted the pendant on its chain, rubbing the diamond with his thumb. His voice grew hoarse. “If you were with me, every secret fantasy you’ve ever held would be satisfied. You would have all the diamonds you could wish for, and your deepest, darkest desires met.”

Bella felt a chill seeping into her bones and wished she hadn’t left her wrap upstairs in the bedroom. She couldn’t help but wonder what price a woman would pay if she agreed to his offer. What price other women had already paid. Bella leaned back against the cushions and Hugo dropped the pendant so it once again nestled between her breasts.

“I’m flattered you would ask me, but I value my engagement to Stephen and do not wish to break it.”

“My loss then, but I think yours as well.” He turned to Seth. “One night then, if that is all I can get. One night, and you will both be free to go on your merry way. I will get to experience the lusciousness that is Anna, and you will make a handsome profit on this relic I wish to possess. The blade that killed the French queen.”

Seth’s gaze remained steady on Hugo. “Done. You pay me my asking price and you’ll get the blade as well as Anna for twelve hours. Anna is not to be bruised in any way. If she is, consider yourself a dead man.”

The hollow pit in her stomach gave an unpleasant roll. Bella didn’t know why she had anticipated a different response. She knew this was part of the mission, but she hadn't expected Seth to acquiesce to Hugo's soul-crushing demand. She felt insanely, intensely angry. Which was stupid. Seth was acting a part, she knew that, but that men had such power over women, and that in the past, no doubt women had been sold to Hugo Montenegro to fulfill his perverted sexual desires, filled her with a rage she struggled to control.

She'd sit next to the monster and pretend it didn't matter, focusing on the conversation that had continued after Seth's casual acceptance of a deal that included bartered sex.

"The guillotine blade, do you have it with you? I wish to see it." The buying sex portion of the negotiation over, Hugo was moving on to the next order of business.

Seth gave a snort of laughter. "You could hardly think I would bring it to your home, a home you have guarded by your own personal army? I have it secured in a safe place."

Hugo rose to his feet, his movements jerky. His suave façade had been replaced by the look of a little boy whose desire for a shiny object was being thwarted. "I want to see it now. It's rumored that there is still blood staining the blade. Is this true?"

"Perhaps, but that doesn't mean it's the blood of Marie Antoinette. Others were likely executed with the same blade after her death."

Hugo sloshed more whiskey into his glass, his knuckles white on the decanter. Bella wasn't sure if he was being ill-mannered not offering a drink to her and Seth because he was upset, or if the thought hadn't even occurred to him. He knocked back the amber liquid, then slammed the glass back onto the sideboard.

"Where are you keeping the blade? I told you before that I want to see it. If I can't see it now, I must see it tomorrow. I will not wait." Hugo's attention had shifted entirely. Where moments before he'd been focused on pursuing her, now he seemed completely absorbed in the grisly relic from the Reign of Terror.

"I'll call my people in the morning. We can set up a neutral location for you to examine what you're considering purchasing. If we can come to terms, I'd like to conclude the transaction at that time. I've already scanned and emailed you the documents to support its provenance."

"If the documents you sent me are accurate, how do you explain that a museum in London claims to have the same blade?"

"What they have is a fraud. They were duped, and refusing to acknowledge that fact is less embarrassing than the alternative. If you don't believe I have the true execution blade, the other party I mentioned is quite interested in purchasing it and has offered a price close to yours. If that's the case, let me know now and I'll be on my way. With my fiancée."

Hugo fixed a stare on Seth, then nodded curtly. "The deal goes forward. I'll expect to hear the location of our meeting first thing in the morning. Once I have procured the relic, I will bring it back here. With Anna. You'll be able to pick up your fiancée the following day."

Chapter Three

Bella stood beside Seth and waited for the elevator door to open. She crossed her arms in front of her, breathing deeply through her nose to try to gain some level of calm. It wasn't working. She tried reciting poetry but couldn't remember the lines. She wanted to tap her foot against the stone floor because physical movement had always provided an outlet for her emotions, but she had to keep her reaction to what had happened buried or she risked blowing their cover. She clutched her arms tighter, every cell in her body vibrating with resentment. She was furious that there were men in the world like Hugo Montenegro. Men who, with impunity brought by wealth, got away with treating women as objects for their personal enjoyment. Her skin crawled at the memory of his touch.

On an intellectual level, she knew women were still exploited as they had been for all human history, and one of the reasons she'd joined the Marshals Service was to bring criminals like Hugo Montenegro to justice. If their mission was successful, he'd soon be back in prison in an eight by ten cell that held little resemblance to the country club prison he'd been housed in before. They'd get him, but dammit, the charges wouldn't include sex trafficking.

The exchange with Hugo brought memories to the surface that weren't easy to live with. There'd been rumors when some older girls had disappeared from the orphanage she and her brother had been sent to, rumors that the girls had been taken to a brothel in Moscow. Bella didn't allow herself to shy away from memories of that time. If she forgot her past, she couldn't honor those who had helped her and her brother survive, often at great sacrifice to themselves.

A big chunk of her simmering anger was directed at Seth. It didn't matter they were undercover. He'd perpetuated the idea that women were commodities to be traded or sold. Playing on Hugo's proclivities might help lure him out into the open where he could be arrested, but Seth hadn't needed to accept the prurient request. That he had infuriated her.

They'd left the room when Montenegro had received a call. It had been no surprise when his voice had turned low and sultry as he greeted the person on the other end of the line as *ma chérie.*

Seth leaned against the wall waiting for the elevator, his hands in his pockets, as relaxed as could be, looking at her with a slightly raised brow that struck her as infuriatingly arrogant.

She uttered a Russian expletive as she glared at him.

"I know what that means, you know." He straightened and raked his fingers through his hair, and she felt marginally better. He wasn't as unaffected by what had transpired as he might seem. The ice man never showed agitation, never made wasted movements that might indicate a lack of control. She liked thinking that he wasn't his usual restrained self. "I don't know what you're so upset about."

She spit out another, even cruder word.

His gaze narrowed and shifted to a spot over her shoulder.

"Take it easy," he muttered in a low voice.

The words were like a match to dry tinder. She drew in a breath to blast him, then heard footsteps as a member of the staff walked past them and down the hall. She felt like a wildfire was raging through her and she had to fight to contain the conflagration before it burned down the house. Imagining stabbing Seth in the eye with a fork helped get her through the interminable wait for the elevator.

The car finally arrived, the door opened, and they stepped inside. It slid shut, and Seth pressed the button to send the car to the third floor where their room was located.

She turned on him in the small space. "Easy? I'm supposed to take it easy? You bastard."

"Yeah, taking it easy is a good idea."

Something about his mildly amused expression, like he was humoring her while she had a snit, served as one last nudge to push her over the edge of her control. Her vision hazed red and she pulled back her arm, fist clenched. He must have read her mind. Before her intention was fully formed, he grabbed her elbows and tugged. Momentum had her sprawling forward into his embrace. He took her with him against the back wall of the car, his mouth clamped over hers. She bit down sharply on his lip. He grunted, swore ripely, then slanted his mouth. His tongue slid past her lips to glide silkily against hers as she tasted blood.

A white-hot flash had anger spiraling into desire, sweeping away the defenses she'd so carefully constructed. Over the past eighteen months, brick by brick, she'd vigilantly surrounded herself with a thick wall of protection against her feelings for him.

He was her partner and her boss, and was therefore way off limits. Not to mention, mostly he behaved like she was a pain in his ass. Except for those rare times when something she did or said made his slate gray eyes flash to silver, sending heat thrumming over her body.

She was a rule follower. With a few exceptions, that's how she'd survived her childhood. The Marshals Service rules said she couldn't have a relationship with her superior. But now her carefully constructed wall was in danger of crumbling around her.

Seth's hands shifted from her elbows, one moving to burn against the skin of her back, the other slipping through the naughty slit in her dress. He paused for a long, ripe moment, making her wonder if he'd pull back and she'd have no way to expel all the pent-up heat. She felt they both teetered on the edge of a monumental decision, then his hand moved, strong and sure under the silky material, smooth against her skin, and she felt her breath leave her body in a whoosh.

Bells warning her she was in the danger zone clanged in her head and were ignored as she groaned against his mouth. His rough, calloused palm caressed the back of her thigh before pulling her tighter against him. She was cradled in the spread of his long legs, and he made no effort to hide his huge arousal.

She shifted angles, pressing heat to heat, rubbing against the hard ridge of his erection. He deepened the kiss, his mouth ravenous on hers, and she had the feeling he'd broken all his self-imposed restraints. She tugged his shirt from his pants and ran her hands under the material, eager to touch his hot skin and hard muscle. Finally having this had her sighing with pleasure. "You feel so good," she murmured against his lips.

He pulled back, allowing a mere half inch between them. "You have no idea."

"I'm getting one."

She dipped a hand beneath his belt as the elevator came to a smooth stop. He grabbed her wrists. "Not here." His voice sounded ragged. "Inside the room."

The door opened and somehow they made it into the hall despite neither one of them letting go of the other. The moment was the cumulation of long months of denying herself her greatest desire. She'd had fantasies about his long, lean body, fantasies fueled by the sparks that raced through her whenever they accidentally brushed against each other, or she found his dark gaze on her.

His appeal went well beyond the physical. Just as sexy was the sharp intelligence that drove her to think through problems, to find solutions, to work harder. Then there was the wry sense of humor that meshed so well with hers.

Add his unshakable love for his family and she hadn't stood a chance against his gravitational pull. She'd come to terms with the fact that she'd fallen face first, head over heels, ovaries in a twist, in love with Seth.

Circumstance had forced her to bury those feelings to protect herself from the hurt that would invariably come from loving a man she could never have. There were times when she almost believed she'd succeeded. Then there were other times when she thought her feelings might be reciprocated, that Seth might feel something for her. He would grin at her and his eyes would warm, and sometimes he seemed to be watching her when he thought she wouldn't notice.

Eventually she'd been forced to admit to herself she was susceptible to wishful thinking. The ice man's control was legendary, and Seth letting his emotions show was like having an earthquake, an eclipse, and being struck by lightning all occurring on the eve of a blue moon.

But on this night, there'd been a cosmic shift and the world had tilted on its axis and she was going to let it ride.

He pushed open the bedroom door, stepped aside to let her precede him, and the minute the door shut and the lock clicked home, he backed her up against the wall. She thought he would dive in once more. She wanted him to dive in, but he took her face in his hands and held her still, studying her with a dark gaze that she felt could touch her soul.

"Seth." His name on her lips was a plea.

His fingers slid into her hair, combing through and scattering pins so it tumbled around her shoulders. “I love your hair loose like this.”

He loved her hair loose? She was never again wearing it up.

He dipped his head and touched his lips to hers, softly at first, then more insistently. Need exploded through her like fireworks. Her lips fused with his as she undid the buttons of his shirt with shaky fingers. He pulled off his tie, and when his shirt opened, she ran her fingers over taut skin, loving the feel of his hard muscle and wiry chest hair.

His mouth moved, and he seemed as out of control as she felt. Once again, he sought the opening in her dress, his hard palms against her skin, her breath catching as his fingers slid perilously close to where she most ached to feel his touch.

She caught the lapels of his jacket and tugged him closer as his mouth moved from her jaw to her ear, the stubble of his beard abrading sensitive skin.

Their positions were reversed from how they’d been in the elevator, and he nudged her legs apart and moved between them, hitching up her dress, the material parting as she took his welcome weight. He pushed against her through layers of clothing, his erection rubbing with exquisite torture and sending her spiraling to the brink of control. When she leaned her head against the wall, he used his teeth to nip at her exposed neck, the brief pain causing her to gasp. He soothed the discomfort with a soft lick of his tongue.

“You taste so good,” he murmured with his lips against her skin.

She reached for the button at his waistband.

He stopped, closing his eyes, his entire body going motionless. “Fuck. We can’t do this.” Then he pulled back and opened his eyes, and she saw what she’d never expected to see. No longer controlled, his eyes burned, sparks of silver flashing through slate gray.

“We are doing this.”

He leaned back his head to take a shuddering breath, the muscles in his arms going rigid. He freed his hands from the folds of her dress and rested them on the wall on either side of her head. “There was a camera in the elevator. That’s why I kissed you. I was afraid you were about to blow our cover.”

Her stomach dropped and tugged her heart down with it. That was it? He’d acted like he couldn’t stay away from her for another moment because there'd been a camera in the elevator? No. She wouldn't accept that. There'd been more to what had happened than an effort to preserve their cover. He'd wanted her too, and his attempt to explain away his reaction sharpened her tone. "Sacrificing yourself for the job? How noble."

His expression turned inscrutable.

With anger layering over being insanely aroused, she wasn't feeling exactly charitable. Seth's cheeks were flushed, his eyes sharp. She would never think of him as the ice man again. Whatever his motivation for kissing her, she could see he was hanging on to control by only the thinnest of threads.

"Like hell you kissed me like that for the job," she ground out. "There was more to that kiss and grope than a show for the camera."

"Okay, maybe."

"Don't be a coward. You may not like me, but at least you can admit you want me."

He opened his mouth, no doubt to tell her that any man would want her, that his was a normal male reaction. She heaved in a breath to fortify herself against his rejection, then his gaze swept down and she felt his quick intake of breath.

She looked down to what had snagged his attention. The bodice of her dress had pulled dangerously low and she felt the insane urge to giggle. Either that or die of embarrassment. She wasn't what one would call overly endowed, just a run-of-the-mill C-cup, but the dress and the magic bra managed to make her look voluptuous, and more than a little decadent with the diamond gleaming in the valley between her breasts.

But that wasn't where his attention was riveted. Her skin burned as his gaze fixated on the dusky areola of one nipple now visible above the shimmery material. He raised a hand and drew a fingertip along the edge of the cloth, tracing the exposed arc, then tugged at the material to uncover the entire nipple. He made a noise deep in his throat that sounded like a wild animal on the prowl.

As if in a trance, he tugged again, pulling down the material to bare her other breast. He brought up his hands to cup both breasts, kneading them, plumping them, then bent his head to take one in his mouth, the roll of his tongue over the tip nearly making her erupt in orgasm then and there.

His mouth was so hot she was surprised there weren't burn marks on her skin as he moved to give his attention to the other breast. While he feasted, she once more reached for the button at his waist, opening his trousers with quick movements.

Ah, there he was. Hard and silky, velvet over steel. She fondled and stroked and had him making that noise again, the vibration deep in his throat. She'd never experienced anything as erotic as the feel of him in her hand.

His mouth left her breasts and his gaze locked on hers. She saw a war raging in his eyes between control and wild abandon.

She'd die if he stepped back now.

"Do you want this?"

She gave a jerky nod.

"Say it, Bella. Do you want this with me right now?"

"I want this. With you. Right now."

He stared long and hard. "Then fuck it."

He picked her up and carried her to the bed and unhooked her bra as she kicked off her shoes. Then he gathered the material of her dress and drew it up and over her body in a silky glide, draping it over the foot of the bed.

He removed her bra and pressed his lips into the swell of her breasts as she pushed down his pants and reached for him once again. He raised his head, his eyes glittering in the shadowy light cast by a lamp in the corner. Something about seeing her naked, but for her turquoise thong, set him off. In seconds he was stripped naked and tumbling them both onto the bed.

In his arms, inhaling the clean scent of him, feeling the strength in his long, lean build stoked the need blazing within her. She loved his hands with those wide palms and blunt-shaped fingers, and he used them to wicked effect, stroking and sliding to bring her to the brink.

She gasped and he shifted to prop himself on his elbows, his thumb tracing the ridge of her cheekbone. Then he was pushing into her. He framed her face with his hands, took her lips with his, and thrust forward.

They both went wild as he plunged into her.

They moved in tandem, the tension, which had always been present between them, shifting and transforming into something new.

She met him, thrust for thrust, responding to his movements, her hands at his hips pulling him in deeper. Harboring a secret love for him explained why their coming together felt more exquisite, more perfect, than her most erotic fantasies. She held him tighter, hoping to lengthen the interlude. But as she was already primed and ready, the strong, sure drive of his body flung her to the top of the surging wave.

He was right there, riding the hard, bright crest along with her, stringing it out to prolong the moment until together they plummeted over the edge and dropped into oblivion.

Seth collapsed on top of her, his weight heavy and welcome. She nuzzled his hand where it cupped the side of her face, his thumb rubbing against the bridge of her nose.

She wondered if her heart might explode inside her chest. She wasn't sure what lay ahead for them, but in that moment she felt giddy they'd moved beyond their armed standoff.

Words she wanted to say were on the tip of her tongue. Maybe she wasn't ready to reveal that she'd been in love with him for well over a year, but perhaps she could work up to that. She could at least tell him that she *cared* for him, that her feelings went farther than simple attraction.

Then his thumb stopped moving and his body stiffened, and not in a good way. He pushed off her to lie on his back, not meeting her gaze, dropping his arm heavily over his forehead.

A moment before, she'd felt comfortably naked. Now she felt exposed.

It'd taken only a split second for the feeling between them to change from intimate to unbearably awkward.

She rolled off the bed, taking the top sheet with her. She yanked it from under his legs and wrapped it around herself. She could no longer bear to be uncovered.

She grabbed the smaller of her suitcases and retreated into the bathroom, carefully turning the lock with shaky fingers.

Chapter Four

The bathroom door's decisive click resounded in the quiet bedroom. Seth pinched the bridge of his nose. He'd screwed up, probably the worst fuck-up in his adult life. He rubbed his fingers against his eyes, images from the past hour replaying in his mind. Yeah, he'd screwed up, but god, it had been amazing. He'd kept his crazy attraction for Bella bottled up so they could have a working relationship. He was her boss, for Chrissake. He'd even managed to keep his response to her in check after he'd kissed her in the car.

But they'd gotten on that elevator and she'd gone off like a rocket in his arms. She'd taken him under, and he'd felt like he was floundering, not even bothering to look for a life raft. He'd managed to gain a slippery grip on control in the bedroom when he'd had her up against the wall. Barely. Then he'd seen the edge of her nipple peeking from under the material and had felt something snap.

He was a drowning man and wasn't bothering to fight the force pulling him under. The control that had been second nature for him had broken clean through. He'd let go and led with his heart, allowing himself a few precious minutes where being with Bella, holding her in his arms and making love with her, was the center of his universe.

For that short span of time, he'd been free.

Denial and control dictated his interactions with Bella, and had done since day one. But from the moment he'd knocked on her hotel room door, this weekend had changed everything. He should've assigned a different marshal to act as his partner for this operation, but he'd wanted Bella.

He always wanted Bella.

They'd posed as an engaged couple and the plan blew up in his face. She'd be within her rights to ask for a transfer, and to lodge a harassment complaint against him. He pushed aside the thought it'd been worth it. Knowing how good it could be between them had shifted the paradigm and there was no going back.

What if they could work it through to the point where they could have a relationship? It would mean a change in their assignments. She could no longer be part of his team. That would be bad. He'd miss working with her. Watching her when she wasn't looking, and enjoying the view. But if it meant they could have a life together, he'd sacrifice almost anything for that. Who knew if she even wanted to be with him for a lifetime. Maybe she'd—

His brain shuddered to a halt. His hand lay motionless on his forehead as reality crashed around him like the proverbial ton of bricks. *Fuck.* He hadn't used a condom. God *damn* it.

For the first time in his life, he'd had sex without thinking about protection for himself or his partner. Which told him how badly he'd wanted Bella. How desire had pushed every rational thought out of his head.

Shit, shit, *shit.*

It felt like every interaction they'd had for the past year and a half had led to the moment when his brain had turned off and his instincts took over. Their sharp disagreements. Those sexy/snarky comments of hers that always got under his skin. The moments where he'd fought to block his reaction or keep from doing what he'd just done, nearly taking her against the wall with all the finesse of a raging bull.

All of it had sharpened the tension between them to the point of rupture, and the sane part of his mind, which considered protection, had been blown away.

He never allowed himself to lose control. Yet that's exactly what he'd done. What if she got pregnant? He scrubbed a hand across his face. Most likely she was taking a contraceptive, or had one of those IUDs. If she wasn't or didn't, and she conceived, they'd get married. That's all there was to it. They'd get married and sort out the rest later.

The door of the bathroom flung open and Bella stormed out. She'd changed into a tank top and some sort of stretchy leggings that fit like a second skin. Her hair was pulled back in a ponytail, and her face was wiped clean of makeup. She looked so fresh-faced she'd be carded if she tried to buy a beer.

"What the hell, Jameson?"

And she was back. Her hands were balled and slammed into her hips. She leaned forward. Her expression screamed furious.

"What the hell what?"

"Don't be funny. It hit me when I was *cleaning up*. You didn't use condom."

Ah. Well. No getting around it. "No, I didn't."

"Why the hell not?"

"Because I wasn't exactly thinking rationally. It's no excuse, but I got caught up in the moment. I don't remember you saying anything."

"It is man's responsibility to use condom."

He couldn't have stopped the grin from splitting his face if she'd pointed a gun at his head. "'It ees man's responsibility'? Do you realize your accent gets stronger when you're angry? You drop your articles and pronounce 'i' like an 'e.'"

His brain was so out of whack he was saying shit he'd never say. He was in for it now.

Color suffused her face as she stalked to the bed. "I'll show you a dropped article, you bastard." She let loose a string of Russian expletives as she launched herself at him, fists swinging. He should've remembered she had a wicked temper when riled. The ripe curse she'd used earlier seemed to be a favorite because it came up a couple times. The rest was lost in the tussle when he grabbed her hands before she could make contact with his face, and then yanked her onto the bed. She pushed and heaved, bringing up a knee in a sharp movement that came entirely too close to emasculating him. He flipped her under him and used his weight to keep her from trying the maneuver again. He reared back a moment before she could sink her teeth into his shoulder. Being buck naked was not an advantage in a fight with Bella Nikolaev.

"Shit, Bella. Stop trying to bloody me. I don't want to hurt you."

"Too bad, because I want to hurt you. Did I say that right? Did I use my article and pronounce the 'i' correctly?"

She worked a hand from his grasp and pinched the skin along his ribs, twisting hard. He swore, scrabbled again for her hand, all the while conscious that certain parts of him liked their situation just fine.

She struggled, squirming to work a leg from beneath him, drawing in a sharp breath when the movement brought his groin against the sweet vee between her legs.

She went still, and shutters dropped over her eyes.

The insane thought crossed his mind that since they'd already done it once, what would it matter if they did it again? Her chest heaved against his and he felt the hard nubs of her nipples through the material of her top. Shit. She wasn't wearing a bra. Once again, his control was slipping from his grasp.

"No. Not again. I don't want you."

He pushed back, his breath sawing out of his lungs. He took in the flushed rise of her breasts and when her thighs spread wider and he settled more firmly between her legs, he was even closer to heaven.

"I think we could argue that point." When he touched her cheek, she turned her head, teeth bared. "Don't you dare."

"I dare as I please."

"Not with me you don't. I don't know if you've had your shots."

"You're a bastard." The color in her cheeks hadn't abated, and she was breathing in shallow gasps. Her blue eyes darkened, edging toward violet, which meant she was as aroused as he was.

"So you keep saying. My mother might disagree. Regardless, you're the one trying the vampire routine."

"Get off me."

"I will, if that's what you want. But surely you've heard of the horse and the barn door."

"That's an American idiom that means it's too late to do the thing that would stop something bad from happening."

"Pretty much. You must've done well in school. In our case it means that we've already done the deed without protection."

"So we might as well do it again? Is that how your tiny brain works?"

"Can't deny that's where it went," he looked down at their position, "given current evidence." The insistent urge to peel off those leggings and let nature take its course had him grappling for control he barely held on to by a thread.

Her chest heaved and his mouth watered at the memory of the tight bud of her nipple against his tongue, which only made him ache for another sample. He closed his eyes to block the image. It didn't work.

Fuck, fuck, fuck.

This relentless craving for her was damned inconvenient and starting to piss him off.

He opened his eyes. "I'm going to let you go. Don't bite me." He saw the calculation on her face. "Or kick me."

He eased his weight off her and flopped onto his back, pulling a sheet over himself since certain parts hadn't yet gotten the memo the lady had said *no*.

"Too bad about your *evidence*, because I don't want you."

"So you said. Might be true intellectually, but physically? You want me bad."

"I hate you."

"Which isn't a denial." He propped himself on an elbow. He could've dealt with the stubborn chin and the defiance in her eyes, but the single tear tracking into the hair at her temple hollowed him out like she'd connected with that knee.

He'd screwed things up between them in the worst possible way. He was the boss. He was in charge. It was his responsibility to fix things. As much as he didn't feel like doing it, he did what he'd done countless time before: he reined in his treacherous emotions and made an effort to lock them into a seldom-used compartment in his head. A technique he'd found vital to keep functioning at his job.

"Are you on the pill?"

She shook her head.

"Using any contraceptives?"

Another head shake.

Shit. "Okay." He didn't think bringing up marriage would go over well at the moment. "We'll deal with a pregnancy if it becomes an issue."

He rolled out of bed, yanking on his briefs. He got clothes from his suitcase and pulled on gym shorts and a t-shirt, then quickly checked his phone. A text from his mom said she was looking forward to him being home, and that she was planning a family get-together.

Family time was good, but at the moment he had a mountain of other shit that needed dealing with. He slipped the phone into his pocket as Bella rose from the bed. He caught the surreptitious swipe of her hand across her eyes as she crossed the room to sit in an upholstered chair that looked too fancy to be comfortable. With her arms wrapped around her knees, those beautiful eyes big and sad, and her luscious hair coming loose from her ponytail, she looked fragile, making his heart twist. He battled back the impulse to scoop her up and hold her close.

Then her brows lowered and she jabbed a finger in his direction. "You didn't *have* to kiss me in the elevator."

Back to that, were they?

"How should I've stopped you from blowing our cover? Montenegro is paranoid and we should expect cameras anywhere in his house. I'd spotted the one in the elevator earlier. There's no audio, but his security would've picked up on you being pissed. For sure they'd have noticed you taking a swing at me. I grabbed hold of you to make it look like we were hot for each other. I had to do something. If this goes sideways, we're in danger, and we risk losing Montenegro and his assets for good."

"That's bullshit. You make it sound so reasonable when it's not. You agreed to sell me for sex. I'd think anyone watching would have understood perfectly why I punched you in the face, then found a rusty knife and cut off your balls."

"I didn't agree to sell you for sex. Jesus Christ." He hissed out the words, frustrated she was succeeding in needling him. "We're on an undercover op. I agreed my *fake* fiancée could be used for sex to benefit the deal."

"Exactly. Which is why you're a bastard. Any woman would've been angry if her fiancé sold her to that monster for sex. I was legitimately angry, but I was still in character."

He stared at the ceiling, hoping for calm. He chose his words and tone carefully. "There's no chance Montenegro will get his hands on you."

"In case you hadn't noticed, he had his hands all over me. You're not much of a fiancé to let that happen."

She scored a point with that one. When he'd walked into the room and saw Montenegro pawing Bella, he'd had to rein in the impulse to break every one of that POS's fingers. "Okay. Stephen Bullock is an asshole. You're pissed. I get that. But you were doing your job like I was doing mine."

“Is there a bug in here as well? That would explain why you had sex with me. How self-sacrificing to stay in character even behind closed doors. Hugo’s security is probably picking up this interesting conversation as we speak.”

“I scanned this room for devices earlier, and installed audio jammers. The suite is clean. But don’t kid yourself. You weren’t telling me to stop, sweetheart, so I’m guessing you got something out of it too.”

She rose from her seat, nose in the air. “I’m going to bed. You can find yourself somewhere else to sleep.”

“Fuck that. That bed is king size and large enough that you’ll have nothing to worry about. If you can keep your hands off me, I can keep mine off you.”

There was a moment where she looked ready to fight him over it, but instead, she lifted the corner of the comforter and slipped under the covers.

She curled onto her side with her back to him, so close to the edge he thought she might tumble off in the middle of the night.

Seth sighed and turned out the light, grateful he wasn’t bloodied or suffering from internal injuries.

Chapter Five

Seth steered the Bugatti around a curve in the road while Bella monitored the GPS on her phone. Working with marshals from the San Francisco office, they'd set up the sting operation to nab their fugitive. They were on their way to a park where Montenegro had agreed to meet them. Morning clouds had cleared to reveal a perfect early summer day and as they topped a hill, the graceful curves of the Golden Gate Bridge gleamed in the distance.

The passing streets held an eclectic mix of architectural styles typical of the Bay Area, but Bella's mind was stuck in the same rut it had been running in for the past few days. The tension between her and Seth, the *awkwardness,* had magnified since Friday night. She was doing her level best to pretend their hot sex never happened, but the effort was fraying her nerves. It didn't help she was still furious with him. She was angry with herself even more. Stupidly, she'd felt their relationship had taken a giant leap forward, and hoped they'd finally admit there was more between them than two people scratching an itch. Talk about being dead wrong.

They'd left Hugo Montenegro's home on Saturday and checked into a hotel near Fisherman's Wharf. Hugo wanted the relic and he wanted Bella, and it appeared that his too-short time in prison had only amplified his need for immediate gratification. They'd decided forcing Montenegro to wait would make him more impulsive and likely to make a mistake in their favor, so Seth ignored the other man's blustering and stalled when Hugo had wanted the deal to be finalized that weekend. Instead, they'd agreed to meet Tuesday morning, so here they were.

Seth had insisted they continue the engaged couple ruse. She got it, and was grateful to leave, though the ruse ended at the hotel room door. They were sharing a suite, not a bed. Yet, even that limited proximity did nothing to lessen her hyperawareness of him. She was starting to resent she noticed every little thing about him. His loose-hipped walk, the way his hair fell across his forehead, the stubble on his jaw in the mornings that made her fingers itch to rub the bristles. Before this assignment, there was palpable tension between them, but they'd become experts at burying their attraction. With the cat out of the bag, they were tiptoeing around each other and that they'd had unprotected sex. On a loop in her brain, she replayed "We'll deal with a pregnancy if it becomes an issue." Deal with a pregnancy? There were a dozen things he could've meant, but as far as she was concerned, if she was pregnant, any decisions were hers alone to make.

Reestablishing their earlier working relationship was crucial. Not easy, but crucial. Before this assignment the constant state of friction between them had made their relationship tense at best, but at least they'd been able to function. Since losing her mind and giving in to her desire, these past few days she worked to keep her emotions in check, tried to stay busy, and made sure any conversations were work related.

But every now and then, the idea she might be pregnant wormed its way to the front of her mind. It was stupid to even think about it. She wasn't due to start her period for another few days, so there was no point worrying. Which, of course, didn't stop the thought from hijacking her brain.

What if she was pregnant? Her world would change, for sure. Being a single mom would be difficult, but having both parents didn't necessarily make children any better off. Her own family was the perfect example. With any other man, the question would be met with more trepidation, but that Seth would be the father made her traitorous heart yearn.

He'd gone along with her assiduously avoiding personal conversations. They talked about their plan to capture Montenegro and the hunt for Seth's father, the domestic terrorist fugitive Richard Jameson. RJ had dropped off the map months before and their team was following leads.

On conference calls with the team, invariably conversations veered toward the personal. Linc and Ellie, Seth's siblings and the other marshals on the team, were also Bella's friends. Bella, Ellie, and Mikayla, Linc's wife, had become increasingly close in the past year, which led to their lives becoming more intertwined. Too often, she and Seth were thrown together socially, something she found stretched her nerves so tight she feared they'd snap.

Three weeks before she'd served as maid of honor, and Seth stood as a groomsman at Ellie's small, beautiful wedding to Judge Sam Creed.

Negotiating all *that* and keeping her distance from Seth was nerve wracking. Especially since she'd catch him watching her, those slate gray eyes giving away not a damned thing. Now the tension between them had ratcheted up by a factor of a thousand. One dose too many of the hotness that was Seth Jameson and she hadn't had the willpower to say *no* when she damn well should have.

"This it?"

Bella yanked her attention back into the game. "Yeah. We take this street through the park and it's on the right."

She refocused to conjure her persona as Anna Novak. Once again she'd dressed the part of a rich man's fiancée. She'd paired loose-fitting pants of a filmy material with suede ankle boots and a knit jacket over a sleeveless linen top. Add in the sapphire and diamond earrings and gold chain to complement the engagement ring, and she thought she pulled it off.

The meeting was to take place at a stone bench outside the Conservatory of Flowers in Golden Gate Park. Montenegro expected to conclude the exchange for the relic and walk off with Stephen Bullock's woman. He was going to be sadly disappointed.

"There's the parking area."

Seth parked the car three spots down from a white van with the advertising logo "Catering by Maria" plastered on its side. The three marshals in the van—equipped with surveillance devices—along with half a dozen officers from the task force who were already in the park dressed as tourists, comprised their backup.

Hugo had insisted on a public location, probably assuming that an open, outdoor setting early in the day would offer him some protection. They'd chosen this time since there were fewer people in the park at this hour, but there was always the possibility someone could inadvertently crash their party. The marshals were ready to deal with any problems, as well as Hugo's hired security.

Seth turned in his seat.

"You ready?"

"Yes, sir."

His gaze went dark, and he nodded. They stepped out of the car and Seth opened the trunk and retrieved the reinforced locking case. Carrying it by the heavy-duty handle, he reached for her with his other hand, lacing their fingers and bringing her to his side.

"Acting like you're in love with me doesn't really make sense, you know," she muttered, deliberately keeping her voice low.

He raised a brow. "How so?"

"Because you've made me part of the bargain. What man allows another man to have sex with the woman he loves?" They walked along the path bordering gorgeous flowerbeds in front of the Victorian greenhouse that looked like a relic of a previous age.

"Back to that, are we?" He caught her sharp look. "Okay, point taken, but we keep going the way we started. As I said, Stephen Bullock is an asshole."

"Yes, he is," she agreed primly.

They spotted Montenegro, flanked by two bodyguards, approaching from the opposite direction. They met at the designated bench and exchanged greetings, Hugo's gaze lingering on Bella before switching to the case Seth held.

Bella didn't know if the avaricious gaze was from desire for her or what was in the case. Seth set it on the bench, went through the steps to unlock it, and lifted the lid.

There, nestled in the foam padding, was the ugly guillotine blade that had beheaded too many French citizens during the Reign of Terror, among them the complicated figure of Marie Antoinette. The diagonal blade was attached with heavy bolts to what Bella thought must be a weight. Hugo examined it meticulously, bending over and holding a jeweler's loupe to his eye, muttering to himself.

"Yes, yes. This dark stain? That must be the blood. It's good that the blade wasn't cleaned." He ran a finger roughly along the edge, then held it up. A smear of blood showed where he'd nicked it. "My blood has mixed on this notorious blade with that of Marie Antoinette." He looked inordinately pleased. "What must she have been thinking, lying there with her head resting in the lunette, waiting for this very blade to drop? One wonders how long consciousness remained with her head severed from her body."

He turned abruptly to Seth. "I don't suppose you also have the blade that killed Robespierre?"

Bella stifled the insane desire to laugh at his hopeful expression. In his home, Hugo Montenegro had seemed dangerous. Now he appeared ridiculous. A glance at his guards sobered her. Both wore mirrored sunglasses and stood watchful on the grass several yards away. In no way were they ridiculous.

If Seth was surprised by Hugo's query, he didn't let it show. "No, but I can keep an eye out. I believe that one has been lost to history."

"That's a shame. I'm pursuing the glass Rasputin drank the poisoned wine from, but that, too, has proven elusive. I'm also interested in the bullet that killed Robert Kennedy. Let me know if you come across either of those items. Acquiring such relics would be exquisite additions to my collection." Bella caught Seth tensing when Hugo reached into his pocket, but he only pulled out his phone. "As agreed, I will transfer the money to the account number you sent me."

Bella didn't let her anticipation show. This was an important step because the marshals wanted to know the source of his money. He might have it shielded, but the money trail could lead them to hidden assets. If they were able to get their hands on Montenegro's assets, the money could be used to pay restitution to some of the victims of his crimes. This was exactly why she'd signed up to do this work. People with money and power shouldn't be free to victimize whomever they chose.

Hugo's gaze rested on Bella and the look in his eyes made her stomach roll. "Once the transfer is complete, I'll take possession of the relic, as I will take possession of the beautiful Anna."

Seth brought out his phone, listened, and said, "It's a go." He reached under his jacket and smoothly withdrew his gun from its shoulder harness. "Hugo Montenegro, I'm Chief Deputy US Marshal Seth Jameson. You're under arrest."

Hugo spun around to find both his guards with their hands in the air as officers surrounded them, weapons drawn. They'd suspected that Montenegro would be armed, and when he reached down to where he likely had a gun in a leg holster, Bella moved quickly. In seconds, she had him face down on the pavement. She wrenched his hands behind his back as he sputtered with rage.

He squirmed, trying to dislodge her, but with her knee in his back he wasn't going anywhere. One of the officers tossed her handcuffs and she snapped them around each wrist. She couldn't help the grim satisfaction. There was sweet justice in being the woman taking down a man who preyed on too many women who didn't have the power to get away or say no.

Hugo Montenegro had been a fugitive from justice and a predator in so many different ways, and once again he'd be locked up, but this time in a cage from which he wouldn't be able to escape.

Seth holstered his weapon. He bent down and took one of Montenegro's arms, she took the other and they pulled the struggling bastard to his feet.

"Motherfuckers! I trusted you. I'll fucking kill you." His voice rose as he fought against his restraints. "I'll disembowel you. I'll eviscerate you. I'll cut you into tiny pieces and feed you to the sharks. You'll both die in pain." He twisted against their hold, screaming the words, spittle spraying from his mouth.

Ignoring the tirade, Seth searched him and, in addition to the gun in a holster strapped to his shin, Seth retrieved an antique folding knife from Hugo's pocket. Two other marshals took custody of Montenegro and frog marched him to the van.

"Good takedown, Bella."

"Thank you, sir."

"Cut it out," he muttered the words so only she could hear.

"I'm a marshal doing my job, sir."

The look he sent her promised retribution.

She suppressed a shiver.

The situation between them had gotten as personal as it gets, but it didn't seem like her efforts to reestablish distance were taking hold. They walked toward the parking area where she tried to hitch a ride in one of the other vehicles but, no surprise, Seth overruled the maneuver and she ended up in the Bugatti with him.

They drove through the busy streets toward the Phillip Burton Federal Building where the Marshals office was located. Her phone vibrated in her jacket pocket. She tapped on the screen, staring at the message as her heart clutched in her chest. She tapped out a response, then turned her head away from Seth, briefly closing her eyes.

"You okay?"

Trust him to notice every damn thing. "Sure. I'm fine."

He probably didn't believe her, but he let it drop.

The rest of the day was spent dealing with the paperwork. Even electronically, the multitude of forms, processes, and procedures was daunting. The diamond engagement ring and other jewelry Bella had worn were returned to the property room, as were the keys to the Bugatti. A steady stream of marshals filed through the office to check out the guillotine in its padded case before it was shipped back to the museum that had loaned it to them.

Seth came into the small conference room where Bella had set up a laptop to work, carrying his jacket under his arm. He still wore his gun and she told herself to get a grip when the shoulder straps of his holster struck her as unabashedly sexy. Even with her current preoccupation, she couldn't turn off her response to him.

She bent her head and busily resumed typing.

"Hey, workday's over. The task force is meeting at a pub a couple blocks away to celebrate Montenegro's arrest. You mind if we walk there?"

"Go ahead. I'll finish this report and then I'm going back to the hotel." She sipped from her now-cold mug of tea and wished for a couple of pain pills for the headache brewing behind her temples. The screen on her phone lit, and with a quick glance she saw only a calendar notification. No text.

The door of the conference room closed and she looked up in surprise when Seth pulled out the chair next to her. "Find someone else to play with, Seth. I'm busy."

"You remember my name."

"Of course, I remember your name."

"Since Saturday, you've been back to calling me *sir*. You know I hate it when you do that, right? Maybe that's why you do it."

"You're my boss, I'm supposed to call you sir."

"Fuck that."

"Okay." She tapped the pad to check the final box on her document.

He grabbed the arm of her chair and swiveled the seat to turn her to him, holding firm when she would have swiveled back.

Deciding she'd only lose the tussle, she went for cool and remote. "I take it you want my attention?"

"Since throttling you is against Marshals Service protocols, we'll talk instead. Tell me what's going on with you, and don't tell me it's nothing."

"Me? I'm typing a report. One you asked for. You, however, are having a snit." So much for cool and remote.

"Dudes don't have snits. The report can wait until tomorrow." His brows lowered. "You haven't answered the question."

"I don't recall there being a question."

"Okay, I'll restate. What's going on with you?"

"Are you asking as my boss about work-related issues?"

"No, I'm asking as your friend about Bella-related issues."

"Then I can't answer you. We're not friends."

He let go of her chair and leaned back. He scrubbed a hand along his jaw, his whiskers making a rasping sound, a rare indication of frustration. "What the hell, Bella?"

The flash of what looked suspiciously like vulnerability hit her like a gut-punch, but she forced herself not to give in to any softening of feelings toward him. Remembering his "that should never have happened" statement after what had been for her a life-altering experience helped. She crossed her arms over her chest and kept her mouth firmly shut.

"Look," he shook his head, "come to the pub with the team. Relax. Enjoy yourself. You can tolerate me for that long."

"You seem to be operating under the misguided notion this is about you."

"So there's a *this.* Something's going on. Tell me."

He stretched out his long legs in front of him like he was settling in for a long chat. She swiveled her seat and clicked a couple of icons to save her work, and closed the file. She'd do better talking to him if she didn't have to look at him.

"I've put in for personal leave. I'm taking the rest of the week off. I finished the report you asked for and I'll email it to you. I've got a flight to Los Angeles booked for this evening."

He sat forward so quickly his chair rocked. She chanced a quick look and found him wearing his *I'm digging in* expression. Damn.

"We made arrangements to fly together tomorrow. Why the change in plans?"

"I'm not obligated to tell my supervisor the reason for personal leave."

"There's fucking more to our relationship than work, Bella."

There it was again, his implication that they were friends. Another low blow. No matter how much she'd like it if Seth truly was her friend, there were some things experience had taught her were better not shared with anyone.

"It's personal."

He grabbed the arms of her chair again and turned her to face him, this time keeping her locked in. His eyes sparked silver as a muscle worked in his jaw. "Are you pregnant?"

"What? No. I mean, I don't know. But it's unlikely. It's too early to tell." Shortly after *the event,* as she'd taken to referring to it in her mind, she'd considered getting a Plan B pill, but had chosen not to for reasons she didn't want to examine too closely.

"You're not taking time off to have an abortion?"

"What makes you think that's what I'm doing? Besides, I'd have to be pregnant to get an abortion."

"Answer the question, Bella."

She was startled to see his control slipping. His knuckles were white where his hands gripped the arms of the chair, and a storm of emotion crossed his face. She was working to reconstruct the wall around her heart and he was battering it down with a sledgehammer without even trying.

"No, Seth. I'm not getting an abortion. Is that clear enough?"

He released the chair. "Okay. Then why are you leaving tonight?"

She pushed back and he released the chair. She shut down the laptop and closed the lid, standing to move around the table and unplug it. "I have to deal with some personal matters. It has nothing to do with you."

He wasn't happy, that was clear from the scowl pulling his mouth down in a frown. But when he rose to his feet, all he said in a gruff voice was, "I'll give you a ride to the airport."

God, he was a good man. Even when he was angry and frustrated with her, and she was leaving without explanation, he still offered to take her to the airport. Keeping him at a distance was vital for her mental well-being, but at every turn, he challenged her resolve.

He'd never admit it, even under the threat of a court order, but Seth was a nurturer. He took care of people. His family, the marshals under his supervision, her. Now he felt responsible for her because of what had happened over the weekend. Her days off would have the added benefit of giving them some much needed distance.

Chapter Six

Seth got off the elevator, glancing in the direction of Bella's desk as he made his way to his office. She wasn't in yet but was due back today. He hadn't heard a peep from her since Tuesday evening in San Francisco. He could admit to himself that it bugged the hell out of him he didn't know what was going on with her. He couldn't help it. They'd been intimate, and for him that intimacy reached beyond sexual. Plus, he plain missed her. With her absent from the office, he'd come to realize how much he counted on her, how often he used her as a sounding board when working out a case, how he subconsciously kept track of her when they were at work. After what they'd shared, their relationship had taken a sharp turn and he was ready to figure out exactly where that turn was taking them.

Leaving his door open so he could see when she came in, he started the coffee, sat at his desk, and turned on his computer. His phone buzzed and he saw his brother's name on caller ID.

"Linc," he said, by way of greeting.

"I've got something."

Without asking, his brother's tone broadcast he was referring to news about their father's case.

"Tell me."

"Three more federal judges have received emailed threats. Two are district court judges in Idaho, the third is in Nevada."

"What do you know?"

"We know the Freedom Defenders have been expanding their recruitment efforts. There's the online presence, but they like their in-person book burnings and rallies, which have stepped up since the spring. They're using those as part of their propaganda machine to engage potential new recruits across the western states. We broke their organization in Oregon, but now others have popped up in Arizona and Idaho, and the one in Nevada has grown. They're bringing in other anti-government groups to affiliate with FD. It's like we're playing whack-a-mole with these guys. The threats against the judge in Reno are the most specific and credible."

"Why target this judge?"

"The situation is similar to what happened with Sam." Federal Judge Sam Creed, now their brother-in-law, had been targeted by the Freedom Defenders. The right-wing extremist group were intent on intimidating judges, going so far as to try to physically prevent those deemed *unfriendly* from sitting on the bench during Second Amendment trials, or any cases dealing with what the group considered challenges to their personal liberties. Seth figured what this group really wanted was to destroy any level of government that got in the way of them living their lives however the hell they wanted. They didn't understand or embrace the concept of the common good. They bullied their neighbors, tore up the land, and brandished weapons at whoever challenged them. The marshals had evidence they funded their efforts through the illegal gun trade, and there'd been rumors of sex trafficking. As far as he was concerned, they were an armed, anti-government domestic terrorist cult minus the religion.

Seth clicked open his email as Linc talked. "The judge's name is Carlos Rebollar and he sits on the bench at the federal district court in Reno. He has an upcoming case dealing, in part, with cattle grazing on public lands. For a couple of generations, a family by the name of MacDonald has been grazing their cattle on property belonging to the American people, and they've been paying pennies for the rights. In the past half dozen years, they haven't bothered paying the pennies. Recently, they were told to pay their past-due bill or their property would be auctioned to pay the tax debt. That seems to have set them off. They're challenging the fees in court, but there's also a lot of bluster on social media about government overreach. To make the issue even more complicated, environmentalists are also interested. A group has brought a suit naming both the government and the MacDonalds. The environmental group is trying to get the federal government to do its job and step up land management to deal with erosion and water issues. They also claim to have evidence that the MacDonald clan has been killing protected animals like mountain lions and bighorn sheep."

"They kill big horn sheep?"

"They've been accused of it. Guess they compete with cattle for resources. The environmental group is arguing that public lands weren't intended to be a free giveaway to ranchers. The ranchers claim a lot of shit, including that it's their god-given right to graze their cattle wherever the fuck they want. Their lawyers are throwing whatever they think will stick into the case.

"The MacDonald clan is part of an organization that has recently changed its handle to FDN, or Freedom Defenders of Nevada. They argue that they're sovereign citizens, that states' rights supersede federal, and that the government is violating their Second Amendment rights."

"Well, shit. How do they figure it's a Second Amendment case?"

"The local sheriff had been pretty lenient but was finally moved to take action when FDN set up roadblocks armed with AKs. The sheriff took exception to his deputies being shot at, and after a standoff, arrested the motherfuckers and confiscated their weapons."

Seth clicked on an email from his boss. "Montrose sent me the rundown. I'll read it later. Where does RJ fit in?" Since everything Linc had described matched what they knew of their father's ideology, he wouldn't be surprised to find Richard Jameson in the thick of it.

"Yesterday, ATF arrested two men at a remote Mexican border crossing driving a semi loaded with bales of alfalfa. Their destination was a town in Sinaloa known to be cartel controlled."

"I'm guessing they were hauling more than hay to feed their horses." Seth put Linc on speaker and walked to the sideboard where the coffeemaker stood. He filled his mug emblazoned with a marshal's star and returned to his desk.

"You'd guess right. Pressed inside those hay bales were enough weapons and ammo to help the cartel do their business for a good long time. We suspect the equipment was stolen from the military. The men were interrogated. Of course, they said they had no idea they were hauling anything but hay bales. Said they picked up the job in Reno and that the bales were already loaded on the flatbed tractor trailer. They also claimed not to have the name of the guy who'd given them the load and the instructions on where to deliver it, other than that he went by Big Dog." Linc paused. "Description matches RJ."

Seth sipped his coffee and let that sink in. As a teenager, he'd been insanely angry when his father had abandoned their family. But next to that anger, somehow he'd held on to a tiny flicker of hope that his dad would come through in the end. That there'd be an explanation for his behavior that Seth could understand. He hadn't wanted to lose all faith in the man he'd once loved and trusted. Seth had wanted his family back, and to have everything right again so his mom wouldn't be sad, his sister and brother wouldn't look like the walking wounded, and Seth wouldn't have to make a too-soon leap into adulthood.

But he'd gotten over all that, and now nothing surprised him about Richard Jameson, who went by the handle Big Dog. Certainly not that he'd turned up the previous year as mastermind of the FD plot to kidnap Sam Creed and Ellie, undercover as his fiancée.

"RJ hasn't joined a church choir. Anything else?"

"Not about that."

"Then what?"

Linc's tone changed. "I talked to Mom last night. She wants you to invite Bella for the Fourth of July weekend."

"To the family thing? Why?" Spending more personal time with Bella? Hell yeah. Spending that time under his family's watchful eye? Not nearly as fun.

"Because it's the Fourth of July. You know Mom and Arch put on a deal. Plus, Mom's all but ready to adopt Bella."

"What the fuck's that supposed to mean?"

"Easy, bro. Bella was at my wedding. Hell, she was maid of honor at Ellie's wedding. Both of you turned up at those weddings without a plus one. Neither of you danced much, but when you did, it was with each other." Seth remembered those dances, especially the slow ones, and the guilty pleasure of having Bella in his arms. Linc rattled on, and Seth could hear the humor in his voice. "Fair warning. Mom thinks you're an adorable couple."

"We aren't a couple, and we damn well aren't *adorable.*"

"I don't know, you seem pretty adorable to me."

"Fuck you."

A movement caught his attention and he spotted Bella dropping her purse into a drawer and sitting at her desk. The thing that'd been wound tight inside him eased.

She was dressed in a conservatively tailored women's dark brown suit, and had her hair pinned at the back of her neck in a schoolmarm bun. Hard to believe he was looking at the same woman who a little over a week ago had worn a dress that had showcased her incredible breasts and was so fucking hot he'd lost his head.

She was still fucking hot, but in a more restrained way. Restrained fucking hot.

"Seth, you still there?"

"Yeah, I'm here."

"You going to ask her? Because if you don't, Mom will."

Seth scrubbed a hand over his face. No one bucked his mom. "I'll ask her. She probably won't come, though."

"Ask her. If she says no, Mom'll call her and convince her to come. Mom said you're both to bring overnight bags so you don't have to drive back from San Diego. She wanted to know if I thought you'd be sharing a room."

Of course that comment made Seth's mind jump immediately to what had happened when they had shared a room. "Jesus Christ. No, we won't be sharing a room. She's not likely to come, so it's a non-issue. Are we done here?"

"Mikayla says hi."

"Tell your wife hi back, and that I'll pay her five hundred bucks if she'll smother you in your sleep."

"She won't do it. She loves me."

"God knows why. Later, Linc."

He tossed the phone on his desk. He hadn't realized the Fourth, his mom and stepdad's annual Independence Day celebration, was coming up so fast. If his mom was scheming to throw him and Bella together, it would make attending the family gathering complicated.

He tipped back in his chair, watching Bella at her desk. She may look prim and proper in the plain suit and restrained hair, but he'd bet the bank there was something going on with her that had nothing to do with work.

After nearly a week off, she should look rested, but she didn't. Her eyes were shadowed and her shoulders slumped. He picked up his cell again.

She picked up hers, glanced at him, then rolled her eyes. "Yes?"

"How come you're tired?"

She swiveled her chair so her back was to him. "You can't call me on my personal phone when I'm at work."

"Why not?"

"Because people working in this office will know, and I don't want to be talked about."

"How would anyone know you and I are talking? Besides, I'm your boss. Talking to you is what I do."

"You're on your personal phone and I'm on my personal phone, not on our official government-issued phones. People will know. And you're looking at me."

"Your back is turned. How do you know I'm looking at you?"

"I can feel it. How do you know my back is turned if you aren't looking at me?"

Another marshal crossed near her desk and she lowered her voice. "These people are my coworkers. They know I don't take personal calls at work, plus they're trained investigators. They'll figure it out."

"Then let's go out for coffee. We need to talk."

"You already have coffee."

"How would you know that if you weren't looking at me?"

He heard her sigh over the line and smothered a grin. "I may've glanced at you when I first came in. For a brief moment."

"Like I said, we need to talk. We'll be back in half an hour."

"I don't want to talk to you."

"Bella, I need—"

A call came through on his office line, caller ID said it was from US Marshal headquarters in Virginia. "Shit. I need to take this. We'll talk later."

The call from headquarters led to a conference call, which led to Seth being swamped all day. They all were. By the time he came up for air it was almost six, and the office was quiet with only a few deputies working late. Bella wasn't one of them. She'd clocked out at five sharp.

He leaned back in his seat, considering his options. He needed to pass on the invitation from his mom. Bella had looked tired. Weren't pregnant women tired all the time? Something was going on that was upsetting her, and not knowing was making him a little crazy. He had a compulsion to make sure she was okay.

Not examining his motives too closely, he loosened his tie, grabbed his coat, and headed for the elevator.

***

In all the time he'd known Bella, Seth never been to her home. A few months ago, he'd been in the area. Curiosity had gotten the better of him and he'd looked up her address and driven by. Now he stopped his car in front of her building, putting it into reverse to parallel park between a Volkswagen and a Prius. The two-story apartment building appeared to have been built in the fifties and looked mid-century cool. Her unit was on the second floor. He went upstairs, found the door to 2D, and knocked.

The last thing he expected when the door opened was to be confronted by a shirtless man who looked like a goddamned Viking warrior. The guy was taller than Seth, at least six-five or six-six. His hair was a shaggy dark blond, with his beard a shade lighter. He had a rough, watchful look that made Seth think he'd had his share of fights. The scar through his left eyebrow and slightly crooked nose weren't trophies from beauty contests. One of those fights had been recent. His right eye was swollen nearly shut and bruises covered his face in varying shades of purple and green. He gripped the doorframe with fierce concentration, like he had to think about staying upright, and his skin gleamed with sweat.

"Who the fuck are you?" the Viking growled.

"I could ask the same of you, pal. This Bella Nikolaev's apartment?"

"Who's asking?"

"I'm asking." Seth pulled out his wallet and thrust his marshal's star and ID in front of the wide, square-jawed face. "Seth Jameson, US Marshal. Where is she?"

The hard glare from the eye that wasn't swollen shut shifted from Seth's credentials to his face. "Why do you want her?"

"Alexei, who is it?" Bella's sharp tone came from behind the guy who stood like a brick wall blocking the door.

The Viking turned, the movement revealing a tattoo of an eagle on his shoulder and a white bandage with a blossoming stain of red taped to the skin low on his back. "It's no one. He's leaving."

"I'm not leaving." The muscle in Seth's jaw twitched.

Bella put a hand to the man's hip as she peered around his back. "Seth? What are you doing here?"

"Looking for you."

"This guy bothering you, *lyubov moya*?"

"Go sit down, Alexei. You shouldn't be up."

Instead of following her order, Viking Alexei pulled her under his arm and pressed a kiss to her hair. Keeping his good eye on Seth, he murmured to Bella, his voice loud enough for Seth to hear. "Have I told you I love you?"

Seth thought his molars could be reduced to powder if he didn't stop grinding them together.

"All the time. Now go." She gave him a push. "Seth is my boss. Stop acting like a possessive idiot trying to make him jealous."

Alexei glared at Seth, then one corner of his mouth turned up. "I succeeded. He thinks he is more than boss." He sent Seth another warning look before releasing Bella. He swayed, then stepped away from the door. "I won't be far."

Seth narrowed his eyes when the big man retreated across the room to lower himself carefully into a deeply padded recliner lined with a blue and white pad, his groan as he sank into the seat audible from the door.

"He's Russian."

"What, did he drop an article? Mispronounce the letter 'i'?" She held up a hand. "Never mind. I don't want to argue with you. He's in pain. I think we all revert when we're in pain." She eyed Seth. "Or are angry."

She'd lost the prissy bun and her dark hair now tumbled in waves around her shoulders. Her colorful top and black leggings looked comfortable and casually sexy. The contrast with her office attire was intriguing.

He kept his expression neutral despite the compulsion to do whatever it took to make what was wrong with her all better. The effort to lock his feelings for her into a corner of his brain no longer worked, and he was starting to question whether he should continue trying.

Since the night at Montenegro's estate, he'd started to question why he should continue to hold himself back. He wanted to see how their relationship evolved. He wanted more.

"You want to tell me what that guy's doing here with you?"

"Alexei is my brother. He was messing with you, trying to make you jealous."

Brother? He remembered her personnel file had listed a brother. The ache in his jaw eased. He could deal with a brother. "He was doing a damn good job of it. Can I come in?"

Her eyes widened at his comment, then she backed up a step and held open the door. He stepped in and looked around. This was where Bella was most herself, and the space felt like her. The furnishings looked warm and comfortable. The walls were painted a pale gold, and cushions decorated the couch with vivid floral patterns he thought might be Russian. The scent of something cooking hung in the air.

She led him to a small kitchen, where she picked up a spoon to stir whatever was in a pot bubbling on the stove.

"What happened to your brother?"

"He was hurt."

"That's obvious." He studied her. "How?"

She didn't look up, instead lifting her shoulder in a shrug as she continued stirring.

He frowned. "Okay, we'll come back to that. First thing, he needs a doctor."

"He does, but he refuses to go. He's stubborn." She raised hooded eyes. "I'm worried about him. I think the wound is infected, but he won't let me take him to urgent care."

"Let me help."

"How?" She turned back to the bubbling pot. "You're not a doctor. I told him if he loses consciousness, I'm calling an ambulance and sending him to the hospital. So of course, he's been fighting to *stay* conscious because he's nothing if not stubborn."

"No hospital." Alexei stood in the doorway to the kitchen gripping the blue and white pad. He held it out to show a wide spot of blood. "I'm bleeding again."

Bella walked to her brother, speaking rapidly in Russian. Seth didn't have to understand the words to recognize the tone, since it was one he'd used with both his siblings—frustration borne from love and concern.

Alexei grumbled and retreated, and Bella turned back to Seth, lines etched between her eyebrows. "You should go. I don't want you to get in trouble."

"For what? Not following the rules and bringing him in if he's involved in something illegal?" Bella froze, only for a fraction of a second, but long enough to let him know he was on the right track. "Sometimes life is messy, Bella. I can deal with it. My question is, can you? You're the rule follower."

"It's safer to be a rule follower. Except when it's my brother, apparently rules don't matter so much to me." Indecision warred on her face, but then she set her chin. "I told him to lie on my bed so I can look at the wound. Will you come?"

Seth couldn't have resisted the plea in her eyes if she'd asked him to sever an artery.

"Of course."

Chapter Seven

Seth followed Bella down a short hall to the bedroom. Her bed had a wrought-iron headboard, which matched the twisted-metal pulls on the dresser drawers. A framed photo of Bella, her brother, and a smiling older couple sat on a bookshelf crammed with hardback books. Alexei lay face down across the bed, the bedcovers pulled back with the blue and white waterproof pads beneath him. The bandage on his back was completely saturated with blood. Seth peered closer at the tattoo on the man's shoulder, an insignia gripped in the talons of the eagle.

Bella knelt on the bed and began peeling off the bandage. She caught her lower lip between her teeth as she removed the bloody pad and exposed an ugly wound. Butterfly sutures held the edges together, and they, too, were soaked with blood. The skin surrounding the wound was red and inflamed.

"Does the skin feel hot to the touch?"

Bella pressed her hand to the area and nodded.

"He's got an infection. I'm making a call." Seth drew his phone from his pocket.

"No hospital. No police," Alexei growled, the words slurred.

Seth eyed the patient. "For the moment, no law enforcement not in this room will know. I'm calling a friend. Markel's a doctor and he'll check you out. If he says you're to go to the hospital, you're going."

"No hospital."

"Hospital is better than dead, man."

Seth went back to the living room to make his call. Markel picked up on the second ring. Seth described Alexei's condition, listened to the response, then relayed Bella's address.

He was pushing the phone back in his pocket when Bella came in. "Will he come? Will your friend come help my brother?"

"He'll be here in a half hour or so, depending on traffic."

"Thank you." She took a shaky breath, her eyes brimming. In all their time together, he'd never seen her close to tears. "Thank you. I've been so worried about him. He wouldn't let me get help."

"You should've called me. You know I'd help, no matter what." Something had changed in their relationship, something he couldn't define, but what he'd said was god's truth. He had her back, no matter what.

"I guess I do know." She gestured to the kitchen. "I made borscht for dinner. It's high in iron and Alexei lost a lot of blood so I thought it would be good for him. I'll save some for him for when he wakes up. Will you eat borscht?"

"Sure, sounds good." Even though she rarely betrayed her origins with her speech, every now and then a turn of phrase or the hint of an accent reminded Seth that she'd been born in Russia and English wasn't her first language. They returned to the kitchen where she ladled beet soup into bowls, opening a foil packet from the oven and placing warm rolls on plates with little pats of butter. When she went to pick up the bowls, he stepped forward. "I'll take them to the table."

They sat at the small table in a corner of the kitchen next to a windowsill lined with potted succulents. Her eyes were on his as he swallowed a spoonful of the savory soup. "Do you like it? Americans often don't like beets."

He nodded. "Yeah, I like it. Did I tell you that my step-grandmother was Russian? The first time we visited her in Chicago, she had a big pot of borscht on the stove. Like your soup, it had carrots and cabbage and potatoes with the beets. It's a favorite." He thought she was relaxing for the first time since he'd come in the apartment.

"That's good." She glanced up at him as she ate her own soup. "You're trying to distract me from worrying about my brother."

He shrugged. "Maybe."

"You don't have to. But I appreciate you'd think of it." After another spoonful of soup, she asked, "How'd you get a Russian step-grandmother?"

He may have wanted to distract Bella, but he found he also wanted her to know something about him. "You met my stepdad, Archer Bollinger, at the weddings."

She nodded. "He's very handsome."

"Mom thinks so. But don't tell him or we'll never hear the end of it. Anyway, he married Mom when I was a teenager. His mom's family immigrated from Russia after World War I, fleeing the revolution and civil war. They'd lost family members to the Bolsheviks and decided to get out."

Bella nodded. "The Bolsheviks were brutal. Conditions only got worse when Stalin came to power." She stirred the soup in her bowl slowly and he wondered where her thoughts had gone.

"What happened to your family in Russia?" Bella had been adopted by an American couple, that much had been in her personnel file. He wanted to know more.

She shrugged. "Our parents were dissidents. They opposed the Soviet government during the eighties. Before they had children, they were involved in protests and had been arrested. My father several times."

Seth smeared butter on a roll while he considered her response. She'd never spoken of her family. She'd always kept that part of her life separate. Those lines were erased when he'd knocked on her apartment door. He was never going back to the way they were before. "What about after they had children?" She shrugged and he pushed harder. "Something must've happened for you to end up adopted by an American couple."

"Yes. Something happened. My dad continued his political work. He would spend months in jail, he would suffer through brutal treatment, then be released, but always with the warning that things could be worse for him if he continued his unlawful behavior. During this time there was a lot of disruption and chaos in Russia. Then he disappeared. My mother thought he would be returned to us after the Soviet Union collapsed in ninety-one, but we never saw him again."

"Do you know what happened to him?"

"All we knew was that he'd been arrested. My mother got word that he'd been sent to a prison in the Ural Mountains, and she decided to try to find him. She took Alexei and me to our grandmother's. Mama planned to be gone only a few weeks, but she never returned. I've done some digging, and I'm certain that they were both killed. My father for his political views, my mother because she wouldn't accept the government's official explanation of his disappearance."

"Jesus. You and Alexei were with your grandmother. She cared for you?"

Bella spooned up soup, swallowing before answering. "If you can call it that. She was poor, was fond of cheap vodka. Mostly, she left us to fend for ourselves. Alexei was only three and I tried to take care of him. She put us in the orphanage when she decided we'd become too much of a burden."

Which would have made Bella only six or seven herself when she was caring for her younger brother. Seth shook his head. While he'd been playing baseball and trying to master algebra, she'd been fighting for her and her brother's survival. Seth had dozens of questions about her past, but was stopped by a rapping on the front door. He rose to his feet. "Let me get it."

He opened the door to a tall Black man, a classic doctor's bag in his hand. His teeth flashed in a wide grin as Seth clapped him on the shoulder and ushered him inside.

"Glad you could make it. I owe you."

"Friends don't owe friends. Especially since you've saved my ass more than once."

Bella joined Seth and he did the introductions. "Bella, this is Doctor Markel Dupont. We did our undergrad together at UCSD and were roommates there for three years. He's the smartest man I know."

Markel turned to Bella. "Don't let this guy fool you. He's the only person I know who reads history books for fun."

"Make that two people. I like reading history too." Bella extended her hand. "Nice to meet you, Dr. Dupont. I'm Bella Nikolaev, I'm also a marshal. Thank you for coming."

"Nice to meet a friend of Seth's, and it's Markel. No thanks necessary. Where can I wash before seeing the patient?"

After Markel had scrubbed his hands, Bella led the way to the bedroom where Alexei had shifted to lie on his side. Bella turned on the overhead light, then Markel did what Markel did best. He soothed his patient and after donning gloves, he got to work.

Bella answered questions and tried to calm Alexei when he growled his displeasure. After several minutes, Markel dug into his bag. "His face will heal well enough, and the bruising should fade in the next week. You did a good job with the butterfly sutures on that stab wound, though the scar won't be pretty. He'd have been better off with a drain, but it's too late for that. I'll replace the butterflies. We're lucky it wasn't any deeper. First, though, he gets a tetanus shot, then a jab of the good juice in his butt, because he's got a nasty infection going."

"Hell no." Alexei's eyes looked glassy, but his vision was apparently good enough to see the syringe Markel was prepping.

Bella said something sharp in Russian, which made Alexei glower at her. "I'm not a baby."

"Show us a butt cheek, my man. After the antibiotics, you'll get the double good juice."

"You said this was the good juice."

"It is, but the *double* good juice is the pain meds. You'll be feeling better and will be out like a light before you know it." After quickly and efficiently administering the injections, Markel took a marker and drew a line around the redness bordering the wound, delineating the extent of the infection.

Ten minutes later, after Bella had coaxed her brother into a more comfortable position on the bed, she walked out with Seth and Markel to the front room.

Bella gripped her hands together, strain evident in the shadows under her eyes. "How bad is my brother? Please tell me the truth."

Seth dropped an arm across her shoulders. He knew how worried she was when she leaned into him.

"The infection is bad, and if you hadn't called me today, he could have gotten much worse and gone into septic shock. He should've been taken to the hospital right away." Seth caught the miserably guilty look on Bella's face.

"The marshal here explained that wasn't your call." Markel shrugged. "If the meds work like I think they should, Alexei should be showing signs of improvement soon, for sure within a day. If they don't and he gets any worse, don't mess around. Call an ambulance and get his ass to the hospital. I'll come back tomorrow evening, and same deal. If the redness has spread past the line I marked or he's not feeling significantly better, he's going to the hospital. That's nonnegotiable. I don't let my patients die from stubbornness." Bella nodded and Seth tightened his hold.

Markel handed her a bottle of pills and a slip of paper. "Here are enough pills to get Alexei through to tomorrow when you can get this script filled. Directions are on the bottle. He can't skip doses."

“Thank you. My brother owes you his life.” She took a deep breath, then released it slowly and Seth felt the tension in her shoulders ease. “I have borscht and dinner rolls. Would you like some dinner, Markel?”

“I’ll have to take a raincheck on that, sweetheart. I’ve got a date with my fiancée tonight.” Markel picked up his bag. He gave Bella a hug because he was that kind of guy, and Seth walked him outside to his car.

“I like your girl, Seth. About time you got serious.”

He was about to deny that he was serious about Bella, but he could still feel her seeking contact with his body as she braced for news about Alexei. “Bella and I are something, but I’m not sure what. At the moment it’s undefined.”

“Yeah? Don’t forget I know you. I saw how you are with her, and you’ve got it bad. I’d say you both do.”

Seth watched his friend drive off in the Porsche he’d put a down payment on with his first paycheck as a doctor, and then climbed the stairs back to Bella’s apartment, thinking about what Markel said. He was right, Seth did have it bad.

He shut the door and Bella came from the hallway. “Alexei okay?”

“He seems to be sleeping easier. The ibuprofen I’d been giving him didn’t ease the pain enough for him to rest. What Markel gave him is much better.”

He’d never thought of Bella as fragile before, but tonight she looked about done in. “Sit. I’ll clean up from dinner.”

She ignored him and walked into the kitchen. “I have to put the soup in a container and wash the dishes.”

She pulled a glass storage bowl from a cupboard and set it on the counter. When she reached for the pot on the stove, he took her hands, holding on when she would have tugged them away.

“You have wine?”

She nodded slowly. “In the refrigerator.”

He got the wine, opened a cabinet, and found a wineglass. He poured it half full and handed it to her.

“Go sit down, drink the wine, relax. I’ll take care of the cleanup.” He tried to make it sound less like an order and more like a request.

Their gazes locked and awareness of the mind-blowing, life-changing sex they'd shared was there between them like something he could touch. It took every ounce of restraint he possessed not to pull her closer and take her mouth with his.

They'd been together only one time, and all he could think was that it wasn't enough. They could be together every night for a lifetime and it wouldn't be enough.

Her cheeks flushed and he knew he wasn't the only one remembering how it had been. What had happened between them had shifted the dynamics of their relationship, and he didn't think either of them was sure where they stood.

But he didn't say anything. "I'll take care of the soup," he repeated.

She nodded slowly. "I'm racking up debts to you."

"You don't owe me anything. Didn't you hear Markel? Friends don't owe friends."

"You called Markel. Doing that might've saved my brother's life. I'm not exactly sure that we're friends, but I owe you."

"That's bullshit. I've got your back, Bella. Always."

Expression solemn, she turned away to walk down the hall. A moment later, he heard a door close.

He rolled up his sleeves and got to work. Since Bella was an organized soul, finding where things were in her kitchen was relatively easy. He stored the soup and bread. Since the 1950s apartment didn't come equipped with a dishwasher, he squirted dish soap in the sink and washed the dishes, leaving them to air dry on a bamboo rack.

He returned to the front room to find Bella curled on the couch, staring out the window into the darkness beyond, her mostly empty wineglass on the coffee table. The sun had set and the sky held a purplish haze.

Seth turned on a lamp and sat beside her. "You flew back to LA last Tuesday, but Alexei's injury isn't that old. What brought you back?"

She hesitated, rubbing her thumb back and forth over the material of her leggings. When she stopped worrying the fabric, she seemed to come to a decision. "Do you want the long story or the short story?"

"I want the full story."

“I thought you’d say that.” She stretched, then settled back into the couch. “There was a boy at the orphanage in Russia, his name was Alexander. We called him Sasha. He was older than me and had been at the orphanage a long time. We were friends of a sort, and he helped me some with Alexei.”

“What was going on with Alexei?”

She continued to look out the window, but he thought she must’ve been seeing images from her childhood. “He was so young, and he had trouble settling into life in the orphanage. He missed our mother. He would be so fierce during the day, trying to be strong, but then at night, he’d be sad. He was a little boy. He’d cry for our mother and wouldn’t sleep. I was afraid he’d disappear, that we’d be separated, so I always tried to stay close to him.”

Well shit. Hard to imagine Bella’s experience as a child, fighting to keep her brother close so he wouldn’t disappear like the other people who’d loved her. A telling clue as to part of the reason she wouldn’t acknowledge a relationship between them. He wondered if deep down she feared that at some point he’d also disappear. “That was a lot of responsibility for a little girl. Go on.”

“The younger boys and girls slept on the same floor, but in separate rooms. At night I could hear Alexei crying from across the hall. I’d sneak into the boys’ room and lie with him on his cot until he fell asleep, then go back to my bed.

“Sometimes Sasha would bring Alexei to me. Even if I fell asleep, I’d wake up early or Sasha would wake me up. We always managed to be in our own rooms before the morning bell sounded. One time I overslept and was discovered in the boys’ room.”

“Were you punished?” Even though his father had been difficult, and at times harsh, until the day he had abandoned his family, Seth’s childhood had been secure.

Thinking of Bella as a scared child in an orphanage made him wish he could go back in time and somehow fix things for her. He put an arm along the back of the sofa, threading her hair between his fingers.

She shifted away from him but didn’t pull her hair free. “No. I was sure we would be, but the matron in charge of our floor decided to arrange a room for siblings. Other brothers and sisters got to move in there too. Alexei and I put our cots next to each other. The matron was a kind woman and truly cared for the children.”

"So things were better?" He picked up another lock of hair, twirling it around his finger.

"Somewhat. There never seemed to be enough to eat, and I don't think I ever felt warm enough, but we survived. I kept Alexei with me all the time so he'd be safe, and Sasha helped protect us from older boys who bullied the younger children. He found my book of poetry my father had given me that one of the mean boys had stolen."

"That's a miserable way to grow up." Her fingers knotted together, and Seth reached for her hand. He brought it to his lap, brushing a thumb across her palm.

"Like I said, we survived. Eventually, we were adopted together and brought to the States to live in Boston. My American parents are the kindest, most loving people in the world. Alexei and I are fortunate they chose us." She sighed. "Anyway, it was Sasha who called me last week."

"He's here in the US?"

She nodded. "He was adopted by a family in Iowa. They're farmers and I think they wanted boys who could work on their farm." She shrugged, her gaze on their joined hands. "Even so, it had to be better than staying at the orphanage. They took him and another boy. Sasha found me on social media a few months ago, and contacted me when we were in San Francisco."

"Why did he contact you?"

"He said Alexei was in trouble and I needed to come back to LA."

Seth wasn't sure if she was aware that as she talked, she'd moved closer, their shoulders again touching.

"He'd been in contact with Alexei?"

"Yes. Sasha wanted to meet with me. He said it was important."

"That doesn't explain the three days off." Seth couldn't help being suspicious that Sasha's interest might be more than friendship.

"I took the days off because I was worried about Alexei and I wanted time to figure out what was going on. We always check in with each other, but I hadn't heard anything for several days. Then when you and I were in the car Tuesday, I got a text, which made me think something was wrong. I'd texted back and tried to call him throughout the day, but he didn't respond. Then Sasha texted me that afternoon. He said he was concerned about Alexei, but wouldn't tell me anything over the phone."

She realized how close they were sitting and shifted away, pulling her hand free and regarding him with a serious expression, lines between her brows deepening as she frowned. "I want to tell you something as a mostly friend, not as my boss."

He drummed his fingers on the cushion behind her head. "Despite what I said earlier, you know I have to do something if what you tell me is actionable. So do you, Bella."

"I know. That's why this has been so hard. I'm caught in the middle of things I have no control over." She stared out the window, and he figured she was thinking through the angles. "Okay, let me say it this way. I met with someone who might have connections to the *bratva*."

"Russian mafia. Shit."

"Shit is right. This person says the *bratva* is pressuring Alexei to join." Which, if Seth was reading it right, meant that Sasha was in with the *bratva* and had information he'd passed on to Bella.

Her gaze turned grim, reminding him that while she may have had the wind knocked out of her, Bella would come back strong. "Later I learned the *bratva* had hurt Alexei and will try again. They told him he could die, or he could join. They said they'd kill him if he went to the authorities."

"He was an Army Ranger?"

"You saw his tattoo."

"Yeah. Was he?"

"He was. He got out of the army about three years ago and joined the Los Angeles Police Department. I've had no reason to question what he was doing." She sighed.

"It's odd that the *bratva* would want him if he'd been a Ranger. They must know it's hard to break the loyalty of that type of soldier."

She shrugged. "They count on Russian ex-pats having greater loyalty to Mother Russia and they can be manipulative and brutal. I was approached when I was going through Marshal training at Glynco." She glanced at Seth. "That's in my file. I reported it immediately. One thing Alexei and I have going for us is that we don't have family in Russia who could be threatened if we don't cooperate. Our grandmother died years ago, and there's no one else."

She breathed deep, held, then breathed out for a long count. He'd noticed her doing that before and wondered if she was practicing a relaxation technique.

"Alexei called me Friday night. He said he was hurt and was in an alley in West Hollywood. Did you know there's a Russian community in West Hollywood?" At Seth's nod, she continued. "He wouldn't let me call the police. I found him and got him into my car. His face was battered and he was bleeding so badly." She closed her eyes for a long moment, then reopened them. "He couldn't even hold his phone, could barely talk. He told me to make a call for him."

"Who'd you talk to?"

"I don't know. Alexei said to tell the man who answered that the plan was working but that he'd be out of commission for a few days. Then he told me to forget the number."

"But you didn't."

She sat up and pulled open a drawer in the coffee table and retrieved a pen and a small pad of paper. She wrote a phone number and held it out. "I'm trusting you, Seth."

"You know you can."

Alexei called from the bedroom and Bella leaned forward with her hands on her knees.

Seth tucked the paper in his pocket. "Sit, Bella. I'll see what he needs."

He understood it as a testament to how tired she was that she collapsed back against the cushion and let him take care of her brother.

Seth helped Alexei to the bathroom, waited to make sure he got back in bed without walking into a wall, then returned to find Bella with her feet tucked under her and her eyes closed. He tugged a blanket from the back of the couch and draped it around her.

For the next two hours, he sat at the little table in the kitchen and, using his phone, did some digging. After calling in a few favors and making a half dozen calls, he had answers to his questions. He returned to the couch, unlaced his shoes, and kicked them off.

With his feet on the coffee table, he leaned back and slung his arm around Bella, nudging her until she lay with her head against his chest.

He set the alarm on his phone and turned off the lamp.

He lay for a long time with Bella tucked against him, staring into the dark.

Chapter Eight

Bella stretched, groaning from the crick in her neck. The arm draped around her tightened, bringing her more snugly into the warm body she was cuddled against. Her eyes popped open and she pushed up.

"Hey there. Slow it down. It's too early." The words were murmured in a sleepy, sexy voice.

"Seth, what are you doing here?" She nudged him in the ribs.

"Trying to sleep." He grabbed her hand and brought it to his lips. The whiskers on his chin rasped against her fingers.

They were lying lengthwise on the couch, which had to have been uncomfortably short for him. She wasn't sure how she'd ended up plastered against him, but she felt like they fit together perfectly. Her arm rested on his chest, her head lay on his shoulder, and one leg nestled intimately between his. The throw barely covered them but she felt plenty warm.

She rubbed her fingers against his bristly beard and he took her hand to bite lightly at her wrist. "You smell good." He licked where he'd used his teeth. "Taste good too."

The temptation to rub against the growing hardness in his pants had her wishing they were alone in the apartment. "We can't do this."

"We can. We've proven that."

He tipped up her chin and then he kissed her, a long, slow, sumptuous kiss that spread through her like light. She hated that one meeting of the lips was all it took to crumble her resistance. Even when she knew he would pull away like he had after they'd made love—no, *had sex*—like every other person she'd ever loved besides her brother, she couldn't prevent herself from responding to him.

He shifted her so she lay fully on top of him. Supporting herself against his chest, she stared into his depthless gray eyes before lowering her lids to hide the vulnerability she feared he might pick up on. Revealing too much was risky. If he thought what was between them was simple sexual attraction, she could deal with it. But if he guessed what was in her heart and then discarded her, she'd shatter into a million pieces. She knew that kind of hurt, and didn't think she'd survive it coming from Seth.

He wrapped his arms around her and pulled her more intimately against him. With a groan, she kissed him, her tongue tangling with his, then bit lightly at his bottom lip, all while moving back and forth slowly over his rigid erection. He slid a hand under the waistband of her yoga pants, cupping her rear and pulling her more tightly against him.

With emotions threatening to push her into an abyss she didn't know if she'd ever be able to climb out of, she broke the kiss and rested her forehead against his chest. "Wait,. Please wait. I can't think."

Her body rose and fell with his as he breathed. "I like it when neither of us think, but okay." His hands rested on her hips.

She jerked up, horror-struck. "My god, I didn't wake up for Alexei. He needs his medicine."

He tightened his grip before she could fly off the couch. "He's fine. I got up a couple hours ago and gave him the pills."

"Is he better? I need to check on him."

His chest expanded beneath her, this time with a sigh. "Go ahead and check on him. You'll feel better when you do."

The pale morning light from the window illuminated his short hair standing on end. She felt the inevitable pull on her heartstrings. Placing her hands on either side of his face, she pressed her lips to his. "You're a good man, Seth Jameson." She rose from the couch and went to check on her brother.

***

Bella tipped back her head, hot water sluicing over her as she rinsed shampoo from her hair. Alexei was sleeping more comfortably. She'd peeked and saw the redness within the border Markel had drawn had receded. Only a tiny bit, but that slight improvement made her almost giddy with relief.

Given the circumstances, she'd slept well, and after waking in Seth's arms, she knew why. Since childhood, she'd always slept lightly, forever alert for any sign of danger. With Seth she felt safe and protected.

He'd done what she hadn't been able to do: gotten medical treatment for Alexei. She and Alexei were as close as siblings could be; their traumatic background created a tight emotional bond. Even when she knew what was best for him, she hadn't been able to override his wishes when he'd refused to be taken to the hospital.

Seth's arrival had come at a critical moment, and he'd gotten Alexei treatment, which probably saved her brother's life. As much as she loved her brother, she hadn't been able to do that for him.

On top of loving Seth and keeping those feelings closely guarded, now she was indebted to him in the most profound way. The only other person in the world she loved was Alexei.

She closed her eyes against a wave of emotion. Loving Seth wasn't something she could act on or expect him to reciprocate. Physically, there was hard evidence—she winced at the pun —he desired her. As her boss, he assumed responsibility for her. Adding in they'd had unprotected sex, his sense of duty would grow exponentially. He said he would always be there for her, but that wasn't the same as having a real relationship.

Not that she wanted one. She closed her eyes, frustrated with her internal conflict. When, after stupendous, mind-blowing sex, Seth had pulled back, she'd been hurt. Deeply. What she should've felt was relief.

She worked conditioner through her hair as she examined her rationale. Certain facts were immutable. Seth being her supervisor was a huge reason they couldn't be together. The other? The reason she should have been thanking him for saving her from revealing her feelings and taking a deep dive into an impossible relationship? She was living proof love was transitory and it was better to protect herself than being crushed under the weight of a kind of disappointment no person should experience.

At some point, Seth would move on. If she wanted to remain safe, it was up to her to make that happen. Never having a serious boyfriend had been intentional. She was careful never to be vulnerable and in a position to be easily discarded. Her parents' political activities had taken precedence over the safety of their children. Her grandmother had turned Bella and Alexei over to an orphanage. What grandparent did that to children who'd lost their parents? Institutionalized, abandoned, and bereft, Bella had lived by her wits to keep her and her brother safe and protected. She'd had no choice since the people she'd counted on to love and keep her safe had let her down.

There'd be no reliving that anguish.

Yet, something critical overshadowed everything about her feelings for Seth. The chance she had conceived. The possibility spun in her mind like a pinwheel, staggering in its implications. The only thing she could be certain of was no child of hers would ever feel unwanted. Her child would never for a moment feel unloved or unlovable.

If she hadn't conceived, any lingering strings attaching her to Seth would dissolve as he moved on with his life, and she hers. For her mental health, never mind her emotional one, it'd be a good idea to ask for a transfer.

Leaving the team and the friends she'd made would be like cutting off a limb, but continuing to work beside the man she loved who didn't love her back would slowly destroy her. Bella understood self-preservation better than most. No way was she going to stay in a situation where she'd wind up more battered and bruised than she felt already.

Going it alone would take its toll since it was possible she was pregnant. While she knew Seth would be responsible—he couldn't help but be responsible—he'd pay child support, start a college fund, send birthday cards and gifts, she had no idea what to expect from him otherwise. She massaged her scalp as she considered what he'd do.

Through work she'd come across plenty of men who'd had no emotional connection to their children. She couldn't see Seth being that guy. She had a feeling that if she and Seth had a baby together, he'd be involved, and they'd have contact through their child for the rest of their lives. She'd have to deal with her feelings for him, but geez, all that contact would hurt.

After a final rinse of conditioner, she turned off the taps and squeezed the excess water from her hair, all the while giving herself a mental finger shaking. She was getting ahead of herself and borrowing trouble.

Wrapped in a towel, she brushed out her tangles, moisturized, then finally gave in to temptation and pulled open the bottom drawer, rummaging behind tampons and pads to the back where she'd stashed a box after a run to the drugstore.

She studied the printed information like it held nuclear launch codes. The manufacturer claimed the test was *ninety-nine percent accurate* and could give her results *six days sooner*. Sooner than what, she had no idea, but she was late for her period by only a few days, which wasn't all that unusual for her. She chewed her bottom lip as she opened the box and studied what looked like a digital thermometer. A slip of paper said that for best results, do the test (pee on a stick) first thing in the morning when urine was most concentrated. She returned the inserts to the box and shoved it back in the drawer. Too late to get the first pee of the day, so she'd wait. Her period could start any time during the day, and that would be that.

She knew she was rationalizing her delay. The reality was she didn't want to take the test because she'd need time to mentally process the results. Doing that this morning wasn't going to happen.

Her brother needed her care, and she had work today. But the big no, *I'm not going to deal with this now*? The potential baby daddy was in the other room.

She wasn't ready to talk to him if the results came back positive, and he was too perceptive not to know something *more* was going on with her.

Delaying the pregnancy test seemed the best plan for the time being.

Calling herself a coward, she dried her hair, put it in a bun for work, and got dressed. She checked on her brother. He still slept, so she left the bedroom door ajar and walked down the hall.

She'd dressed in her usual demure and professional work attire, which Seth had goaded her about on more than one occasion.

He turned from where he'd been standing in front of an open cupboard. His gaze traveled over her and heat simmered in that all-encompassing look. She looked down to make sure she hadn't accidentally left her blouse unbuttoned to reveal the lacy edge of her bra.

Nothing was amiss. "What?"

His grin shot an arrow of heat to her belly. "After seeing Anna Novak in that hot blue dress, knowing what you're hiding under those straitlaced clothes is downright sexy."

"This outfit is *not* sexy. It exceeds the professional dress standards laid out by the Marshals Service."

His grin widened. How had she ever thought of him as the ice man? "I'm the one looking, and I say it's sexy because you're purposely trying not to be sexy. The flip-flops make the outfit."

"You make no sense. And I change into heels before I leave the apartment."

"Heels are definitely sexy."

"You're such a guy." She smothered a smile and gestured to the open cabinet. "What are you looking for?"

"You don't own a coffeemaker."

"True." She reached past him into the cupboard to pluck a carton from among the canisters of tea. "This is the best I can do." She tore open the box and handed him a packet from inside, then lifted the lid on a jar on the counter to get a teabag.

Seth took the carton from her and frowned as he read the label. "Freeze-dried coffee? Does anyone drink this anymore?" He'd taken off the button-down shirt he'd slept in and wore a white t-shirt untucked. With his hair sticking up and his morning beard shadowing his jaw, he looked adorably rumpled.

"It's either that or find the closest coffee shop. Alexei likes one that's down the street about five blocks."

Seth continued scrutinizing the label on the packet. "This contains caffeine. It'll do."

Bella busied herself filling the kettle and putting it over the flame, then opening a bag of bagels. She plunked two bagels on a cutting board and handed Seth a serrated knife. "Slice and toast."

"What's going on here?" Alexei's rough voice came from the doorway and had her turning to study her brother.

Despite the surly tone, which wasn't unusual for him any time before nine a.m., he looked clear-eyed. Relief flooded through her. He no longer looked deathly pale beneath the bruises that still colored his face, and he wasn't holding on to the doorframe for support. He'd pulled on an old college t-shirt she kept in her dresser. Paired with plaid boxer shorts, he didn't quite hit his normal level of intimidating, though the narrowed gaze he aimed at Seth showed he was trying.

Seth leaned back against the counter, long legs in front of him and arms crossed over his chest.

"Breakfast is going on here. How are you feeling?" she asked Alexei.

"Like I might not die." He nodded toward Seth. "What's he doing here?"

"Seth stayed last night." Her raised brow dared her brother to make an issue of the situation. "Good thing he came. It's because of him Doctor Dupont came by. You could have died."

The teakettle whistled and Seth turned to pour steaming water into mugs. Alexei scowled, but jerked his head toward Seth. "Okay. Thanks, dude."

Seth turned back to face him, gaze direct. "Your sister and I have a thing going. That a problem for you?"

"We do *not* have a thing going."

The hot look Seth shot her had her reassessing the validity of that statement. "You seeing anyone else?"

"No, not that it matters."

"Good. We'll see where this goes."

"Oh, we will, will we?" A spike of anger had her stalking toward him. "First off, I don't date arrogant men, and second, we don't know if I'm pregnant, so you're getting ahead of yourself."

"This isn't about you being pregnant."

"Pregnant? You got my sister pregnant?"

"I am *not* pregnant," Bella said between her teeth. At least she didn't think she was. How had this conversation gotten so off track? "I choose who I date, Seth Jameson, and I don't follow orders in my personal life."

With the bagels in the toaster oven, Seth returned to his spot leaning against the counter, looking relaxed and like nothing was bothering him while Alexei glowered, fists clenched like he was ready to take a swing.

"Alexei, *back off,*" she hissed.

Seth sipped from his mug, not even grimacing as he drank the instant coffee. He ignored her brother and addressed Bella. "Like I said, this isn't about you being pregnant."

She didn't know why his mild tone irritated her so much and made her want to kick him in the shin.

She opened her mouth to respond when Alexei cut in. "You got my sister pregnant. You marry her."

"Agreed."

"What?" She gaped at them, gaze flying from one to the other. "Are you idiots? Newsflash, we're not in the Dark Ages. *If* I'm pregnant, I can and will take care of myself and my baby. I don't need to get married, and I don't need you buffoons interfering."

"Guess we'll figure that out when we know." She thought Seth was being diplomatic until he added, "But here's another newsflash. *If* you're pregnant, I take care of you, and I take care of our child. That's nonnegotiable."

Alexei nodded like it was the most reasonable thing in the world.

"You want this freeze-dried shit that identifies itself as coffee?" Seth held up a packet for Alexei.

"If that's all there is," he grunted. "I'll have a bagel, since you're toasting them."

"What, now you're pals? How about we have coffee and a bagel and pretend we're modern men who respect women? I can't keep up." She wished her hair wasn't in a bun, because then she could tear it out by the roots. She needed something to shock her system back to reality, because somehow this crazy train she'd been riding for the last week had come off the rails.

"I respect women," Alexei muttered. "But married is better for you and the child if the man is good."

Seth was wise to keep his mouth shut.

Shaking her head, she got plates and set them on the table while Alexei leaned heavily against the doorjamb and Seth put another bagel in the toaster oven.

The smell of toasting bread permeated the air to combine with the aroma of fresh peaches as she finished slicing them into a bowl. Alexei laid his hand on her shoulder, then dipped his head to drop a kiss to her temple. He murmured in Russian, and she nodded.

Of course she'd forgive him. It was too much work to stay angry. The likelihood she was pregnant after that one time was low, so, she decided, she didn't have anything to worry about.

Probably.

Making breakfast and enjoying her brother's recovery nudged her toward an unexpected feeling of contentment.

Seth thought he was right about every damn thing and assumed too much; her brother was bossy and tended to be high-handed. But for the moment, Alexei was on the mend and she was oddly happy to be preparing breakfast with the two most important men in her life.

She reached out and plucked up the hem of Alexei's shirt. "I want to see how it looks." She knew she was looking for reassurance that he was recovering, but she liked tangible evidence. Occupational hazard.

The white bandage was unstained. The redness around the bandage continued to look healthier than it had the night before. "It looks good, Alexei."

"I'm getting better, *sestra*." He turned to lay an arm across her shoulders in a half hug.

"Sister, right?" Seth asked. "I've been learning Russian."

"*Da*," Alexei replied with a grin as he released Bella.

"You are not learning Russian." Bella stared at Seth.

"I am. Conversational, with slang and swear words. There's an app for it." Seth hitched a shoulder. "I practice in the car when I'm driving to work. This way when you swear at me in Russian, I'll be able to understand what you're saying."

Bella felt her heart give a slow, lazy roll in her chest. He couldn't keep doing that. Adding more little things to make her love grow even brighter, testing the fortifications she'd erected to keep those feelings safely walled off.

Chapter Nine

Bella set the peaches on the small table, then brought over the cream cheese and plum jam. Seth poured hot water into a coffee mug for Alexei, and they sat at the table nearly knee to knee.

Licking plum jam from his thumb, Seth leaned back in his seat, stretching his legs to the side of the table. He nodded at Alexei. "You're working with the FBI."

Alexei sipped his coffee, then bit into his bagel, his expression carefully neutral as he chewed.

Bella paused, her loaded knife hovering over her bagel. "How do you know this?" If Seth said Alexei worked with the FBI, then Alexei worked with the FBI.

"I suspected, then did some digging. I have a couple contacts and gave them a call. Word is the *bratva* has been laundering money through nightclubs in West Hollywood, and using them as fronts for prostitution rings. The FBI has created a task force with a special LAPD unit. They're intent on crippling the *bratva*. Part of the plan is to infiltrate the organization." He looked at Alexei as he said the last part.

"But Alexei was beat up because he refused to join, he—"

Realization dawned and Bella turned to her brother. "You're playing hard to get."

He shrugged, slouching in his chair and rubbing a hand over his face, an indication that his energy was beginning to flag. "Let's hear what the marshal says. He seems to have all the answers."

"I have some. My guess is you allowed yourself to be set up. You were attacked by a seemingly random individual who demanded money to make you think you were being mugged. Am I right?"

At Alexei's nod, he continued. "Things got ugly and you got knifed. But it's a shallow wound. Your bad luck is it got infected. A member of the *bratva* would've rushed to your aid to help fight off the aggressor. He'd act like he's saved your life. Now you're indebted to them."

Alexei nodded again.

"Did you know the person who knifed you?"

Alexei shook his head at Bella's question. "The marshal is right. It was probably someone with the *bratva*. The guy who came to my rescue was for sure."

"It's a classic manipulation. Now you'll let them convince you. Once they think you're a convert, you'll be the inside guy keeping tabs on the *bratva* for the LAPD."

"Basically, yes."

Bella brought the kettle to the table, along with the instant coffee packets. "Sounds dangerous." Worry made her throat tight.

Alexei shook his head at the offer of more coffee. "What I'm doing is dangerous? What about what you do? You should be an accountant or a dentist. Not working at an agency where you could be hurt."

"You're the one who was knifed, who called me when he was bleeding and couldn't risk going to the hospital."

Her brother ran a hand down her arm. "Don't be mad at me. I couldn't tell you. If this operation is successful, we could save many women who are being exploited by the *bratva*." Alexei rose to take his plate and mug to the sink. "I'm applying to the FBI. This task force gives weight to my application. Go to work, Bella. I'll be fine today. I'm going back to bed."

Bella returned to the table when Alexei left the kitchen. The understanding in Seth's expression had her swallowing a lump in her throat.

"He's smart, Bella. He'll be careful."

"He's part of me. He's my only blood relative."

"Some of the people I care the most about are marshals, so I get it." The way he said it made Bella think that maybe he was including her in that group. "Most of the time it's not dangerous. But sometimes it is."

She pushed back her plate and picked up her mug. "Why'd you come here last night? You never said."

His gaze locked on hers, and her pulse quickened. At one time, she'd thought his impenetrable expression meant he didn't feel emotions, but now she knew that was his way of hiding them. She was beginning to suspect he kept a mountain of feelings strapped down tight, and that she was one of the few people he let see them.

"Several things. Most important? I was worried about you."

She had to tell herself worried wasn't the same as caring, and that as her boss, he'd see worrying about her as part of his job.

"Now you know why I came home early and took the days off, so you don't have to be concerned about me. I'm fine, and I think Alexei will be, thanks to you."

"You should've told me what was going on." His head tilt said *Am I clear?* "Another reason I came by was to deliver an invitation from my mom. She wants you to come to the Fourth of July thing in San Diego."

Bella set down her bagel. "How would you define a 'thing'?"

"The usual for Fourth of July. Arch will barbecue a mountain of burgers. Mom will make her potato salad, which by itself is worth going for. There'll be watermelon and corn on the cob. Linc, Ellie, and their spouses will be there, along with friends and family, and whoever else Mom invites.

"Arch organizes ping-pong tournaments and pool games for the kids. From the backyard, their house has a great view of the valley, so after dark we sit on the deck and watch the city fireworks show. It's a good time."

"That sounds more like a family thing. It's nice of her to invite me, but I don't think so."

"She wants you to be there, and, if it helps persuade you, I want you to be there."

Bella sipped her tea. "That's kind of you, and I'm sorry if this puts you in an awkward position. Send her my regrets and you'll be off the hook."

Seth was shaking his head. "You don't know Margaret Bollinger. My mom will hound you until you say yes. She's got a thing about having all her ducks together, and she considers you one of her ducks. Since the fireworks won't start until after dark, she told me you're to pack a bag and stay the night." He chewed the last of his bagel. "Ask Alexei if he wants to come. He'd be welcome. Mom would love to have him."

"How can that be? She doesn't know him. She doesn't really know me. We met at the weddings, and she was welcoming and kind. I thought you and your siblings are lucky to have her and your stepdad, but she and I had only a few conversations."

"Apparently, it was enough for her to decide you'd do for her eldest son."

She fumbled her fork, dropping it with a clatter against the bowl of peaches. "What do you mean, 'I'd *do*'?"

He held her gaze. "According to Linc, Mom noticed you and I went to the weddings with no plus one, and we only danced only with each other."

Panic clutched at her throat. Had she somehow given away her feelings? She'd need to be much more careful. "That's not true." She tried not to let anxiety seep into her tone.

"What part?"

"The dancing part. I danced with other people."

His gaze narrowed. "Who else did you dance with?"

"That little boy wearing the cute blue tuxedo and bow tie asked me. I think he's your cousin's son."

"That would be Christian. He's nine. He doesn't count."

"He's a charmer, but okay. Then there was that other cousin of yours at Ellie and Sam's wedding. He has gorgeous green eyes and he's close to my age."

"Gorgeous green eyes? Who the hell has—are you talking about Micah? Did he hit on you? He's only what, twenty-two or twenty-three? I didn't see him dancing with you or I'd have told him to get lost."

"Why would you do that? He was sweet, and obviously looks up to you. He's interested in joining the Marshals Service. We talked about that, and he plans to give you a call for advice."

"He's not sweet. The kid was a terror growing up." She smothered a smile when he scowled. "Whatever. You're officially invited."

That wiped the smile off her face, because while she was friends with Seth's siblings, and enjoyed spending time socially with them and their spouses, it sounded too much like she and Seth would again be thrown together as they'd been at the weddings. Those events had given her a painful glimpse into a life she could never have. No way would she torture herself more at a family barbecue.

She looked at the clock on the wall. "Oh, wow. Look at the time. We need to get to work. You'll want to get home to shave and change clothes."

"Good evasion, Deputy Nikolaev, but Mom will pin you down." His expression shifted. "I want you to come too, so think about it."

She sighed. "Okay, I promise to think about it."

"Good enough. Before I go, I need to bring you up to speed on Richard Jameson." She nodded. "I talked with Linc yesterday after you left the office." He relayed information about the threats to federal judges, and how the description of the man who'd organized the shipment of weapons into Mexico had matched RJ. "We knew the Freedom Defenders in Oregon were smuggling weapons into Canada, so it's not a surprise to find their affiliates are supplying arms to the cartels in Mexico. Regardless, this gives us a good idea what he's up to."

Bella ran water to fill the dish basin and Seth came to stand beside her. His expression didn't give much away, but he exuded a certain tension, which prompted her to ask him something she'd often wondered about. She knew the details of Richard Jameson's case, but she didn't know how Seth felt about it. "Are you angry with him? I'd be angry if he was my father."

He put the cream cheese and jam back in the fridge. When he turned toward her, his expression was guarded.

"He's just another fugitive."

"No, he's not. He's your father. He abandoned your family. That must hurt."

"That's not the issue. Here's the plan for this week. Ellie has developed a contact inside a militia group in Washington, so she's working that angle, learning what she can from him. Linc is in Nevada delving into the threats to the judge in Reno. Since it appears RJ was involved in shipping the load of weapons hidden in the hay bales to Mexico, and because that load originated in Reno, that's where we're focusing our attention. Today, you and I are combing through bank records to see if we can find financial links between Freedom Defenders and the Mexican cartel. If there have been other gun sales, I want to know about it. It'd be nice to pin international gun smuggling on their asses."

Not really surprised he'd deflected her question about his dad, Bella rinsed the plates and set them on the drainer.

"I need to go. You're dressed for work," he eyed her outfit, "but you can work from home today if you want to stay close to Alexei."

"No, but thanks. I want to make sure Alexei has everything he needs here, but I'll be in."

He gave a brief nod. "Okay, then I'll head out. I'm stopping at my apartment, then I'll be at the office."

He sat on a chair to put on his shoes and button his shirt.

"Thank you. For everything."

He stood and surprised her by dropping a swift kiss on her cheek before heading for the door, a gesture that made her heart yearn.

***

Seth sat at his desk, staring at the paper in his hand. After leaving Bella, he'd swung by his apartment for a shower and a change of clothes, and to pick up his mail before fighting LA traffic to get to the courthouse, where the US Marshals office was located. One letter stood out from the usual junk mail. It bore no return address and was postmarked Modesto, California. He reread the handwritten message, holding it carefully by the edges when instinct told him he'd be better off jamming it through the shredder.

Give up, Seth. You're not man enough to find me and never will be. Maybe that's my fault. If I'd stayed, your mother would never have married that asshole Bollinger and he would never have brainwashed my offspring and pushed them to join the feds. You think I don't know I'm the reason you're a marshal, and your brother and sister are marshals? I was sorely disappointed to learn you kids chose to follow Bollinger. What made you think you could ever find me? Instead of being adults I can be proud of, you betrayed me. I had important work to do, work that couldn't wait, and I had to leave to do it. Asshole Bollinger could never find me and neither will you. Be warned, if you keep trying, all hell will break loose. I have created an empire, which is destined to retake our land for the true Americans. If you keep after me, you will bring the wrath of God upon you and everyone you care about. You are my blood and your loyalty should be to me. Join me in my fight to rid this country of the scourge of unrestricted immigration and a government that has strayed from the Constitution. I don't want to hurt you, but if you try to thwart me, I will do what I must to see the fruition of my plan. If you don't stop harassing me, the deaths of many people, including your brother and sister, will be on your head. Heed my words. Richard Jameson

Seth stared at the printing, the same slanted scrawl his father always used. The signature struck him as odd. He didn't know why he expected the letter to be signed *Dad.* Not that Seth had thought of him as that for years. Seth and his siblings had settled on RJ years ago. The man had abandoned his family, leaving home for work one morning, and never returned. In and of itself that would've been reason enough to spur seventeen-year-old Seth to hate his father, but they soon learned his crimes were more egregious than abandoning his family,

Three days after RJ's disappearance, US Marshal Archer Bollinger had appeared on the doorstep of their suburban San Diego home. A home his mom told him and his siblings they could no longer afford without their father's income.

Seth still remembered the sensation of being gut-punched while standing at his mother's side as she listened to Arch explain why the US Marshals were hunting the fugitive from justice, Richard Jameson.

Before his disappearance, RJ had been charged with federal crimes, accused of systematically embezzling money from the government agency where he'd held a managerial position. The sick feeling in Seth's stomach had worsened at the devastated look on his mother's face. They'd had no idea that his father had been in trouble, much less that charges had been filed against him.

One upside—there weren't any flashy cars or jewelry bought with his father's ill-gotten gains to be confiscated. Rather, it appeared the stolen money had been diverted to help fund an anti-government militia group.

Learning what his father had done was a bone-deep betrayal of everything Seth had been raised to believe in, and what he thought his father believed in: honesty, integrity, and loyalty. Seth had been brought up on those values, and his father had violated every one of them.

No matter how hard Seth worked to obliterate it, there was always that insidious voice in the back of his head telling him that he was no better than his father. Someday Seth would fuck up and show the world that blood was stronger than ideals, and he too could be corrupted.

For years, he'd been quietly feeding the burning rage he kept hidden deep inside him. Spewing it out wouldn't help and wouldn't change anything. He was the eldest, and it'd been his responsibility to pick up the pieces.

His baseball coach had been disappointed when he'd lost his starting first baseman, but the money Seth earned flipping burgers had been more important than playing varsity baseball. His mother had objected, but the reality was, they'd needed the money.

He'd corralled an equally enraged Linc, helping his brother channel his anger into football, and Seth made sure he was there for Ellie when his sister had been lost in the miasma of betrayal.

There'd been many late nights when he'd felt helpless as he lay in bed hearing the muffled sobs coming from his mother's bedroom.

It'd taken only a few weeks for her to square her shoulders and set about rebuilding her family. She'd arranged for every one of them to see therapists. God, Seth had hated those sessions. He'd endured them, and maybe they'd helped some. He'd come to realize that there'd been signs his father had been dealing with issues Seth hadn't understood, and from which his mom had likely been shielding her children.

Regardless, he'd been glad when the sessions were done. They'd moved into a smaller house and learned to economize. He'd been offered a scholarship to Stanford, but that dream had no longer seemed relevant. He'd wanted to take classes at the local community college so he could continue to work and be close to home to support his family, but his mother had been adamant he attend a four-year university. They'd compromised, and he'd gone to UC San Diego.

Through it all, Deputy Marshal Bollinger had been a constant, unflappable presence in all their lives.

While Arch had been looking for RJ, he'd fallen flat on his face in love with Margaret Jameson. When they'd eventually married, Arch had brought a steadiness to the family and had helped guide the Jameson kids into adulthood. It was from him Seth had learned the true meaning of honor, and how to be a man.

Seth's chair creaked as he leaned back. RJ had betrayed his family and his country, and Seth was determined to prove he was a better man. Sometimes, it didn't seem to matter he and his siblings had made something of themselves, something that counted. He stared at the words his father had written and felt those old emotions churning, waiting for a weak moment to tear Seth down and make him feel like he was nothing.

He let the letter drop onto the desk and stared at it, fighting an internal battle. There was that voice in the back of his head that said he could make the letter with those hateful words disappear. He rose from his seat, took out his phone and snapped a picture of the letter, then, after scanning it at the copy machine, he went to the supply room to retrieve an evidence envelope.

Back at his desk, he put the letter inside the envelope, sealed it with evidence tape, and used a Sharpie to fill out the required information. He walked it to the evidence tech and watched as it was logged in, aware of the ache in his jaw where his muscles, rigid with anger, clenched his molars together.

Back in his office, he pulled his phone from his pocket. His sister picked up on the first ring.

"Hello, big brother."

"El, how soon can you get a flight south?"

Ellie dropped the lighthearted tone. "Soon. I'm in Portland, and there's a flight to LA that leaves in an hour."

"Good. Be on it. I need you and Linc here today."

Chapter Ten

Bella sat at the large conference table in the Marshals' office, her laptop in front of her, the late afternoon sun slanting through the blinds. Ellie sat next to her busily texting as they waited for Seth to join the team.

Before leaving Alexei, she'd gotten a text from Linc's wife, Mikayla, urging her to come to the Fourth of July party at the Bollinger home. Then, while walking out of the corner café with an iced hibiscus tea, her phone buzzed. Answering it, since she knew she'd be hounded if she didn't, she'd talked to Margaret Bollinger for twenty-minutes.

Seth's mother was sweet, friendly, and unwavering. They'd chatted about this and that, and before she knew it, Bella found herself agreeing to attend the family Fourth of July celebration.

Once again, she and Seth would be thrown together socially. It didn't help that their relationship was in this strange place. They'd been lovers, but they weren't lovers. They were friendly, but they weren't exactly friends. She was in love with him, but he wasn't in love with her.

Her shoulders slumped as she traced a finger through the condensation on the outside of her cup.

"You gave in, didn't you? You're coming to the barbecue." Linc leaned back in his seat, a takeout coffee cup in his hand and a grin on his craggy face.

She gave him a wry look. "What do you think? Is anyone ever able to say no to your mother?"

"Not that I know of. She can be kind of scary when she wants something."

"Mom's not scary, she's determined," Ellie commented, not looking up from her phone.

"Your point, El. Hey, you texting Sam?" Linc asked his sister. "Tell him I've been breaking in my hiking boots and got a cool backpacking stove. It's lightweight and heats food super-fast."

"Tell him yourself. Then he can tell you about the new water treatment gizmo that he absolutely had to have. You guys have geeked out about this trip."

"Seth said he's figured out the best tents to get. I need to order mine. September will be here in no time and we'll be heading for the backcountry."

Ellie set down her phone, rolling her eyes. "Hiking to the top of Mount Whitney is not that big a deal. Lots of people do it. Some even do it in a day. It's not Everest."

"You're only saying that because this is a guys' trip and you're not a guy. Anyway, we're doing more than Whitney. We're hiking at least forty miles of the John Muir Trail."

"I don't want to go tramping through the woods for forty miles. Trust me."

Linc sent her a shrewd look. "No, you probably don't. But it bugs you that it's a guys' trip."

Ellie inclined her head regally toward Bella. "Let's plan something for the same week the he-men are *mountain climbing*." She used air quotes around the words.

"Hey, it is mountain climbing," Linc protested.

She ignored her brother and said to Bella, "Let's organize a girls' week. I've got my eye on a cabin in Mammoth in the eastern Sierras. It's got a deck and an awesome view of the Minarets. It'll be me, you, Mikayla, and Mom, Arch is going with the must-have-a-penis group." Ellie grinned at Linc's scowl. "Mammoth is awesome. There are a bunch of lakes connected by a network of bike trails. We can rent electric bikes, or hike, or spend all day lazing on the deck breathing in the mountain air and reading if we want. When we're done doing the fun stuff, we can hang out at the cabin and drink wine, eat tacos, and play Scrabble. You in?"

"I'm absolutely in. That sounds great."

"Hey, I want tacos."

"You'll be eating freeze-dried spaghetti and granola bars, so enjoy that," Ellie told her brother with a smirk.

Seth strode in with a stack of papers in his hand. He'd shed his suit jacket and turned up the sleeves of a blue shirt past his elbows.

With a maroon tie knotted at his throat, and his gun in its holster at his shoulder, he looked like what he was: a solid, reliable chief deputy.

Okay, a hot, sexy, solid, and reliable chief deputy.

Was it only last night they'd cuddled together on her couch?

He passed a sheet of paper to each team member. Bella scanned the photocopied letter. It was addressed to Seth, and the signature at the bottom identified the sender as Richard Jameson.

"This arrived at my home address in yesterday's mail. The envelope was postmarked Modesto and dated three days ago. Take a minute to read it."

Bella read through to the end before glancing at Seth, whose face held his usual closed expression. He'd resisted talking about his feelings about his father, and he wasn't giving much away now.

"The fucker," Linc muttered. "He's trying to mess with your head. I want to know how he got your address."

"Our father is an asshole, and it's not too hard to find a home address, even a US Marshal's," Ellie added.

"There's a lot in this letter." The quiet command in Seth's voice refocused the conversation. "RJ rambles, but main points are that all of us, but mostly me, are a huge disappointment to him, and if we don't back off, people, including Linc and Ellie, will die and blame for that will be on my head."

"He's got an agenda and the team is interfering with it." Bella studied the letter. "How I read it is that we've been successful in disrupting his organization in Oregon and he's angry."

"I think Bella's right," Ellie said. "I'll repeat what Linc said. He's trying to mess with your head, big brother. He's pulling the disappointed dad card to get you to back off."

"He can't think I will."

"He doesn't know us anymore, Seth. His memory of you is as a teenage boy." Ellie's blue eyes were clouded. "I saw him for only a few minutes when we came face-to-face in Oregon, and my takeaway was that he is emotionally closed off from us. He doesn't care about his children at all. He had no problem ordering me killed."

"I think this letter gives us a clue on how we can bring him down," Linc said.

"Go on." Seth leveled a stare at his brother.

"What if you contact him, act like you're going rogue? Tell him you want to meet with him."

"He'll never go for it. He's a federal fugitive. I can't see him willingly meeting with a US Marshal, even if it is his son," Seth argued.

"He might." With all eyes turning to her, Bella went on. "I agree with Linc. For one thing, RJ expects that ultimately you'll have the same lack of integrity he had. We play to his ego, and while I'm not arguing with Ellie's assessment that he's distanced from you, I think there's a different way of looking at it."

"Go on."

"Ellie says he's closed off from you, his children. I agree. He no longer loves you as a father should."

"If he ever did," Ellie muttered.

"I believe he is still emotionally invested in you, or he would've never written the letter. He's vulnerable because of his ego. It bugs him you three became US Marshals like his nemesis, Archer Bollinger.

"Arch may not have been able to nab RJ, but he arrested his close associates, and he made it more difficult for RJ to operate, and forced him to go underground for a number of years. RJ sees him as more than a rival. Arch is the enemy who married your mom. That makes the dynamic even more volatile.

"He sees you following Arch's footsteps as a personal betrayal. If he could get you to join him and turn your back on the marshals, Arch, and your own family, then he's won a huge psychological victory. That may be too enticing a prospect for him to ignore.

"Add to that, it bugs him you don't respect his cause. He wants you to join him to fight for what he believes in, and if he can convince you, he's scored another victory."

She took a breath. "I think Linc is right. We figure out how to contact him and then convince him you're genuinely interested in his cause. The temptation of meeting you face-to-face might be too great for him to resist."

Seth frowned, staring at the copy of the letter in his hand, then gave a curt nod. "Okay. We'll explore that avenue."

***

Bella sat at her desk staring at the computer screen, worrying her bottom lip, scanning through images on the screen. Her brother was healing, which was a relief. No, she hadn't taken the pregnancy test. She wasn't avoiding knowing. Well, not really. She was avoiding knowing and not telling Seth. She wasn't ready to face him, especially after the caveman conversation he'd had with her brother. As she'd always done, she was being careful to protect herself. Yet, even with all the changes a pregnancy would bring to her life, deep in her heart she wanted Seth's baby.

Calling herself a coward, she pushed those thoughts aside so she could focus on her job. Since the team met to discuss the letter, she'd spent the past two days searching for clues where RJ was hiding out. If the guy wanted Seth to join the dark side, why hadn't he included something handy like an email address?

After an afternoon spent reviewing surveillance footage from a post office parking lot in Modesto, all she had was stiff shoulders and no leads. The office had quieted as most of the other deputies and staff had quit for the day. Ellie had flown back to Oregon to work on her contacts there. Linc, who was bunking at Seth's apartment, had been in the office most of the day and had taken off an hour ago.

Bella planned to leave soon and pick up takeout from her favorite Chinese restaurant for her and her brother. Alexei had started spending a lot of time on his phone, and wanted to get back to work.

He had a job to do, and his time holed up in her apartment where she knew he was safe would come to an end. She sighed. She wanted him to stay with her a little longer. She knew he wouldn't. He'd accuse her of being overprotective, but his injury had shaken her.

The night before, they'd talked about his role to infiltrate the *bratva*, and while she understood why he was doing it, nothing was going to stop her from worrying over his safety.

He was set on the mission and ultimately joining the FBI, and she'd learned long ago that getting her brother to change his mind once he'd settled on a course of action was like trying to stop the Santa Ana winds from blowing. It wasn't going to happen. Relief at his recovery felt like a giant weight had lifted from her shoulders. She would still worry about his mission, but at least he was no longer bleeding and nearly septic.

Bella clicked the mouse, scrolling through more feed from the date they estimated the letter had been sent. If they could identify the vehicle of the person who'd mailed the letter and trace its registration, they might have an avenue for tracking down Richard Jameson.

She knew the letter could've been mailed from anywhere in Modesto, and the sender never had to set foot in the post office. But tracking down every possible avenue meant scanning image upon image.

In Oregon, RJ had been driving a white truck with dual rear tires. He'd likely ditched that vehicle, but she still prioritized checking for any similar trucks that came into the post office parking lot, as well as vehicles registered in Nevada. The person mailing the letter might've driven over the Sierras to get the letter postmarked in a location designed to throw them off the search. She studied every white man who matched RJ's age and body type. So far, she hadn't come up with any matches.

A sound had her looking over her shoulder. Seth walked toward her desk. "Got anything?

She shook her head. "There are plenty of men who match RJ's general description, but so far not one of them is driving a vehicle with out-of-state plates. If we assume he drove to Modesto so the letter would be postmarked from there to throw law enforcement off the trail, then we're looking for a car that's not registered to an address in the vicinity of Modesto."

"Someone else could have mailed the letter for him." Seth came to stand behind her.

"Which is why I'm looking at all the vehicles, but focusing on those I think are most likely."

"Did you check the camera footage from the evening before? He could have dropped the letter in a mailbox after the last pickup for the day."

"True." Bella tapped on the field to call up footage from the previous day.

"You can do this tomorrow, Bella. It's time to go home."

"I'll leave in a few minutes."

"Bella."

She glanced up at him. He leaned against her desk, the look on his face making her catch her breath. His expression didn't give much away, but enough that she understood there was no going back to where they had been before.

No matter how hard she tried, the walls between them were crumbling. She didn't know how she'd exist if she ever let him fully in, and he left her. There was too much risk she'd end up like she had as a child, orphaned and struggling to survive. But she was a fighter, not a whiner. She answered him in the same tone he'd used. "Seth."

The corner of his mouth curled up. "You're using my name. That's an improvement. Let's go. I'll walk out with you. Tell me what you want, and Linc and I can pick up takeout and bring it to your place. Markel said he'd come by and give Alexei one last checkup. I'll call him to see if he wants to eat with us." His fathomless slate gray eyes studied her and she had the feeling if they weren't in the office, he wouldn't be so restrained. "What do you say? You want to spend the evening together?"

She found herself nodding while chiding herself for giving into the temptation of spending more time with him. "I want to go through this next file. I'll leave in half an hour. I promise."

***

Seth stood with Linc on Bella's doorstep as she eyed all the bags hanging from their hands before stepping back and holding the door wide open. They walked past her, Seth leading the way to the kitchen, where he and Linc piled the bags on the table and started unpacking them.

Bella looked at the array of containers, brows raised. "That smells amazing, but did you order everything on the menu? That's an incredible amount of food."

"You know Linc eats like an underfed teenager, and we wanted to make sure there was enough for leftovers."

"Even Linc can't eat this much food."

"Hey, I'm a big guy. I need a lot of fuel."

Alexei wandered in. "That dinner? I'm starved."

"Speaking of someone who eats like an underfed teenager."

Seth caught Bella's expression. She looked so damn relieved her brother was feeling better, which reinforced how frightened she'd been. She made the introductions while Seth opened a cupboard to take down plates.

A knock sounded at the door and Seth followed Bella when she went to open it. Markel stood with his black bag in one hand and a grocery bag in the other. “Hey, lady, and my man, Seth.”

Bella smiled and backed up so Markel could come in. “You’re in time to join us for dinner.”

He set his doctor bag on a side table and gave Bella a one-armed hug. “Thanks for the invite.” He held up the grocery bag. “I’ve got beer, already chilled.”

Markel checked out Alexei’s wound and declared him on the road to recovery. Seth had watched Bella as the diagnosis lightened her eyes at the news that her brother was truly better.

They were all in Bella’s living room. Alexei had taken the easy chair, and Linc and Markel brought in chairs from the kitchen table. They held their plates as they ate, beer bottles on the floor beside them. Seth sat elbow to elbow with Bella on the couch, the coffee table pulled close. She picked up his beer to set it on a coaster.

Across the room, Linc gestured with his chopsticks, as he tried in earnest to convince Markel and Alexei to join the guy backpacking trip.

Bella wound lo mein noodles around her chopsticks, swallowing a bite before saying to Seth, “I think I found the person who mailed the letter for RJ.”

His gaze traveled over her. Her hair tumbled around her shoulders and the purple top she wore outlined her breasts. “Tell me.”

“A woman with Nevada plates dropped an envelope in the outside collection box fifteen minutes after the last collection the evening. She drove a silver Honda Civic with plates registered to a Vivian Cochran with an address in Reno. She owns a duplex at the same address, but she doesn’t appear to reside there.”

“Did you come up with a photo?”

Bella picked up her phone from where it rested on the table and tapped the screen. Seth leaned toward her and she turned the phone so he could see. It struck him if their relationship were strictly professional, they wouldn’t be sitting so close that he could smell the soap on her skin.

Vivian Cochran's driver's license had the usual stats: fifty-four years old, five foot four, one hundred and thirty-five pounds. She had hazel eyes, and while her hair was noted as brown, the photo showed Vivian with her hair bleached blonde.

Seth set down his beer. "What makes you think she's the one who mailed the letter?"

"A couple things. Her husband was the leader of a local chapter of a white nationalist group. Donald Cochran killed himself three years ago after a gunfight with the feds. He was facing charges in gun trafficking and was suspected of assaulting a Sikh man whom Cochran had accused of being an Islamic jihadist."

"The fucker thought the Sikh man was Muslim."

"Apparently he wasn't only racist, he was ignorant."

Seth shook his head. "What else you got?"

"Before Vivian married Cochran, she'd been married to a member of a similarly affiliated motorcycle club. That marriage ended in divorce."

"She has a type, and she's been part of the same world RJ belongs to."

"Exactly. There's more. Her car has popped up several times on automated license plate readers in locations around Lake Tahoe."

"Which means she, or someone using her car, is spending a lot of time there. It could be where RJ's staying. Forward this photo to me and the rest of the team. First thing tomorrow, write up what you have and send it to me. I'll assign Linc to track her down and pay her a visit, see what she knows." He paused. "Good work, Bella."

Her gaze met his and held. Seth felt like he was being drawn in, drowning in a sea of deep blue. He didn't like they hadn't nailed down the status of their relationship. As far as he was concerned, they were together. But Bella was holding herself just out of reach, keeping a distance between them that had the potential to become a chasm if he couldn't find a way to close it.

It'd been nearly two weeks since the night they'd spent at Montenegro's castle. He'd known he wanted to be with Bella for a long time. After that night, he was certain. With their work relationship it would be difficult, but he wanted a chance to work it out.

"Hey, Seth." His brother forced Seth to tune in to the conversation across the room. "Tell these two that backpacking food isn't so bad."

"Backpacking food sucks." Seth leaned back against the cushions. "But the mountains, the stars at night, and the fresh air will make the experience worth it."

Linc rolled his eyes. "Way to back me up, man." He turned to the other men. "Okay, maybe the food isn't great, but we'll bring fishing gear and we can have fresh trout cooked over the open fire, and what Seth said about the outdoors experience is spot on."

"I like sleeping in a bed with a soft mattress and no bugs crawling on me," Alexei commented, shaking his head.

"I'd rather rent a place at the beach," Markel added. "Spending a week soaking up the rays sounds a lot more fun than getting chased by bears."

Linc sighed in apparent disgust. "Where's your sense of adventure? You're a couple of babies."

Alexei casually gave Linc the middle finger. "Call me when you have a civilized vacation planned."

Seth glanced at Bella. She gave him the smile he was becoming addicted to, and then spoke in an aside. "Alexei embraced the conveniences of life in America from the first moment we got here. He has a special appreciation for American bathrooms. I don't think you'll get him to sleep outdoors, or do anything outdoors that can be done indoors."

Her phone chimed, and Seth saw the name Sasha on the screen with the first words of a message written in Russian. She grabbed her phone and leaned back against the cushions, reading for a moment, then busily texting.

Seth bit back on the irritation that made him want to grab the phone and text the guy to fuck off. Bella having connections to someone in the *bratva* could bring a shitload of trouble down on her. As a deputy US marshal, associating with a member of a known criminal organization was verboten. It was more than enough of a reason for her to avoid him, but Seth couldn't deny on a more personal level, it annoyed the shit out of him that she was getting texts from someone she had a history with, and who had made a point of reconnecting with her.

He raised his brow in question when Bella put down her phone, but she ignored him, and stood to take their empty plates to the kitchen.

Chapter Eleven

Bella woke to a sharp knocking on her front door. She glanced at her phone to check the time and saw she'd missed several texts from Seth. She knew who was pounding on her door bright and early on a Sunday morning.

She stumbled to the door, peeked through the peephole, then pulled the door open. "Why are you here?" She crossed her arms in front of her and couldn't help the scowl she knew was on her face. Seth in jeans, a deep red cotton shirt with the sleeves rolled to his elbows, and scuffed leather boots was too much gorgeousness for her system to handle this early in the morning.

"If you checked your texts, you'd know."

"I was asleep. I don't check texts when I'm asleep."

"Let me in, Bella." He never used to let emotion show in his eyes, but this morning instead of flat gray, they glinted with humor, and when his gaze traveled over her, appreciation. Which made her remember that she was wearing an oversize t-shirt, which hung off one shoulder and barely covered her butt.

He held two lidded to-go cups, one dangling the tag of the tea she liked. She reached for it but he pulled it back.

"Damn it," she muttered, giving up on any thought that she'd get him to leave. "Fine. Give me my tea and you can come in."

He handed her the tea, and she turned around to shuffle into the kitchen. He followed, setting down his cup and snagging the bag of bagels from the counter. She watched as he got a cutting board and serrated knife from a drawer.

"Can I get you anything else, maybe your slippers or the Sunday paper?"

He shot her a grin that made her toes curl. "You know you're kind of grumpy in the morning?" She ignored him, instead sipping from her hot tea. He placed the bagels in the toaster oven and turned to lean back against the counter.

"Your brother here?"

"No, he insisted he was well enough to go back to his place. He—"

That was as far as she got. Seth snagged her tea and set it on the counter, then grabbed her hand to tug her forward.

In less time than it took to form a coherent thought, she was leaning against six foot plus of warm male who smelled of coffee and the outdoors.

He placed his mouth on hers and she melted like warm chocolate. This was a bad idea, there were reasons they couldn't be involved, but that didn't stop her from slipping her hand under the collar of his shirt to feel the warm skin of his neck while opening her mouth to his kiss.

He reached under the hem of her t-shirt to run his hands down her backside, pulling her into the cradle of his legs against the heat of him. The kiss was teetering on the brink of something more when he pulled back, drawing in a deep breath as he rested his jaw against her temple to whisper in her ear, "Good morning, Bella."

She dropped her head into the crook of his neck and breathed him in. "Why do you do this to me?"

"Do what?" He spoke in a low murmur.

"Make me want you. I'm not supposed to want you like this."

"Right back at you, darlin'."

Searching for a measure of calm, she said, "I should get the cream cheese from the fridge."

"Yeah." Instead of loosening his hold, he pulled her more snugly against him, his arms like a security blanket wrapped around her, keeping her safe.

Being held by him made her yearn for something she'd told herself was impossible, and made what was becoming a difficult situation even more complicated. She still hadn't started her period, and her plan had been to do the pregnancy test first thing that morning. That wasn't going to happen. Seth's being here put her plan on hold. If she was pregnant, she needed time to think through all the implications before talking to him. From what he'd said to Alexei, she was afraid he'd insist on getting married. Seth had a forceful personality, and she wasn't about to let herself be swept along with what he wanted until she was sure of her own wants and needs.

The toaster oven dinged and he loosened his hold. They went about getting breakfast on the table, and Bella was painfully aware her efforts to act like there was nothing between them were for naught. Their relationship may have been hard to define, but it was something, and at some point they'd have to deal with it, pregnant or not.

They sat across from each other at the little table, and it felt so normal to be sharing the first meal of the day with him. He spread cream cheese on his bagel, then handed her the knife. "We're heading to Reno today. Our flight leaves in two hours."

"Something's happened."

"Yeah, something's happened. Judge Rebollar's teenage son has gone missing."

Bella's brain was starting to wake up. "What do we know?"

"Parents say the boy, Anthony, has been testing boundaries lately. Took the mom's car without permission, missed curfew a few times, that kind of thing. But he's still tight with his family. Dad wasn't taking any chances after getting those threats and had security installed around their house. The system was on all night but didn't catch anything."

Bella sipped her tea, setting it down slowly as she considered the situation. "Inside job?"

Seth shook his head. "Linc thinks Anthony knew enough about computers to get around the system. Turns out he's got a girlfriend, and as both kids are fifteen, their parents don't let them date. Best guess is the kid had a meetup planned with the girl but it went sideways."

"Has Linc talked to the girl?"

Seth nodded. "She's denied meeting with Anthony, but Linc's read is she's scared. Her parents have threatened to send her to live with relatives in Mexico if she doesn't obey their rules, and they won't let her be interviewed unless they're present. She's clammed up and he won't get anything from her with her folks there. Linc's confident she knows something. He's working on getting the parents to ease up so the girl will talk."

"Could be Anthony and the girl had a fight and he's staying with a friend until he cools off. Kids do stuff like that. Why are you thinking this is more than star-crossed lovers, albeit young ones?"

"According to the judge, Anthony's never been gone all night, and he's not with the girl. Since he's the son of a federal judge who's had threats made against him, and who has a controversial case coming before his bench in three days, we're assuming the worst unless told otherwise."

Bella nodded. "Give me thirty minutes and I'll be ready."

***

Early in the afternoon, Bella and Seth walked into the hotel in Reno where Linc had booked a suite. On the hour-and-a-half flight, they'd worked from their laptops, purposefully sitting in the last row of the plane so no one could look over their shoulders. Seth's demeanor changed when they got to the airport. The man who'd shown up at her door that morning with a quick grin and her favorite tea, the man who'd kissed her like it was full-on sex, had been replaced by the no-nonsense seasoned marshal intent only on doing his job. For so long, she'd viewed him only in his role. It was the only part of himself he'd allowed her to see. It gave her a glow inside to know when they were alone, he was letting her see the more human side of him. For the time being, whatever was personal between them had been locked away and he was focused on the job.

The suite had only two bedrooms, and since she had no intention of taking the pullout sofa bed in the common area, she rolled her suitcase past the bedroom that had Linc's bag on the bed to claim the other room. When she came out, Linc turned an iPad on the coffee table so they could see Ellie on the screen.

Bella pulled a chair from the small table while Linc sat on the couch. Seth paced the room, still in the jeans and cotton shirt he'd been wearing when he'd shown up at her door, but now armed with his gun in its shoulder harness.

"Linc, you're up first. Update us on Anthony."

"No news on the boy's whereabouts. I've had more luck with the girlfriend, Serena. It took convincing her parents not to send her to Mexico to get her to cooperate and tell me what she knows. She finally confessed she and Anthony had plans to meet up last night around midnight. Dad wasn't happy to learn they'd done this before. Anthony texts her when he's outside her house, she comes out, and they go to a park a couple blocks away. Serena fell asleep waiting for him to text, and when she woke up this morning there was nothing from him. Poor kid's in tears and worried sick about her boyfriend."

"How does he get to her house?" Bella asked.

"Rides his bike, and then they ride double to the park. The judge confirmed his son's bike, a top-of-the-line mountain bike, is missing, as is Anthony's cell phone. The cell is either turned off or destroyed because it's not sending out a signal."

"His parents must be frantic," Ellie said.

"That's an understatement, but they're holding it together." Linc rose from his seat and crossed the room to the kitchenette where he opened an undercounter mini fridge. He returned with chilled bottles of mineral water and an apple. He passed the bottles to Bella and Seth and took a big bite out of the apple.

"Anything from FD, or any other group claiming they have Anthony?" Seth unscrewed the cap on his water, taking a deep swallow.

Linc shook his head. "Nada. The judge is watching his email, we're monitoring social media platforms where these types like to hang out, but there's been nothing. Local cops are doing their thing, checking with Anthony's friends, getting access to any security cameras that might've caught a kid on a bike."

"Okay. What about Vivian Cochran?" Seth's phone vibrated and he looked at the screen, brows dropping in a frown.

Linc chewed and swallowed before responding. "I went by the duplex at the address Bella found. All the tenants know is Vivian Cochran is their landlord and is hands off about it. She has a local handyman do the maintenance, and a lawn service keeps up the outside. They had nothing of note to offer. That said, the next-door neighbor had a lot more to say. Turns out the neighbor, Netty Pierce, who's African American, has had a few run-ins with Cochran."

Linc bit into the apple, talking out of the side of his mouth while he chewed. "Miss Netty's a hoot. She's has a pack of little yappy dogs, sings in her church choir, and has twenty-six grandchildren, seven great-grandchildren, and it sounds like every last one of them dotes on her."

Linc held up his hand at Seth's expression. "I know, get to the point. I may have spent an hour talking to her, but it got us some information. Turns out one of the duplex units became available for rent and one of her granddaughters submitted a rental application. She wanted to live close to her grandmother because Miss Netty's turning ninety in a couple months, though you wouldn't know it from the size of the garden she's got behind her house."

"Still haven't got to the point," Seth growled.

"Point is Vivian Cochran didn't accept the application, and didn't accept Miss Netty's son's application last year."

"What race are the current tenants?" Ellie asked from the iPad.

"White. Miss Netty isn't one to take racism without fighting back. One of her grandsons is a lawyer and the family has filed a housing discrimination lawsuit against Vivian Cochran. Discrimination against blacks in housing jives with her affiliation with known white supremacists. That's what I got," Linc concluded as he took another bite of his apple, then sent the core sailing into the trashcan, raising a fist in triumph when he made the shot.

Seth gave a curt nod. "We need to track down Vivian Cochran. She's got a history of hitching her wagon to men with racist affiliations. Could be that she and RJ are together." He shrugged. "If not, they move in the same circles and she may know where he's hiding." Linc nodded. "Moving on to RJ, an email came in from him a minute ago." He tapped on his phone, waited a second, then tapped a few more times. "Check your texts. The email is encrypted, but I took a screenshot of the message and sent that to each of you."

Bella found the text and began scrolling down.

"Blah, blah, blah, more of the same," Ellie muttered from the iPad. "He's still trying to manipulate you. Tell me you're not falling for all that 'my eldest son is a disappointment to me' crap."

"I'm not." Seth took another swallow from his water bottle. "Do you see this line he wrote? 'Good people have taken measures to protect our country from the mongrel hordes who have infiltrated the judicial system and are corrupting the government.'"

"That's the same kind of shit he always says," Linc muttered.

"But what if this time he's referring to something specific? What if his followers are the so-called good people and Judge Rebollar is one of those who RJ believes had 'infiltrated the judicial system and are corrupting the government'?" Seth asked.

"Rebollar is an immigrant."

Seth's gaze lasered in on Bella. "What do you know?"

She scrolled through the page on a website she was reading. "I found his bio on a professional organization for lawyers. His family came from El Salvador in the seventies, and he gained citizenship under Reagan's amnesty law that was passed in eighty-six."

"Then it's an even better fit. We're going to focus on whether RJ or other Freedom Defenders kidnapped Anthony Rebollar. We're also looking for a connection between the MacDonald clan and FD. If RJ's involved, we'll nail his ass."

Linc leaned forward in his seat. "RJ says he wants to meet with you." He looked up from his phone screen to zero in on his brother. "Set up the meeting, we arrest him, and get him to tell us where they're holding the boy."

"Now that we have a way of contacting him, yeah, we'll set up a meeting, but not to arrest him. RJ hasn't shown any inclination to cooperate. We arrest him and we could be writing that boy's execution warrant. It's better I make him think I'm interested in meeting with him, but with another goal in mind. Bella and I will work out an email to send him and make sure we leave enough crumbs for him to think I'm disgruntled and open to discussing his fucked-up ideas with him. I think he'll go for it."

Ellie said, "Okay, but one more thing. My contact has a buddy who was in with the Oregon branch of Freedom Defenders before we dismantled that organization. The buddy says Big Dog, aka RJ, has moved somewhere near Tahoe, on the California side. Since Reno's not far from Tahoe, arranging an in-person meetup is feasible. This also puts him and our friend Vivian in the same general area."

Seth nodded. "Good. They run in the same circles. I'll see if the IP address on the email will tell me where it was sent from. If it's from around Tahoe, we'll know we're on the right track."

"If RJ agrees to meet with you, that'll be further evidence," Ellie commented.

"Yeah," Seth said, "The more we know about RJ, the more—"

"Got something." Linc was staring at his phone. "Local PD says they've recovered Anthony's bike. A local homeless guy riding a high-end mountain bike caught their attention. The bike is registered and it belongs to Anthony."

"Homeless guy say where he got the bike?"

"Yeah. Says he found it behind a gas station that's on the likely route Anthony would've taken to get to Serena's house. PD is getting a warrant for surveillance footage from the gas station and the Chinese restaurant next to it."

"Shit," Seth muttered. "Any chance the homeless guy has Anthony?"

"Local LEOs don't think so. The guy is known to them. He has mental illness and claims the bike was left behind the gas station because God wanted him to have it. They've had only minor problems with him in the past. To verify, they checked where he's camping and other than having over a dozen Bibles in his tent, there's nothing there. There's more about the bike, though. Cops say scratches on the frame and scraped rubber on the handle grips indicate it hit the pavement hard." Linc sighed. "Working theory is that Anthony was forced off the bike, possibly being sideswiped by a car, and someone grabbed him."

Bella's stomach gave a slow, queasy roll. Vulnerable children always hit her hard. She could relate. Thinking about the terror a fifteen-year-old would experience being kidnapped off the street in the middle of the night, her fear over what he might be going through brought back too many memories. She sipped from her water bottle to ease her stomach.

A notification popped up on her laptop screen showing results for a search she'd initiated. "I've got something too." Seth inclined his head and she went on. "I searched property holdings in and around Reno, Lake Tahoe, and, since we got a hit from an automated plate reader there, from Truckee, a town that's roughly twenty miles north of the lake. I also searched for Donald Cochran. Cochran was Vivian's second husband and the white nationalist who assaulted a Sikh man," Bella reminded the group.

"And killed himself rather than be arrested," Linc added.

"That's him." She scanned through the search results. "There's a property owned by Donald Edward Cochran listed as being delinquent on property tax payments. Could be she's keeping a low profile by not informing the county her husband is dead." She tapped on her keyboard to bring up another screen. "I've got a map up. The Cochran property is about halfway between Truckee and Lake Tahoe, there's five acres with one dwelling and several other structures. It backs up to the Truckee River."

"You see a property history?" Ellie asked.

"Yes. It appears the property belonged to Donald prior to marrying Vivian. She was never added to the title."

"Do we know if Donald died with a will?" Linc tore open a small bag of peanut M&Ms and popped a couple in his mouth.

"I haven't dug that far." Bella shook her head when Linc held out the M&Ms. "But minus something like a prenup or children from a previous marriage, the property likely went to Vivian when he died."

"Could be," Linc went on, dumping candy into Seth's outstretched hand, "this is where she's been living."

"Can you pull up a satellite image?" Seth asked.

Bella waited until a picture popped up. "Here it is." The area was hilly with lots of tall trees and the Truckee River flowing along one border like a silver ribbon. "It's a big piece of property. The satellite image shows the closest neighbor is across the river, downstream about a hundred yards. Nearest neighbors on their side of the river are over a half mile away. That kind of setup might be interesting to someone like RJ looking for a place where he doesn't have anyone close by who might notice what he's doing."

"Can you magnify the structures?"

Seth dropped a hand on her shoulder as he bent forward, his head close to hers. Telling herself to ignore the tingles, Bella zoomed in.

Seth studied the screen before straightening. "There were a lot of vehicles on this property at the time the photo was taken. This image could be months or years old, but it's likely more recent than Cochran's death three years ago."

"It gives us a place to start. Why don't we knock on the front door, see who answers and how they react to a bunch of marshals on their doorstep?" Linc suggested.

Ellie fluttered her hand and made a sound like *pfft*. "Yeah, let's do that because we want to tip our hand and let Vivian and possibly RJ know we're on to them."

"Okay, then we play dumb. We go in dressed like a couple of hikers, pretend we're lost and ask for directions. We see what pops."

"Excellent plan," Bella picked up an eye roll from Ellie as she spoke to her brother, "until RJ happens to be there and guess who's at his door, the sons he abandoned twenty years ago."

Linc sighed. "Damn. Shot down again. Since I'm the idea guy right now, here's another one. How about we send up a drone and use modern technology to have a look-see?"

"We'd need a warrant, and at this point, I don't think we have enough to get one." Seth stood with his hands on his narrow hips, his brow furrowed. "Here's what we'll do. Top priority is finding the boy. The Reno Marshals' office is helping us coordinate with local LEOs. Linc, you're focusing solely on tracking down anything that comes up related to Anthony Rebollar. Bella and I will finesse our response to RJ. Once that's sent, we'll pursue finding Vivian Cochran, looking for anything to tell us if she's connected to RJ. Ellie, I want you to dive deeper into both the plaintiffs and defendants in the environmental case coming before Judge Rebollar. Look for any chatter that might be linked to a kidnapped boy. It's a long shot, but we need to pursue it.

"If this is what we think it is, Anthony was taken by the Freedom Defenders, my bet is they'll contact the judge today. They've let the parents worry and get anxious. When they think the judge is primed, they'll make their move. Their goal is to sabotage the case coming before the judge, and they can't do that if they don't make their demands known. Meanwhile, we tighten security around others involved in the case and bring in more marshals to protect the courthouse."

Ten minutes later, Ellie signed off, and Linc had left for a meeting with detectives from the Reno PD. Bella and Seth sat at opposite ends of the small table, both with laptops open in front of them. Seth had snagged a couple tangerines from the supply of groceries Linc had stocked in the kitchenette and began peeling them. He set a small pile of tangerine segments on a napkin at her elbow, then sat at his computer, eating tangerine.

Bella sighed. That was one of the reasons she loved the entire Jameson family. They were innately generous and so casually caring of one another. Somehow she was lucky enough they'd widened their circle to include her.

She read the shared document on her screen, studying the changes as Seth worked on his reply to the message from RJ.

"Since the kidnapping, I'm reconsidering my position on whether he'll meet with you or set you up. You're a US Marshal, he's a federal fugitive. He's too smart to put himself in a position where you could arrest him. I don't trust he's not doing this to hurt you."

"I think he'll meet with me. He's the one who brought up that I should come over to his side. But, like we discussed, we write this carefully, play to his ego, make him think there's the possibility I could go over to the dark side.

"The other part of this is that he thinks he's smarter than me, and everyone else. He'll figure he can stay one step ahead." Seth shrugged. "If he goes for it, we're winners; if he doesn't, we've lost nothing but a little time."

"Unless he says yes, but has something else planned for you."

Chapter Twelve

Seth steered the rented SUV through morning traffic, such as it was. Compared to LA, they were cruising along. The sun was bright in a cloudless blue sky, reflecting off the windows of the tall hotels in the casino district as they headed away from downtown toward the suburbs. It'd been warm when he and Bella had stepped outside, and temperatures were likely to hit well into the nineties by noon. Linc had left early, then had called to report, as he'd predicted, Judge Rebollar had received an email making demands in exchange for Anthony's return.

They were on the way to the Rebollar home to meet with the judge and his wife, and the Reno PD detective assigned to the taskforce.

Which was exactly where Seth's attention should be focused. But, as was becoming the norm over the past few weeks, the woman riding beside him was playing havoc with his concentration.

He could smell her scent, which reminded him of his mother's flower garden in the spring. The urge to pull over and haul her into his arms was difficult to resist. Compartmentalizing his feelings was a necessity to do his job. Since the weekend at Montenegro's palace, he couldn't help thinking of her as *his*. As a permanent part of his life. As someone he wanted to be with every damn day.

They'd made love that one time, and it had been, hands down, the most incredible encounter of his life. From that moment their relationship had taken a monumental turn. His need for her was as essential for life as oxygen, and it meant he was no longer able to push his desire for her into a corner of his brain.

He'd been pretty successful doing that for the past year.

While his obsession with Bella was always there on the periphery, at least he'd been able to function. One lapse. One hot and satisfying lapse, and thoughts of her permeated his every waking moment, and most of his sleeping ones. His frustration was stoked on a near daily basis when he woke from erotic and explicit dreams featuring the woman sitting beside him wearing the blue dress that had driven him fucking crazy. He spent nearly every day aroused and aching.

Take Sunday morning. Showing up at her door hadn't been necessary. When she hadn't responded to his texts, he could've called her. She would've answered her work phone. But no, he'd seized on the excuse and shown up at her apartment.

He was blending the personal with the professional.

He steered the car to the off-ramp, pulling to a stop at a signal. He caught Bella clenching her fists, her face in profile as she gazed out the window.

"You okay?"

She turned, and per the norm, he felt a charge when her blue gaze settled on him. "Of course. Why wouldn't I be?"

"Cases involving kids bother you."

He caught her shrug before returning his attention to the traffic beginning to move through the intersection. "Cases involving kids hit everyone hard."

"Sure, but you always seem to be more affected." He accelerated around a slow-moving box truck. After what she'd told him of her childhood, he had better insight as to why. He drummed his fingers on the steering wheel, then finally asked the question that was never far from the surface.

"It's been a couple weeks since we were together."

"So?"

"So, have you started your period?"

He could feel her glare. "You can't ask me that. *If* I were pregnant, I would follow official protocols in informing my superior at the appropriate time." She crossed her arms in front of her, a classic defensive gesture.

"Damn it, Bella." He slowed and veered to the left to give a group of bicyclists more space. "Don't shut me out. I'm not asking as your boss, I'm asking as your boyfriend." Which was the wrong thing to say. He knew it the moment the words left his mouth. Just because he thought of himself that way didn't mean she was on board with the idea.

Her gaze turned lethal. “Did you skip a step or ten, Seth? How did we get from having sex a couple weeks ago to you being my boyfriend?”

He’d already blown it, so he figured he might as well play his hand. “You haven’t been paying attention if you haven’t noticed the steps. They may not have been conventional, but they’ve been there.”

“Oh, you mean the step when you told Alexei that we have ‘a thing’?” She used her fingers as air quotes. “Are you talking about that romantic moment? Or maybe you’re imagining all those dates, you know, with walks on the beach and candlelit dinners, those dates we’ve never gone on.”

He turned into a subdivision with well-kept two-story homes, many with what looked like native-plant landscaping. Arriving at their destination, he parked on the street, turned off the engine, and shifted in his seat to face her.

“Maybe we haven’t done those things, but how about what happens every time we kiss? What about when you slept in my arms and how it was when we woke up together? How about every time I look at you I’m pulled in a little deeper until all I can see is you?” He wanted her to understand, and worked to keep his frustration under wraps. “Look, I know our relationship has been anything but typical, but we have a relationship beyond our professional one. What we need is to have an honest conversation, unfortunately, that’ll have to wait. But, Bella, while we’re waiting remember this. When I look into the future, I see you with me. That’s what I want. You’re going to have to decide if it’s what you want too.” He sighed. “Will you spend the day with me? The next free day we have. Will you spend it with me?”

She nodded slowly. “I’d like that.”

Tension released the hold it had on his heart and he gave her a half smile. “Good. Let’s go meet the Rebollars.” As they walked up the sidewalk to the entrance of the stone-fronted home, it hit him that she hadn’t answered his question.

A diminutive woman with a lined face opened the door and, after Bella and Seth presented their badges, she introduced herself in careful English as Carmen, Anthony’s grandmother.

They entered a wide foyer of a warmly decorated home. Pottery and paintings displayed what Bella recognized as vibrantly colorful indigenous art from Central America. They were led into a dining area adjacent to a spacious kitchen with wide granite counters. The grandmother left them to climb the stairs to the upper floor.

A couple sat at the table and Bella recognized Judge Carlos Rebollar from his photos. His hair was grayer, and his face was more haggard. He sat erect with squared shoulders, and struck Bella as dignified. She thought he looked remote until she caught the haunted look in his eyes. This man was terrified and holding it together the best he could. Expression grim, he clasped hands with the woman sitting beside him, her face reflecting the anguish of a mother with a missing child.

Linc stood near the sliding glass door, which opened to a deck and pool. He was talking with a woman with hair spiraling in black curls to her shoulders and a badge hanging from a lanyard around her neck. Linc stepped forward and made the introductions. The woman with the badge was Lieutenant Keisha Browne, a detective from the Reno PD who'd been assigned as the department's lead on the taskforce.

Maria Rebollar let go of her husband's hand and stood. Her dark eyes were shadowed, and Bella wondered if the woman had gotten any sleep in the past thirty-six hours. She clenched her hands tightly in front of her. "Welcome to my home. I appreciate you are all here to help find my son. Let me get you some coffee." She indicated a corner of the counter where a coffeemaker stood next to mugs arranged on a tray. "Or, if you'd prefer, I can put water on for tea."

Bella stepped forward. "If you'll tell me where your kettle is, I'll put the water on, Mrs. Rebollar."

She shook her head and led the way into the kitchen. "Call me Maria. Being busy keeps my mind from dwelling on how scared my Anthony must be."

"Tell me about your son."

The woman busied herself filling the kettle and set it on the stove where she adjusted the flame. When done, she leaned against the counter, folding her arms tightly in front of her.

"You asked about my son. That's good, because knowing him might help you to find him. Anthony is my baby. He has two older sisters. They're both in El Salvador visiting their grandparents for the summer. We haven't told them their brother is missing. It is better to tell them when he's been returned safely to us." She spoke precisely in accented English. “Even though his father and I tried to be strict with him, I am afraid we spoiled him.” She swiped her hand under her eyes. “He’s always been a sweet boy, so good-natured. He gets his way through charm. He uses it on his sisters and his teachers, and he has such a way about him. He is a good boy.”

“Have you met Anthony’s girlfriend, Serena?”

Maria wiped under her eyes again, and when she spoke, her voice reflected the strain of holding back her tears. “No, we haven’t met her. Her family moved to Reno a year or so ago, so she wasn’t one of the kids Anthony went through grade school with. We thought he was too young to date. We wanted him to focus on school.”

She took a deep breath and let it out slowly. “I understand her parents feel the same. Anthony made the varsity soccer team last year, the only freshman on the team, and he was excited about it. We thought being in honors classes and with sports, he had enough on his plate. Then he met Serena and was infatuated. First love hits you so hard. We knew he spent time with her when they were at school, and that was okay. We were glad when it was summer. We thought being apart would cool the romance some.”

She sighed. “With cell phones these days, it’s so easy to be in constant contact. It turns out Anthony was being dishonest and sneaking out at night to meet with her.” She shook her head. “Hindsight is always twenty-twenty. We would have been better parents if we’d let him invite her over where we could keep an eye on them. If we’d done that, he wouldn’t have been out at night where he was in danger.”

“You were trying to be good parents and do what you thought was right.”

“My job is to protect my son, and I failed.”

“You aren’t to blame. Anthony made a poor decision, yes, but the people who took your son are to blame.”

The water in the kettle began to boil and Maria turned off the burner. Bella chose a tea bag from a small basket and poured the hot water. She didn’t think she’d convinced Maria, but she hoped the mother would eventually forgive herself.

If Bella’s mother or grandmother had been even half as concerned about Bella and Alexei’s safety, her life might have turned out differently. She was happy to be where she was, and with her career. She wouldn't trade knowing Seth for anything, but she wished getting to this point hadn't been such a painful process.

The group gathered around the table where Judge Rebollar passed around papers from a stack in his hand. "This is the message that was emailed to me early this morning." He nodded toward Linc. "At Marshal Jameson's direction, I requested proof of life." His voice cracked at the words. "We haven't heard anything since then."

Seth spoke. "Judge, I'd like permission to look at your computer. I want to see if we can retrieve the IP address this email was sent from."

"Please, call me Carlos. And yes, of course, you have my permission."

Bella thought he'd gladly sacrifice his own life if that's what it took to get Anthony returned home safely.

Linc nodded at the look from Seth. "I'm on it."

"I'll take you to the office where the computer is." Maria led Linc out of the room.

Bella took the paper Carlos handed to her and read through the email he'd received, not surprised at the virulent racist language.

In the space of three paragraphs, Judge Rebollar was referred to as an illegal, a wetback, and a border hopper. The message included a rant about the Fourteenth Amendment and the need to revoke birth citizenship because mongrel hordes were defiling the country. The author claimed his organization had kidnapped Anthony to get the judge's attention. Previous warnings had been ignored and taking the boy had been a matter of necessity.

The author didn't identify him or herself by name or group, other than broadly as one of many "true American citizens fighting tyranny." Their goal was to stop what they claimed was government overreach by whatever means necessary. They condemned the actions of the environmental group, threatening to blow Judge Rebollar, the "tree huggers," and Anthony to "hell and back again" if their demands weren't met.

"Our assumption that this had to do with the MacDonald case was correct," Seth said.

"The case the environmental group brought named the federal government and the MacDonald clan. They want Judge Rebollar to dismiss the case with prejudice so they can't bring that case back to court again. Ever," Bella said.

"Linc told me who you all think is behind the kidnapping of young Anthony. You got anything more specific?" Keisha asked. "Whoever wrote this sounds like they're on the nutty side of the loaf."

Seth gave a short laugh. "That's apt."

"There are similarities with emails from RJ." Bella's gaze was on Seth, who was still scrutinizing the email as she spoke. "There's the use of the word 'mongrel,' which RJ has also used. He's targeting a federal judge, and there's the references to explosives, which we know is a preferred weapon. Freedom Defenders, and RJ specifically, have used explosives against federal courts. The group also blew up Sam's car," she said. She turned to Keisha and shared, "Sam Creed is a federal judge in Oregon. I think this situation has a lot of similarities with that case and with emails to other federal judges that have been turned over to us."

"RJ is Richard Jameson, Seth and Linc's dad, right?" Keisha asked. At Bella's nod, Keisha muttered, "That's got to suck. There was a buzz about that in the department when we heard what marshals were assigned to this case."

"It does indeed suck," Bella agreed.

Maria rushed into the room, a paper clutched in her hand she brought to her husband. "It's Anthony. They've sent a picture of Anthony." The couple stood close together, examining the image of their son. Maria's hand shook as she held the paper. "He's been hurt. Oh Carlos, they hurt him."

"But he's alive, and these are injuries he can recover from. Look at him, he looks strong. Our boy looks strong."

Linc came in. "This is the kidnapper's proof of life." He gave everyone a copy of the email containing the photo. There was no text, only the image of Anthony Rebollar, hair tousled, gaze defiant, holding a newspaper in front of him so the front page could be seen. What looked like a nasty scrape was evident on his forehead above his left eyebrow, and the cheekbone under his right eye looked swollen and bruised.

"This is the front page of today's newspaper."

Seth stared at the image. "Anthony looks like he's resisted, fought back. That's good from a mental standpoint. But we don't want him to do something that gets him hurt any more than he has been."

"Our son's never one to accept injustice," Carlos said, his eyes still on the image of his son. "When a student was suspended from his school for fighting a young man who was bullying another boy, Anthony rallied other students in protest. He wrote an article for the school newspaper and got many students and even a few teachers to sign a petition."

Seth's phone buzzed and he took it from his pocket to glance at the screen before responding. "That kind of temperament would make him more likely to fight against his captors. He could have gotten the scrape on his forehead when he came off the bike, but the bruising around his eye? Someone hit him."

"This email and the previous one have the same IP address," Linc stated, his gaze steady on his brother. "They also match the IP address of the email sent by RJ."

Seth stood stoically, absorbing Linc's statement before giving his brother an almost imperceptible nod. Bella thought he'd needed a moment to accept their father had reached another, deeper level of depravity.

"What does that mean?" Maria asked.

"It means we have a clear idea who took Anthony, and we have a direction to pursue to get him back."

The team left the Rebollar home and stood for a moment on the driveway. Seth gave orders for the next few hours. "Judge Rebollar will inform us immediately if more emails come in. Lieutenant Browne, I'd like you to take another run at the girlfriend. Anthony was snatched by someone who knew he was leaving the house at night. Find out if he talked about meeting anyone new, or if he'd mentioned anything he'd noticed that was out of the norm, like someone following him. I'd also like an update on the bike. It was dusted for fingerprints, so find out if that turned up anything."

"Sure thing. I'll get back to you with whatever I find." Keisha gave a good-bye wave and crossed the street to her car.

After her departure, Seth turned to his brother. "You work with the local marshals at whoever's in the judge's circle. Talk to the family, the grandmother, the sisters, any close friends. We want to learn if anyone noticed anything, no matter how small the detail. So far Freedom Defenders has been direct in their approach, but we want to cover all bases."

"What will you and Bella be doing?" Linc asked.

“We’re still working the RJ angle. If he’s got the boy, we’ve got to figure out where the bastard is. We’ve established a link between RJ and the kidnappers. RJ’s connection to Vivian is inconclusive, but I’m going to find who I need to talk in the Reno office to get a warrant to send up a drone over the Cochran property.”

Chapter Thirteen

Bella sat at the table in the hotel suite, elbow to elbow with Seth. He always managed the team the same way. He'd give orders, sometimes pairing Linc and Ellie together, other times having them work independently, while she and Seth were almost always partnered up. She'd thought that was common procedure when she'd first been hired and was on probation. The chief deputy would naturally partner with the least experienced marshal on his team.

Once she was past her probationary period, the arrangement hadn't changed. Looking back, she wondered if there were more instances than she was aware of where Seth might've been revealing feelings for her, but she hadn't been reading him correctly. Those times when she thought he didn't trust her, she wondered if he'd wanted to be with her. The thought warmed her and gave her something to think about.

Their laptops were humming on the table in front of them, but at the moment, they were both staring at the screen of Seth's laptop. The image they'd received that morning of Anthony's battered face had added a renewed sense of urgency to finding him, and the county sheriff in California had been more than willing to help them obtain the warrant. Now that sheriff's department was using their drone to look at the Cochran property. Seth was on the phone to the operator as the drone images came through to his laptop. There was always a risk that the hovering machine would be spotted from the ground, but so far, no one had appeared on the screen.

The house was a rambling structure with a covered patio that looked out over a yard that sloped to the river. Tall trees grew around the house, which limited what they could see.

The operator panned over other structures. There was a small shed, which might hold tools, a carport provided shelter for a backhoe, and a large metal structure big enough to store heavy equipment or several automobiles. Behind the shed was an area that looked like it was being used as a firing range with an old, rusted truck riddled with bullet holes. The ground shimmered with reflecting sunlight, likely from shattered glass bottles used for target practice.

“Can you circle the big metal garage-like building so we can see all entrances?” Seth asked the drone operator.

The drone revealed a smaller door on side of the building, plus two side-by-side wide rollup doors. As they were watching, a car approached on a dirt road and the image widened as the drone gained altitude. The drone operator spoke through Seth’s phone on speaker. “Sorry to have to pan out, folks. This drone is quiet, but not so quiet that if someone got out of that car they couldn’t hear it and realize they’re under surveillance.”

Bella’s knee bounced, and she moved forward in her chair. “That car is silver and could be a Civic. It might be Vivian Cochran’s.”

The car disappeared under a tree behind the house where the back end of a white truck was visible. A minute later a woman appeared carrying bags, possibly groceries, in the gap between the tree and the back of the house.

“Get as close a shot of her as possible,” Seth directed.

Seth took a series of screenshots before the woman disappeared through a door next to the covered patio. While the drone continued its examination of the property, Seth sent the screenshots to Bella’s computer. She clicked to pull them up and zoomed in as far as she could without distorting the images. The woman was shorter than average, looked to be medium weight, and had light hair. Bella wondered if it was bleached blonde. Seth leaned closer to study the images and Bella caught a whiff of him. So distracting.

“She seems to match the description of Vivian Cochran, and the car looks like the Civic at the post office in Modesto,” Bella said. “If those are groceries, we’ve found where she’s living.”

Seth’s brows dropped down. “Yes, but we still don’t know anything more about whether Anthony’s being held there, and if RJ is there.”

As he spoke, the drone returned to the back of the house where the woman had stepped outside once again. She disappeared under the tree, then reappeared carrying more bags. For the next five minutes, the drone flew over the property, until the operator said,

"I've got three minutes before I need to bring the drone back or run the risk of running down the battery."

"Copy that," Seth replied. "Is that the only drone you have? How long does it take to recharge?"

"Our other unit was recently damaged. This is the only one that's currently usable. It takes over an hour to recharge."

"Okay, I think we're—" Seth held up a hand. "No, wait, there she is again. Can you watch her for a couple more minutes? I want to see what she's up to."

"The drone is yours for two more minutes."

They watched her walk across an open area on the north side of the house, carrying a box. When she got to the big garage, she pulled keys from her jacket pocket. Even with the distance they could see the bright red puffball key fob. She unlocked the door and disappeared inside.

"I think that could be Vivian," Bella said. "It looked like something covered in foil in that box. Maybe food. If Anthony is in that building, she might be bringing him something to eat."

"Or that could have been a totally innocent woman walking to her garage with a box of whatever. We don't have enough for a warrant to enter the property."

Bella didn't know she was chewing on her lip until she noticed that Seth's gaze was locked there instead of on his computer screen. Her belly hitched. "Focus, Seth."

They might be neck deep in an investigation, their concern for Anthony's safety dictating that finding him was their primary focus, but despite all that, the magnetism between them was ever present, waiting for a break in concentration for it to rear its head.

"Easier said than done," he muttered, but returned his attention to the laptop. The woman stepped outside the garage, the box now empty, and crossed the open area to return to the house.

"You're clear to bring back your drone," he told the officer on the other end of the line. "Let me know when it's charged in case we want to have another go." He thanked the other officer and signed off.

***

Bella felt as if she'd had a double hit of espresso with an extra shot of caffeine. Seth and Linc were in a huddle, discussing how Seth would handle the meeting with RJ. She and Seth had worked to get the tone just right in the email, and must have succeeded. RJ's response had been almost eager. Another exchange of emails and they'd solidified arrangements for a meeting. Which was why Seth was standing in the small living room of their hotel, dressed in jeans and a bomber-style jacket unzipped over a black t-shirt.

"I think I should go with you," Linc insisted. "RJ is working some angle, and I don't like you going in without backup. He agreed to this meeting too easily."

Seth was shaking his head. "Having both sons show up might set him off. He contacted me, and if he's working an angle, I'll figure it out."

"Not if you're ambushed," Linc stated.

Seth kept talking as if what Linc said didn't matter. "I think he's eager because we dangled the hook he feeds off. I'm unhappy with my job, and I'm open to hearing what he has to say. He knows it would be a major coup for him with his *followers*, and a personal victory if he could entice me to join his side. He took the bait. I don't want to spook him before I can find out about Anthony."

"Who cares if having both his sons show up spooks him? He could have his own backup with AKs. You don't know what you're walking into."

"I'll deal with whatever it is. I'm not going to jeopardize what we might get out of him by deviating from our agreement." Seth put a hand on his brother's shoulder. "You want to put a fist in his face and take my back. Got it. But not this time."

"I could be the backup." Bella was on the receiving end of a double dose of intensity as both the Jameson brothers lasered their attention on her.

"RJ doesn't know who I am. I could pose as Seth's girlfriend who wanted to tag along to the bar."

Seth scowled. "A US Marshal doesn't go to a meeting with his girlfriend. RJ won't buy it. I'm going in alone. That's the only way this will work."

"You're being stubborn," she said calmly, but felt anything but. "There's got to be a way to mitigate the danger."

Seth gave her his *I've made my decision* look. Linc asked, "You got both your phones, personal and official?"

"Yeah, I got 'em."

"Good. If RJ decides a Chief Deputy US Marshal is too big a prize to resist, at least if you have your phones, we should be able to find where they dump your body."

"Nice," Seth muttered.

"Here's another idea," Bella offered.

She wouldn't be so jittery if she was doing something productive, something that would help to ensure Seth came back alive and in one piece. "I'll go to the bar early. You know, just another girl at the Easy Rider on a Monday evening. I've seen enough photos of RJ. I'll recognize him. Once I identify where he's sitting, I'll find a seat where I can observe. That way if there's an issue, Seth isn't on his own."

"Easy Rider is a biker bar and you're too classy for anyone to believe you're a biker babe. You'd stick out like a sore thumb." The scowl on his face told her she was on the losing side of the argument.

She had to try anyway. "Give me an hour and I can be a biker babe."

Linc elbowed his brother. "I bet she could. Get her a short leather skirt. You know, black with silver studs, and a lacy thing under a leather jacket. She'd look hot."

"Fuck no." Seth turned to Bella, eyes blazing. "You go into that bar alone, you'll be pegged as looking for a hookup. Every unattached male will be hitting on you. Hell, even the attached ones will be hitting on you. You'll draw too much attention, which is exactly what we don't want."

Bella sighed in exasperation. Seth wasn't going to budge. "Then Linc and I will hang out somewhere nearby. I looked at a street view. Easy Rider is at the edge of a warehouse district in South Lake Tahoe. There's not much around there, but I did find an all-night diner where Linc and I can hang out. It's not a great solution, but at least you can call us and we'd be nearby if you get into trouble. I think that's the best plan."

He studied her, then gave a curt nod. "Okay."

Linc's phone chimed, and he pulled it from the pocket of his jeans, collapsing onto the small sofa as he texted.

Bella moved to stand in front of the window. Their room was on the twelfth floor and the granite slopes of the Sierra Nevada mountains to the west glimmered in the late afternoon sun. Despite the early summer heat, there was still snow on the peaks. She turned her back to the view when Linc spoke.

"That was Dave Fuller. He's the lead marshal from the Reno office. A witness has come forward who claims they saw Anthony the night he was taken. They're bringing him in and I want to be there. I'll be back in a couple hours."

Bella turned back to her perusal of the mountains, not surprised when Seth came up behind her. He slipped his arms around her and pulled her against him. He bent his head to rest his cheek against her hair, his chest expanding against her back as he breathed.

"You okay?"

She shrugged. "I'm worried about your meeting with RJ."

"I have to do it. I'll be fine."

"I know, but I can still worry."

He lowered his head farther and nuzzled the curve of her neck. She closed her eyes and leaned her head against his. It didn't seem to matter there were unresolved issues between them. In that moment, it felt like all the uncertainties were stripped away and they were simply Seth and Bella. Two people whose insatiable need for each other was laid bare.

She tilted her head to give him better access and as he moved his mouth to the underside of her jaw, she was acutely aware of the growing hardness pressed against her backside. She turned in his arms and then his lips were on hers in unrestrained hunger.

The heat that raced through her shouldn't have been surprising. It seemed they only needed to touch and she went up like a match to dry tinder. His hands swept down her waist, cupped her ass, and pulled her closer. Bella moved against the hard ridge of his erection, eliciting a groan.

He pulled back slightly and tipped her head up with his thumbs. "Do you want this? I sure as hell do."

She stared into his eyes stormy with emotion. Into his face, which she trusted in all matters except those of the heart. Being with him again could put her mental well-being in grave danger. It would leave her vulnerable, and she knew she couldn't take losing him.

But there was also the voice in the back of her mind saying maybe it would be worth it. Maybe being with him, for however long whatever was between them lasted, would be worth the heartache when he left her. Then she remembered that moment of devastation when she realized her mother was never coming back, and only months later, holding Alexei's hand as their grandmother drove away. She'd never be able to move past the love she felt for him if they continued to be intimate. Eventually, he too would leave her, and her heart would shatter.

"I think you better stop."

He stopped stroking her rib cage. "That doesn't sound like a hard no."

"It is. I'm sorry. I can't risk it."

"Risk what?"

She closed her eyes. She might as well say it. If he understood, then he would leave her alone. At this point, what did it matter if she bared her heart? Opening her eyes, she said, "Loving you."

She didn't think she could have shocked him more if she'd told him she was joining a traveling circus as the painted lady.

"You love me?" The disbelief in his voice would have been comical if he wasn't slowly breaking her heart.

She opened her mouth to reply when the hotel door swung open and Linc strode into the room. "The car has a flat, and can you believe it doesn't have a spare? The rental company is sending out a—" He stopped abruptly, his gaze traveling from his brother to Bella who were now standing three feet apart. "Am I interrupting something?"

"No, of course not," Bella replied, forcing a smile that threatened to splinter her face.

"You know, I'm interested in what that witness has to say," Seth growled. "I'll go with you."

Linc glanced at his brother, then back to Bella. "Okay, sure. Whatever you want."

Chapter Fourteen

Seth paused inside the door of Easy Rider and took a slow look around. Motorcycle exhaust pipes served as handrails, a sign on the wall read “Hawg Heaven Highway,” and a couple of flaming skull posters hung on the wall. He guessed biker bar interior decorating was SOP since all the dives looked the same. The big guy behind the bar seemed more likely to plant a fist in your face than pour you a drink, and made Seth wonder if the man’s choice of defense under the bar was a baseball bat or a shotgun. In the dim light, he skimmed his gaze over the people sitting hunched on barstools, most of them staring into the glasses in from of them. The clientele was mostly male and gray-haired. Booths lined the walls where a few couples sat nursing their drinks. People came to a place like this for serious drinking, not for the ambience.

Seth glanced into a room to the left of the door. Two men were playing pool and looked like they’d come straight from central casting with leather vests over bulging beer guts, wallet chains hanging from their pockets, and stained beards. The taller of the two chalked his grimy pool cue while the other set up the table. An old-fashioned jukebox belted out a Creedence song, and John Fogerty’s wailing competed with the cue ball clack making the break shot.

Seth had deliberately arrived early. He wanted the advantage of picking his seat and observing if RJ arrived with anyone. Seth headed for an empty booth in a back corner where he wouldn’t have to watch his back. He caught the attention of the only waitress, who gave him a once-over as he ordered a beer and took a seat. That his seat also afforded him a view of the TV over the bar wasn’t a hardship. He watched as the Dodgers’ third baseman tagged out a player on a forced run, then winged the ball to first for the double play, retiring the side. He wondered if Bella liked baseball.

The station went to commercial, and he slouched back in his seat. He couldn’t get Bella’s voice out of his head. She was at risk of loving him? She'd dropped that bombshell, and before he could recover enough to form a coherent thought over the thundering in his ears, Linc had barreled in with all the finesse of a camel at a tea party.

Why was loving him a risk? He didn't know the answer, but he knew those few words changed everything. Now he had a starting point to work from, and there wasn't a chance in hell he was going back to where they'd been. He and Bella were going to see this thing through. As far as he was concerned, they belonged together.

And he'd better get his head back in the game before he blew this operation.

Dudes wearing leather over beer guts seemed to be the preference at Easy Rider as a few more came in and ordered their drinks at the bar before joining the players in the pool room.

Seth was sipping from a longneck when the door opened and two men entered. Neither of them was RJ, but their attire and demeanor instantly snagged Seth's interest. Both had shaved heads, full beards, and wore black leather jackets with heavy boots. Tattoos of swastikas and other symbols denoting white supremacy covered most of their exposed skin.

The shorter of the two, a stocky man with a thick neck, sported iron crosses inked across each eye. But what caught Seth's attention was the stylized "F" inscribed on his right cheek, with a "D" on the left. Freedom Defenders for sure.

FD guy scanned the room. His gaze latched on Seth and after a hard stare, he turned to the other man, a giant who had to top out at over three hundred muscle-bound pounds, and said something before they started across the room.

The bartender saw them coming and took a baseball bat from beneath the counter and set it on top of the bar in clear warning. The stocky man waved Godzilla to the bar, where a patron hastily vacated a stool to put distance between himself and the skinhead.

FD guy approached Seth. He placed a hand on his hip, pulling back his jacket in a move no doubt calculated to reveal the holstered pistol on his belt. Nevada was an open carry state, but California was not. The bar was barely a mile over the state line in California. Seth had spotted a couple other armed patrons, and guessed the guy behind the bar wasn't bothered by the violation of state law.

Seth studied the man coming toward him. The skinheads probably thought the tats made them look intimidating, but Seth thought that much ink looked a little OCD, like once they got started, they didn't know how to stop.

"You Jameson?"

"Who's asking?"

"Answer the fucking question."

Seth considered him. "Yeah, I'm Seth Jameson. Who are you?"

"Hell no, I'm not telling an asshole US Marshal my name. You can call me Dub."

"Okay, Dub, why are you and Godzilla here? The deal was I would meet with Richard Jameson. Only him."

"You'll meet with him, but not here. Think he would risk you having a team ready to grab him? Big Dog hasn't stayed ahead of the marshals all this time by being a dumbass."

"What about you, Dub? You a fugitive too? Though I guess that would make you the dumbass if you agreed to meet with me." Dub hesitated and Seth figured he'd hit the truth dead on. "Guess Big Dog didn't mind risking you meeting the marshal."

"Go fuck yourself. You don't know shit about me other than that Big Dog trusts me to fetch you." He jerked a thumb toward the backdoor. "Let's go."

Seth raised the bottle to his lips and took a slow sip, then set it down carefully. "I haven't finished my beer." He gestured to the bar. "By the looks of it, your pal Godzilla is just getting started." Seth couldn't have timed the comment better. Dub looked over as the bartender placed a lowball glass half full of amber liquid in front of the big man. "Looks like he's settling in. Have a seat so we can talk over our options."

Dub muttered an expletive and strode to the bar where he growled something at Godzilla who gave a defensive shrug and a scowl. Seth took the opportunity to tap out a quick message to Bella and Linc.

RJ a no-show. Sent two skinheads to bring me to his location. Wait for update. He hit send and slid his phone back in his coat pocket before Dub returned to the table.

"Let's go, asshole. I've got orders to take you to Big Dog."

"I told you, that's not what I agreed to. You don't really exude trustworthiness with those freaky crosses over your eyes, you know?" He took another sip of his beer.

Dub slid into the opposite seat, and then leaned forward with his elbows on the table. "Listen up, asshole. Big Dog said you might be reluctant. Said I should persuade you however I see best." He cracked his knuckles making a sound like popcorn popping. This asshole watched too many mafia movies. "I'll start by explaining the setup, and I'll say it real slow so you can understand. I'm in charge, and you'll do what I say. Me and Pete are here to transport you to a secure location. Before you can speak to Big Dog, you'll be searched for weapons and electronic devices. Once he's done with you, we'll bring you back here." The ink over his eyes stretched as he raised his brows. "You follow all that, pretty boy?"

Seth shook his head once. "No fucking way. I said I'd meet with my dad. I'm not going anywhere with a couple of dipshits decorated like pathetic clowns. No deal."

Dub grinned, showing stained teeth. "I'll say it a different way so you get the full meaning. Big Dog wants to meet with you, so that's what's going to happen. He sets the conditions, not you. You can leave here under your own steam, or Pete and I can carry you out of here. Either way, you're going. That's what Big Dog wants, and he's the boss." Dub's grin widened. "He said to get you there, but he didn't say what kind of condition you needed to be in."

Seth leaned forward, studying the other man's face. "Man, did that hurt when they inked around your eyes? I arrested this guy once who had the whites of his eyes tattooed. Can you believe it? The whites of his eyes were tattooed red. That had to hurt like shit. Where else you got ink?"

"What the fuck, man. You understand English? I gave you two options. Pick one, or I'll pick for you."

"Sure, I'm taking option three." Seth snaked out a hand to grab Dub by the front of his shirt and yanked him forward.

Seth kept his tone reasonable. "Don't even think of drawing your weapon, you fucker, because under this table I've got a forty caliber Glock pointed right at your dick. You make a move I don't like and I'll blow that tiny dick off and there won't be enough of it left for you to jack off with."

With his peripheral vision he could see the big man at the bar give a startled jerk when he figured out something was going on at the booth. He paused with his glass halfway to his mouth and appeared to need a minute to process what he was seeing.

"Wave off Godzilla, because the minute he starts over here, I shoot you, then I shoot him. Got it?" To make his point, Seth jammed the muzzle of the gun into Dub's crotch. Dub uttered a muffled scream and his face blanched. The big guy pushed up from his stool.

"Stay back before he shoots me," Dub wheezed.

Only one other patron in the bar seemed to notice what was going down. He hastily threw a couple bills on the bar and scuttled for the door.

Seth shoved Dub back in his seat. He sat back himself, resting the Glock on his thigh. "Your dick's still in firing range, so no sudden moves, *asshole.* Keep your hands on the table where I can see them."

"Big Dog's not going to like this."

"He'll have to deal. Tell me where he wants you to take me, then I'll decide if that's where I'm going."

Dub leaned forward. "I told Big Dog he couldn't trust you. You may be his kid, but you're a marshal and you'll double-cross him. He thinks he can bring you over to our side, but I know you'd arrest his ass the second you had a chance. At least he listened and agreed we wouldn't take you to the compound."

Seth kept his face expressionless at the mention of a compound. That was exactly where he wanted to go. He used the gun under the table to nudge Dub. "Get to the point."

"*Fuck.* He'll meet us at a turn out on the highway on the other side of the lake."

"Why there?"

"It's someplace no one's going to bother us," Dub sneered. "It's also where there's a five-hundred-foot drop-off to the river. I could kick your body over the side of the mountain and no one would know where to look for you."

"Way to sell it, shithead. I'm not meeting my old man there."

Seth's mind raced to figure out a way to salvage the situation. It was obvious Dub didn't support RJ meeting with Seth. Could be that Dub was RJ's top lieutenant and felt his position would be threatened if Seth were brought into the organization. He needed to believe he'd get positive intel if he were going to risk a meeting. He eyed the man sitting across the narrow table and gauged how he could get more information out of him.

He brought up his phone and, one-handed, snapped a photo of Dub. "Should've smiled, man, I could've sent you a copy to include with your Christmas cards." Seth shot him a mock-quizzical look. "Do skinhead punks like you even do the holidays? You know, that time of year when good people share love and joy? What do skinheads do, send their moms wishes of hate and dystopia?" He hit send. "Thanks for that pic, by the way. I'll check to see if you're in the system."

"You think you're a fucking genius, don't you?" Color rushed back into Dub's face under the ink. "You think because you're a big-shot marshal, you hold all the cards? We've got a card you want, asshole. Keep up with the attitude and you'll never get that card back."

That caught Seth's attention. "What are you talking about?"

"Guess you don't have all the answers after all. I'll lay it out for you. We've got something that you want. If you want any chance of getting it back, you'll cooperate."

"You're bullshitting me. You've got nothing I want."

Dub reached for a pocket and Seth made sure the man felt the muzzle of the gun pressed against his kneecap.

"I'm getting my phone. You think I'm bullshitting you? I got proof."

Dub pulled his phone from his pocket. He tapped a few times, then turned it so Seth could see. Anthony Rebollar stared at him from the small screen, expression defiant, eyes scared, and blood smeared under his nose.

"Got your attention, didn't I, asshole?"

Seth nodded slowly.

"Guess we got the attention of that fucking judge too. We're going to make things right in this country. You want this kid to stay alive, then you're coming with us. Got it?"

There wasn't any choice. "Yeah, I got it."

Seth put a ten under his empty bottle. They filed out the backdoor of the bar, Dub in front of Seth, and Godzilla behind him. They crossed the parking lot to the farthest corner where an older model, dark-colored Suburban sat parked in the shadows next to a Dumpster.

Confirmation that RJ and the Freedom Defenders had kidnapped Anthony changed the game. Seth had to figure out where they were holding the boy. His gut told him RJ was linked with Vivian Cochran. There'd been a white truck parked under the tree behind her house, and the last time they'd seen him, RJ had been driving a white pickup.

Weak evidence, but it was a start. When the drone had caught Vivian crossing the yard to the big metal garage, Bella had said Vivian had been bringing food to Anthony. Seth needed to do more than talk to RJ; he needed to get to the compound and gain access to that garage. A plan was formulating in his brain. It would be painful, but there was a possibility it could work.

Dub turned to Seth when they stopped beside the Suburban. "Give me your phone."

"No."

Godzilla opened his mouth in what was likely supposed to be a smile, silver-capped front teeth gleaming faintly in the light above the backdoor of the bar. He looked like he chewed nails for breakfast.

Dub shook his arms like he was loosening up before a boxing round. "Give me your fucking phone."

Seth braced himself. He should probably turn over his phone, but it didn't sit right. "No."

"Asshole has more guts than smarts." Dub lashed out with a fist, lightning fast. Seth ducked that one, but not the sharp jab thrown by Godzilla that snapped his head back. A hand to his back slammed Seth face first against the Suburban.

"Sweet, I get to frisk the cop," Dub gloated.

Godzilla kept a heavy hand on Seth's neck as Dub searched him.

Seth's phone was snatched from his pocket and his stomach sank when his Glock was taken from the holster at his shoulder. Shit. There was nothing good about this. Dub continued his search. Seth held his breath, then let it out in a hiss of frustration when his marshals-issued phone was discovered in the inside pocket of his jacket.

Dub chortled with glee. "A gun and *two* phones. Must mean you're a special kind of asshole. Not going to help you though."

Godzilla loosened his hold and Seth shrugged him off. A barking dog ringtone sounded from Dub's phone. Eyes on Seth, he put the phone to his ear.

"We got him, boss." He listened, nodding like the person on the other end of the line could see him. "Will do."

Dub disconnected and, in a casual move, tossed both of Seth's phones into the Dumpster. "Now we're ready to go. Dear old dad is waiting."

***

The big Suburban took a turn at a dark intersection, driving straight into what looked like a black hole, headlights providing twin cones of light in front of them. Despite the wide swath of stars, the moonless sky didn't offer much light. They'd left the developed area around Lake Tahoe, skirting the lake on its western side before taking a winding road heading north. Seth had spotted a sign. They were taking the road linking Tahoe to Truckee. Trying to think past the ache to the side of his face, he brought up a mental map of the area and figured they were in the general vicinity of the Cochran property.

Seth wished he had a bag of ice. He couldn't see shit from his right eye because of swelling where Godzilla's huge fist had hit with the force of a freight train. The big guy sat on the driver's side of the backseat, but angled toward Seth, a forty-five resting across his lap. Dub drove, whistling under his breath as he sped into the darkness.

"How'd you guys get involved in this skinhead bullshit?" Seth asked conversationally.

"Shut up, asshole," Dub growled.

"No, really. I want to know. I'm always curious how the criminal mind works."

"We're not criminals."

"Don't talk to him, Pete." The glow from the dashboard caught Dub glancing in the rearview mirror.

"Come on, give me a break. I want to understand. Were you bullied in school and becoming a skinhead made you feel powerful? It'd explain those impressive tattoos. It's like wearing a blinking neon sign saying *I'm a badass, don't mess with me.* That's a powerful thing. I bet those bullies would give you respect if they could see you now."

"I wasn't bullied."

"I told you not to talk, dumbass."

Seth shifted so he could see Pete more clearly in the shadowy interior of the vehicle. "Seems like you're still hanging with bullies." Seth nodded toward Dub.

"I said I wasn't bullied. Kids at school left me alone 'cause I could kick their asses."

"So maybe you were bullied at home. Your dad beat up on you?"

"My dad didn't stick around. Mom beat the shit out of me pretty regular, though."

"Shut it, both of you," Dub snarled.

Seth ignored him. "Man, that sucks. Guess we have that in common. Not the mom part, but being abandoned by our dads."

"Yeah, it sucks. I played football in high school and my dad never came to one of my games."

"I get it. I played varsity baseball and my dad stopped coming to my games, too."

"You played baseball? That game's too slow. I like football better."

"That's fucking it." Dub slammed on the brakes and the Suburban fishtailed before sliding to a stop at the side of the road. He spun around in his seat. "No more, you hear me? Get a clue, Pete. Asshole here is trying to do what they call building a rapport." He gave the words extra emphasis. "He's not your friend, he's not your therapist. He's a fucking Deputy US Marshal, and he's Big Dog's kid. That should be enough to keep you from spilling your goddamn guts. And you," he swiveled to point a finger at Seth, "lay off, or *I'll* beat the shit out of *you* and tell your dad that you tripped over my fists. Got it, asshole?"

"That's Chief Deputy."

"What?"

"I'm a Chief Deputy US Marshal, not a Deputy US Marshal. Bit more of a mouthful, isn't it? Comes with a nice pay raise, though."

Dub lunged over the seat. This was the part where things could go sideways, and Seth had to hope for the best. He evaded the flailing fists, but he couldn't evade Godzilla and his forty-five. He caught Seth across the temple with the butt of his gun.

Seth felt his head explode, and with blackness closing in, hoped his plan worked.

Chapter Fifteen

Bella stared out the window of the diner. Lake Tahoe glimmered between the buildings across the road, reflecting lights from the marina. She'd like to visit the area during the day when she was free to enjoy the mountain scenery she'd gotten a glimpse of from their hotel window. Despite the warm summer days, nighttime temperatures in the Sierras were regularly in the forties and, as the diner's door swung open to admit a gray-haired couple, both using canes, she was glad she'd packed her heavy zippered jacket.

She sipped from the mug she held in both hands. The green tea had cooled and wasn't working to settle her stomach. Seth had sent them a text, and then the photo, which had eased her worry somewhat, but she couldn't get rid of the feeling something could go wrong and Seth would be in danger. There were too many uncontrollable variables, which could sabotage the success of the operation.

RJ was notoriously unreliable, and the emotional dynamics between Seth and his father made the situation all the more volatile. She and Linc were too far away to provide backup, and the thought brought on a bout of nausea, which had been eating at her stomach for the past hour. Coming to a decision, she set down her mug.

"We should go to the bar."

Linc looked up from his phone. "Explain."

"Seth might need us. We already know that RJ isn't there so we don't have to worry about you being recognized. We go in as a couple looking for a drink, and we're there as backup if necessary."

Linc considered her suggestion. "He'll kick our asses if we mess up the operation."

"How are we going to mess it up?"

"For one, there's a chance RJ could still show up, though I think if that had been his plan, he wouldn't have sent the skinheads. I can pass as a dude who goes to a biker bar, but you, sweetheart? My brother called it. You're too classy for a joint like that. You'd stick out and people would notice you. Seth doesn't need that kind of a distraction."

She narrowed her eyes. "Give me a minute." She grabbed her purse, rose from her seat, and disappeared into the bathroom. She returned five minutes later and was gratified to see Linc's jaw go slack.

He recovered quickly. "How the hell'd you do that?"

"A little lipstick, hairspray, and I stowed the jacket in my bag. It's not a little leather skirt with silver studs, but I think I'll do."

After their conversation in the hotel room, she'd put a couple of things in her big purse, just in case. Bright red lipstick and hairspray to tease her hair worked to give her what she thought of as a sexy, vampish look. She was already wearing slim black boots with skintight jeans, and while she'd miss the added warmth, removing the jacket and half unbuttoning the bright plaid shirt underneath revealed her lacy camisole.

"Hell yeah, you'll do. Seth will swallow his tongue." At her startled look, he closed his eyes. "Shit, sorry. I shouldn't have said that, but sometimes I wish you two would get out of your own way."

"What's that supposed to mean?"

"It means I care about both of you and want to see you happy." He raised a hand when she opened her mouth. "That's all I'm going to say about it. Let's go."

Linc held open the door and they stepped out into the chilly night. In minutes they were in the car with Linc behind the wheel as Bella engaged the app on her phone to locate Seth's devices.

"His phones show him still at the bar."

"Good."

They arrived at the half-full parking lot and Bella was somewhat reassured to see Seth's rental parked near the backdoor. Linc put the car in park. "Let's go, sexy girlfriend."

She raised her brows in mock horror. "'Sexy girlfriend'? That's all you've got? I'll have to ask Mikayla what in the world made her think you were the one and only for her."

"Hey, I was on my game with her. Nothing like beating off an attacker and rescuing the girl to get her to fall for you. Just ask her. Now she loves me best." Linc's smile was as goofy as it was endearing.

They walked to the front of the bar. Linc laced his fingers through hers as they approached the door.

They stepped into the sounds of a bar at its evening peak. There was the clack of pool balls interspersed with the thud of darts hitting a target. A big-screen TV over the bar showed a guy in a blue uniform hitting a baseball that was caught by a guy in a red uniform. Linc tugged her into the room. Scanning the booths and tables, she rubbed a hand over her stomach when she realized, unless he was in the bathroom, Seth was gone.

The waitress motioned them to a table as she cleared off empties. They sat, Linc flashing a smile at the woman whose name tag identified her as Deb. Her face showed lines that might put her in her forties, but Bella guessed she might actually be younger. Deb gave Linc a tired smile back before lugging the bus tub behind the bar.

Linc leaned forward. "I'll check for the signal from Seth's phone. You talk to the bartender, see if you can learn anything."

Bella approached the bartender, and minutes later returned to the table. Her voice was clipped in frustration. "The bartender says he hasn't seen anyone matching Seth's description. Same response when I asked him about the skinheads. He says he runs a clean place and no skinheads come in here."

"He's lying."

"Yeah, he is. My guess is he keeps his clientele happy by minding his own business."

"The locator app says both Seth's phones are still in the area. We didn't check his car when we came in, so I'm heading back to the parking lot to do that."

Bella spotted Deb disappearing through the swinging door of the women's bathroom. "Okay, I'll meet you there."

Bella pushed through the door to the small restroom. Deb stood smoking a cigarette, blowing smoke through the small window opened to the outside. Bella bent over the sink to wash her hands, catching Deb's eye in the mirror.

"Could you help me out? I'm looking for someone I think was here earlier this evening." Deb lifted a brow as she took a drag on the cigarette. "He's late thirties, about six two, dark brown hair that falls over his forehead, intense gray eyes. He would have been here in the last hour."

Deb gave an incredulous laugh. "You mean tall, dark, and hotter than sex on a stick? That guy?"

Bella couldn't help laughing. "Yeah, that's him."

"What, are you collecting all the good ones? The hot guy you're with not enough for you?"

"I guess it's my lucky night, at least if I find the guy I'm looking for. Have you seen him?"

"Yeah, I saw him." Deb blew another steam of smoke toward the window. "Looked all cool and steely-eyed like Gary Cooper in *High Noon*."

"I don't know it."

Deb hitched a shoulder. "I watch old movies with my dad. He likes the westerns."

Bella made a mental note to check out the movie. She was always trying to fill the holes in her knowledge of American pop culture. "Did you see when the man left?"

"Yeah, I saw when he left. I saw who he left with, too. Those two were bad business. Had tattoos all over their faces and heads like a couple of freaks."

"When was that?"

"About twenty minutes ago. The three of them left out the backdoor. The one you're asking about paid for his beer, though, and left a decent tip."

Bella thanked Deb and left the bar to find Linc climbing out of the Dumpster in the corner of the parking lot. His tone was grim when he held up two objects in his hand. "He's not in his car, and his phones were tossed in the trash."

She swallowed hard as her nausea ratcheted up her throat.

***

Seth woke feeling like his head was a pressure cooker ready to explode at any moment.

He opened his eyes, or rather, his eye, to dappled sunlight. He was lying back on a bed. At least he was on a bed, and a cursory glance suggested he was in a bedroom. Memory of the night before had him pushing up, then regretting that movement as pain spiked.

"Bottle of Tylenol is on the table next to you."

The voice came from the man sitting in a chair next to a window. His hair was white and he had a face craggier than it had once been, with deep grooves bracketing either side of his mouth. His long, lean build was the same as Seth remembered. It was a shock to see what he might look like in thirty years. His father had lived hard and showed it. Seth hoped fate would be kinder to him.

His father stared at him with blue eyes Seth remembered from childhood. As a kid he felt like that stare could look right through him. A memory slammed into him. He'd been only six or seven, and was violently ill throughout a long night. He woke in the morning to find his father had stayed in a chair beside his side all night.

"Dad." Emotions he didn't want grabbed him by the throat and threatened to choke him. Seth thought he'd effectively cauterized any leftover feelings he might've had for his father, but they'd slipped under his guard, ready to undermine his control.

His father rose to his feet. "Take the meds, son. We'll talk when you don't feel like shit."

That rough, deep voice was another unexpected wrench back into the past. Yelling at him from the stands to slide into third, telling him that strong men didn't cry, explaining how it was Seth's responsibility to watch after his siblings. The last memory came with a jolt. It had never occurred to him his father had telegraphed abandoning his family.

Fast approaching seventy and with a slight rounding to his shoulders, Richard Jameson still exuded an aura of strength. Take him back a hundred and fifty years, and he'd fit right in with the gunslingers of the old west. He wasn't wearing the black hat, but he had a holster slung low on his hip, the pearl-handled grip of a revolver gleaming dully in the light coming through the window.

He left the room, closing the door behind him. Muffled voices came from the other side of the door, but Seth couldn't make out what was said. He boosted himself onto one elbow and reached for the Tylenol, gritting his teeth against the motion. Even that much movement made the world spin like he was on a carnival ride.

He didn't recall getting hit in the ribs, but they ached like a son of a bitch. He downed the pills with a half bottle of water and lay back against the pillow, closing his eyes to slow down the spinning. He'd give himself a minute, then he'd get up and deal with whatever came next.

The next time he opened his eyes the light had changed and he realized he'd slept for hours. *Shit.*

Swinging his feet over the side of the bed, he was glad his vision had settled. He took a quick survey. He likely had a concussion and should rest his brain, but that would have to wait. He was missing the bomber jacket, but still wore his clothes and shoes from the night before and his empty holster was draped over the footboard. It looked like they'd carried him in, tossed him on the bed, and called it good. He crossed the room to peer out a window, taking a moment to push it open.

His team had called it. A white pickup and silver Civic were parked under a pair of tall pines, and across the yard were the storage shed and long metal garage with its twin rollup doors. Beyond the garage the property sloped to the river. He could see water gleaming through the trees. He'd been taken to Vivian Cochran's property.

From the sun's position, he guessed it was late afternoon. He had to think the Cochran property would be the first place Bella and Linc would think to look for him. Locating Anthony was Seth's top priority, but once the boy was safe, Seth was going after Richard Jameson and the Freedom Defenders were going down with him.

Seth used the john attached to the bedroom, wincing when he caught his reflection in the mirror. His right eye was swollen shut, and the skin had split over a lump that was raised below the hairline on his forehead. Godzilla'd had a heavy hand with that forty-five.

Seth splashed water on his face, rubbing to remove the blood that had dried into his hairline. When the water ran clear, he dabbed his face with the towel. He left the bedroom, and saw a woman sitting in an easy chair with a laptop resting on a tray.

She glanced up, and then gave him a once-over. "You look like him. I'm Viv." Like in her driver's license photo, Vivian Cochran's hair was dyed blonde. She looked short, a bit overweight, and had painted fingernails that clicked as she tapped on the keyboard of the computer.

"I'm Seth." He was trying to figure out his status. Was he a prisoner? A guest?

"Rick gave those two boys hell for the condition you were in last night."

He didn't say anything. Calling Dub and Godzilla boys was like calling his Glock a squirt gun. Seth took note of the layout of the house.

The bedroom he'd been in was to the left of the living room, and a hall to the right suggested more bedrooms in that direction. He guessed wide openings to either side of the back wall of the living room would be to a kitchen in the rear. The floral patterns on the couch upholstery and the wallpaper reminded him of the décor in his grandparents' home when he was a kid. Dated but clean. Not that he'd expected Nazi flags or a copy of *Mein Kampf* on the coffee table, but there was nothing about the place that would lead someone to guess that it served as headquarters for a white nationalist terrorist organization.

"Guess you'll want something to eat."

"Where's RJ?"

"RJ? That's what you're calling your dad?"

"Got to call him something, and Dad doesn't fit anymore. Where is he?"

She shrugged, then powered down her laptop and shut the lid. A door opened and closed somewhere in the house. "There he is now. Follow me. There's hot coffee, and you can make yourself a sandwich if you're hungry."

"Thanks. Does RJ live here?"

"He does. We're not married, but we've been together for a year or so. Rick helped me through a hard time when my husband died."

Seth followed her into the kitchen.

RJ settled himself at a kitchen table, dropped heavily into a ladderback chair, and rubbed his knee. His gaze was on Seth. "He doesn't need to know any of that."

Vivian poured coffee into a heavy mug and set it in front of RJ. "I'll get your pills and some water." She returned a moment later with a vial of pills and an uncapped water bottle.

RJ gave Seth a look that seemed almost sheepish. "For arthritis. Got it in my knees. Doc says I need knee replacement surgery. At night I add pills for high blood pressure and cholesterol. Can you believe your old man's getting old?"

Seth shook his head, struck by a feeling of unreality. If his life hadn't taken a hard turn when he was eighteen, it might have been his mom bringing the pills, and he might have been sitting down with his dad. Instead, the man at the table was a stranger whom Seth had gotten half his DNA from. Weird thought.

RJ lifted his mug to sip. “You drink coffee?”

“Yeah.”

“Then get yourself a cup and sit down, boy. We need to talk.”

Chapter Sixteen

Seth opened a cupboard, looking for a mug, and made a quick study of the kitchen. Most interesting was a row of hooks by the door containing sets of keys, one of them on a bright red puffball key fob. A plastic zip bag with what looked like a peanut butter and jelly sandwich cut into neat squares, a banana, and a bag of Famous Amos chocolate chip cookies sat on the counter. Vivian hastily stuffed the lunch into a paper sack and took a can of Coke from the refrigerator. "This is for one of the guys we have working here. He forgot his lunch." She quickly disappeared out the kitchen door.

Maybe there was a worker who hadn't brought his lunch, but it could also be for a boy being held captive. From the window, Seth watched Vivian until she disappeared from view.

Seth poured coffee, and since the fixings were out, put together a pb&j. RJ came into the kitchen to refill his cup, limping slightly.

Throughout Seth's childhood, this man had been a giant, and it was a shock to see he now stood inches taller than his dad. Big and strong, Richard Jameson had a scathing tongue that could cut through a boy's confidence with laser precision, leaving it in tatters.

Even as a child, Seth had been aware his mother had tried to shield him from the worst of his father's criticisms, and that his father had singled out his eldest child for harsher discipline than his siblings.

Seth had been held to impossibly high standards, which were ever-changing and unattainable. He had a moment of insight, and realized much of what he'd achieved had likely been driven by a desire to prove he was better than his father: more honest, hard-working, decent, and dedicated.

Whatever flaws RJ possessed, Seth had compensated by working harder to prove that those weren't his flaws, that he was a better man.

RJ stopped in front of Seth. "Got taller, didn't you?"

"Yeah, I got taller."

"What about Lincoln? That boy was born long."

"This why you wanted to meet, to catch up with news about the family?" Seth made an effort to even out his tone, but accumulated anger from the past twenty years was hard to rein back.

RJ returned to the table and Seth took a chair across from him.

"It's natural for a man to want to know how his sons turned out, don't you think?"

"Not when you abandoned them without a backwards look, no, I don't think your interest is natural. You haven't asked about your daughter. The daughter you ordered killed."

"She tell you I ordered her killed? She always had a quick temper, that kid. But you always knew where you stood with her. You, on the other hand, kept shit bottled up. When you finally lost your temper, you went off like a rocket. That time when you were twelve or thirteen and I'd told you to wash and wax the car. You did a shitty job and I made you do it again. You were so pissed, you backtalked me. Had to take a strap to you to teach you a lesson."

Seth noticed RJ didn't deny having ordered his followers to kill Ellie. Whatever this meeting was about, it wasn't about family. "You were an asshole who beat his kids."

"Watch your tongue, boy. You needed to be taught discipline. You should thank me for it. You got me in trouble with your mother that time, though. Said she'd kick me out if I laid a hand on any one of you ever again." He shrugged. "She'd have done it, too. I wasn't ready to leave at that point, so I found other ways to keep you in line."

Memories flooded in, dark and painful. Seth needed every ounce of that discipline to control the temper that rose up fast and fierce, wrapping around his throat and squeezing until it hurt to breathe.

His father had taught him that leading with his emotions led to pain, and that pain didn't have to be physical. He'd learned it was better to keep what you were thinking or feeling inside, safe and walled off. He supposed RJ was right and Seth could thank the old man for that.

He sipped his coffee, considering how he was going to finesse the conversation. He needed to find a way to gain credibility, gain the possibility of acceptance. He needed to find an opportunity to get that key and gain access to the garage. If Anthony was being held there, Seth would free him. Then he was going to bring down the hammer on RJ and every traitor working for him.

RJ leaned back in his chair. "I named you boys after Americans I admired. You're named for Seth Bullock, who brought law and order to Deadwood. Your mother decided to name Ellie after Eleanor Roosevelt, which, in retrospect, was a poor choice as she was part of the New Deal that led our country on the road to socialism."

"Your point?"

"My point is that Seth Bullock was no saint, but he stood for something important and lived by a code. You're sacrificing your life working for the feds, upholding laws passed by corrupt politicians. It's not too late to make your life mean something."

"By doing what, joining you in your noble crusade?"

"It is a noble crusade. I've sacrificed a lot for it, including my relationship with my family."

Seth was now able to see out of his right eye, but he was having trouble thinking past the pain in his head that had started throbbing like a sore tooth.

"You said in the email you wanted to meet with me. Why?"

RJ took a moment to sip his coffee. "I'm a fugitive, you're a fucking US Marshal. Better question is why you agreed to meet with me."

"To bring you in, of course."

"You think you're going to arrest me? I've got your gun, boy. My guys would beat the shit out of you again if I told them to. How are you going to arrest me?"

"It might not be now, but I will. That's a promise."

"That doesn't answer my question, does it? What's your real motivation? Why meet with your fugitive dad when you know you're not bringing me in? I'll tell you what I think. The reason is because you want answers from me." He leaned back in his chair, gaze steady. "You want to know how I could have abandoned my family, left my kids, and left my wife." His expression turned sly. "Some say I stole from the government, planted a couple bombs. How is it that your dear old dad could have done those things you think are so reprehensible? That's what you really want to know, isn't it?"

Seth took a bite of sandwich, taking his time while chewing and swallowing before responding. "I figured all that out a long time ago. Your family never meant shit to you, and you're a racist bigot who doesn't possess an ounce of integrity." He shrugged. "Those answers are easy."

"Just because I don't want our country overrun by foreigners doesn't make me racist."

Seth had to choose his words carefully and searched for a nuanced response. RJ would never buy it if Seth suddenly embraced the white nationalist ideology. He needed to give him enough crumbs for RJ to warm to the idea that Seth would consider joining his side.

"I don't want my country overrun by foreigners, either, but I don't plant bombs in courthouses."

"Sometimes there has to be sacrifice. Think about the men who signed the Declaration of Independence. John Hancock signed his name big enough that the king didn't have to use his eyeglasses to read it. If the Revolutionary War had gone differently and the British had won, every one of the men who signed that document would have been hanged for leading a rebellion. At some point, history will look back on my people as the founding fathers of a new revolution. You can be a part of it."

"There's no way you can succeed."

"Not as long as I have the US Marshals on my ass. You could get them to back off."

"I can't trust you."

"That's where you're wrong. You can trust me. I did what I did because I have integrity. I believe in the fundamental ideals of our country, in the principles of freedom and liberty that are enshrined in the Constitution. I committed myself to stop those who want to hijack the government and create a socialist nightmare where the races are mixed and our freedoms are trampled under the heels of Marxist revolutionaries." He eyed his son. "You should want that, too. You should want to protect our country from hordes of immigrants who are leeches, sucking the life out of the hard-working people who create jobs."

There were landmines all through RJ's diatribe and Seth had to step carefully to navigate through them. He needed to say the right words, and if Seth could finesse it, find the opportunity to search for Anthony. "The question is how far is too far? What actions are too reprehensible? And since when is it up to you to decide who gets to be in our country?"

"Not me, the Constitution."

"I'm not saying you don't have a point, and maybe I agree with some of it. I'm worried about the direction the country is going, and that American culture is being appropriated by outsiders." He sipped his coffee and lifted his shoulder in a shrug. The words soured in his mouth when he thought of Bella and Alexei, and Anthony's parents, immigrants to the United States, and all they and others had brought to it. "There's not much I can do about it."

RJ's expression turned calculating. "You can do something about it. Being a marshal, you have more influence than a lot of people. I have some literature for you to read. You should talk to some of our people."

Seth gave a disbelieving snort. "You mean like Dub and Pete? If they're the best you've got, you're scraping the bottom of the barrel."

"Dub and Pete are useful as foot soldiers. No, you need to talk to other leaders of our organization. They're the ones who can provide the intellectual foundation that you're looking for. The foot soldiers are good at repeating the slogans, spreading the word. They're your racists and they're thugs, but they're useful to me. It's the generals you need to talk to."

Seth leaned sat back in the chair, his legs stretched out in front of him. "I'll listen to what they have to say." He narrowed his gaze. "But tell me, am I a prisoner here, or can I leave when I want?"

"You're not a prisoner. If you'd cooperated last night, we'd have had our meeting and you wouldn't have ended up here and in the condition you're in." RJ sighed heavily, sounding like a man with a lot of trouble on his mind. "We're holding a general meeting this weekend. Those men I want you to talk with are gathering here, some coming from out of state. I want you to meet them."

Seth nodded slowly. "Okay. Out of curiosity, where exactly am I?"

"Don't worry about where you are. We'll blindfold you when you leave here and you'll be taken back to the bar where your car is. When you join us this weekend, we'll pick you up." RJ paused. "I want you to stay for a bit. Give us a chance to talk."

The kitchen door opened and Vivian entered, Dub following her into the house. Daylight enhanced the impact of the tattoos over his face and head.

Vivian poured herself coffee and brought it to the table to sit next to RJ. She was a wild card, an unknown dynamic. Seth watched her carefully, trying to gauge what part she played in the operation. Dub, on the other hand, was a known entity.

"Everything good?" RJ asked.

Vivian gave a nod. "Got something to talk to you about, though." Her gaze moved from Seth back to RJ. "Later."

Dub opened the refrigerator and took out a chilled can of Coke. "Everything's as good as it can be with this outsider here. I can take care of him for you, Big Dog." Dub kicked the leg of Seth's chair. "How's the face, asshole? Looks painful. Can't say I'm sorry, though."

"You belong in a freakshow, dude. Scare any little kids today with that face?"

Dub leaned against the wall, his arms crossed over his chest. His mouth turned up in a smirk that Seth wouldn't have minded removing for him.

"Shut up, both of you." RJ pointed a long finger at Dub. "My son might be an asset. He and I are having a conversation. He's interested in our fight."

Vivian's brows lowered, and suspicion laced her tone. "He's a marshal. He's interested in arresting you."

"Yeah, he's a marshal, but he's also my son. That means something."

"He threatened to blow my dick off." Dub reached out a foot to push at Seth's chair again.

Vivian stared hard at Seth and he stared right back until she looked away, shaking her head. "He's playing you," she told RJ. "I don't trust him, either."

"Mom's right, we can't trust him. He's an outsider and could bring a shitload of trouble down on us." Seth kept his expression carefully neutral, not letting his surprise show. Dub was Vivian's son? That was a twist he hadn't expected.

Dub rattled on. "Let me and Pete take care of this guy. That's the only way to make sure he's not a threat to our movement. We don't want any chance he could come after us. We'll do the job, then take his body into the backcountry where it'll never be found and where it can't be traced back to us." Dub cracked his knuckles and Seth again had the image of a low-level mobster.

In a practiced move, RJ pulled the pearl-handled pistol from his holster and laid it on the table. He leaned forward as he glared at Dub from under bushy eyebrows, his voice as deadly as the implied threat from the unholstered six-shooter. "You lay a finger on my son and you won't survive the day. I'll plug a couple bullets through that simple brain of yours and watch you bleed out. Leave Seth to me. If he becomes an issue, I'll take care of him myself. Until then, you're to keep your hands off him, and everyone else, for that matter." The last words were said with pointed emphasis.

They may have been talking about his potential murder, but it was RJ's final comment that had Seth's interest piqued. He was certain RJ was referring to Anthony, and his words gave Seth an uneasy feeling.

Dub raised his hands as if in surrender, but his gaze shifted to his mother. That silent communication made Seth think they were up to something, something RJ was unaware of. There were undercurrents upon undercurrents, and Seth wished his head and ribs didn't hurt like a bitch so he could think more clearly.

RJ gestured toward Seth. "Viv put a clean shirt in your room earlier. Go ahead and take a shower if you want. We'll talk again later."

It was a clear dismissal, and he guessed RJ wanted to hear what Vivian had to say. Not seeing much option, Seth went to the room he'd passed the night in. A gray t-shirt and heavy flannel overshirt were folded on a chair by the door. He pulled off his boots and started the shower running in the miniscule bathroom. Then he opened the bedroom door a crack, listened carefully, and slipped into the living room.

Vivian's voice carried from the kitchen. "Rick, a buyer is interested in the military weapons we have, including the grenade launchers. They want to come tomorrow."

"Tomorrow's not good."

Her voice firmed. "It'll have to be. We need the money, and I don't want to put them off. Another letter came from the county saying they're going to seize this property if I don't pay the back taxes."

"The fucking government is always messing with people's rights." This came from Dub. Footsteps had Seth tensing, ready to retreat back to the bedroom. He heard water running in the sink and listened warily.

"Who are the buyers?" RJ asked.

"The guy who sent the email says his name is Zeb Petrov, though there's no way that's not an alias. Only an idiot would use his real name. They contacted me through a dark web connection," Vivian said. "I'm contacting a couple other people I know who'll be able to tell me if this guy's organization is legit. So far, he is. The word I'm getting back is that he's from the *bratva*."

Seth felt his insides freeze. The *bratva*? What did that mean? RJ made a garbled comment that ended with "fucking Russians," then spoke louder. "Do they have cash?"

"They say they do," Vivian responded. "They want the weapons quick. They say they have some of their people in Reno. I've heard the *bratva*'s involved in the casino business. Anyway, since that's close, they said they could send their buyers here around midmorning."

"I don't know. Sounds rushed to me. Could be a setup." RJ's voice sounded strained, and Seth remembered his father rubbing his knee.

"I'll vet them," Vivian said. "The *bratva* are a good connection. We've got that shipment coming from Washington next month, and if this works out, maybe we could do more business with them. Selling to them is easier for us than trying to smuggle weapons across the border to Mexico."

"I bet we could sell them a shitload of military equipment." Dub sounded eager. "Russians are white. I bet they'd agree with our beliefs, too."

"Let me get my laptop." There was the scraping sound of a chair sliding on the floor. "I'll check if they've gotten back to me."

Seth slipped back into the bedroom. He carefully closed the door, his mind racing as he considered the ramifications of what he'd heard. His team's working assumption had been that RJ was in control of the Freedom Defenders movement, but Seth wondered if RJ's control might be tenuous.

Seth stripped down and stepped into the shower, gritting his teeth when hot water streamed across the injuries on his face, though the water eased the ache in his ribs. A wide, purple bruise, about the width of the sole of a boot, was clearly visible on his right side. The cowards must have kicked him while he was unconscious.

Trying to focus beyond the pain, he processed the new information. The purported contact from the *bratva* added a new twist. If his hunch was right, the *bratva* popping up suddenly as part of the equation had to have something to do with his team. He couldn't be positive, but the coincidence glared at him as too unlikely.

If Bella, Linc, and Ellie had devised a plan to gain access to the compound, then he had to work it from the inside. Most urgently, he had to figure out where Anthony was and come up with a plan to keep the boy safe in case events turned violent.

He thought ahead to when Anthony was free and RJ was behind bars. Seth wanted this done and behind him. Only then could he have an honest conversation with Bella.

Being bashed in the head and taken captive weren't the best circumstances for clear introspection, but he knew some things for certain. He wanted a future with her. If she was pregnant, they'd get married as fast as he could arrange it. Regardless, he was going to do it right with a ring and a proposal, the whole deal. The thought of baring his heart to her scared the shit out of him, but that's what he'd have to do to have Bella with him the rest of his life.

Bare-chested and buttoning his jeans, he stepped out of the bathroom, coming to an abrupt halt when he heard low voices in tense conversation. He stepped closer to the open window and recognized Vivian and Dub.

"Rick says if the judge does what we tell him and dismisses the case, we have to release the little brat. We can't do that." Vivian's voice was low and urgent. "The kid has seen the weapons. He knows what we look like. If he goes free, he can identify us. We'd be in deep shit."

"What are we going to do about it?"

"My contact with the *bratva* says he's sending three of his people tomorrow in the late morning to check out the merchandise. I want to be ready."

Dub said something Seth couldn't completely make out, then Vivian responded, "I'll check them out before telling them where we are. No way am I letting people on my property until I'm sure they are who they say they are. They want to see the weapons before handing over a hundred thousand in cash. If they're satisfied with what we've got, they said they'd come back with a box van to transport the merchandise."

Seth eased closer to the open window, staying out of view.

Vivian continued, "Rick's going to be sleeping heavy tonight. I've got some sedatives, and he takes whatever pills I give him. I'll give them to him with his blood pressure meds before he goes to bed around eleven. That'll keep him out of the way and he'll never know. Once he's asleep, that's when you're going to get the boy. Take him to that quarry behind Little Mountain. The water is deep there. Do what needs to be done and put weights on him so his body stays at the bottom."

"I'll get Pete. We'll take care of it."

"Not Pete, Dub. Only you. You've got to do this yourself. You and I can trust only each other, like always. Understood?"

"Shit. Okay." There was a shuffling of feet. Seth didn't dare move. He didn't want them to realize the window was open.

Dub spoke, resentment lacing his tone. "What about Big Dog's asshole son? Big Dog acts like his shit don't stink, that his kid is going to help the cause. What about me? I've been working my ass off all along, doing the dirty work. I don't get respect for what I've done."

"Rick's blind when it comes to his kid."

"Then what are we going to do about him? He could really mess up the deal with the *bratva*. He's playing the old man. I swear it."

"Yeah, he's playing him, telling him what he wants to hear. No way in hell a guy who is a chief deputy is going to be our inside man with the marshals. I need to think about it. Maybe I can slip sedatives in a Coke or his coffee at dinner. If we could knock him out, you could take him to the quarry, too. Throw him in with a few weights and he'd drown."

"What do we tell Big Dog when the kid and his son disappear?"

"Leave that to me. If he doesn't like the answer, we can take care of him, too. He's about used up his usefulness."

Seth heard the rustling of footsteps. He chanced a quick peek out the window. Both had their backs to him and Dub was pulling keys from his pocket. "Pete and I are heading to town in a bit."

“Dammit, Dub, I need your help here. What’s so urgent that it can’t wait a couple days?”

“I want to hang out with my bros.”

“You’re going to buy weed.”

“So? It ain’t illegal anymore. My stash ran out, and I still want to hang with my bros.”

She shook her head. “Be back soon. As soon as Pete’s asleep, I’m counting on you to follow through with our plan. We need to move fast.”

Chapter Seventeen

Seth pushed out the screen, then climbed through the window. He'd feigned nausea and skipped the chicken strips and instant potatoes Vivian had prepared. Her fake concern turned his stomach. She'd brought him a pill she claimed was for nausea, and then watched with her beady eyes as he drank from a can of Coke. The chime of an incoming text had sounded and Seth had used the moment of distraction when both RJ and Vivian had been looking for their cellphones to drop the pill into her glass of wine.

The situation had gotten weirder. RJ was treating him like his long-lost son, but when he'd mentioned that he wanted to take a walk after dinner, both RJ and Vivian had said it wasn't a good idea. Vivian went so far as to mention that there'd been a mountain lion spotted a few days before and it wasn't safe. He'd claimed exhaustion and retreated to his room. Earlier, he'd noticed the door could be locked from the outside, and wasn't entirely surprised to hear the quiet click as the lock was engaged sometime later.

Now he stood outside the window in the shadow of the tall pine, the key to the garage safely tucked in his pocket, the red puffball key fob he'd separated the key from still on its hook so it wouldn't be missed. He'd also swiped the keys with the Honda insignia and a small flashlight he'd seen on a desk. Before dinner, Dub and Godzilla had sped off in the Suburban and, despite "the plan," had yet to return.

Vivian and RJ had retreated to a room on the other side of the living room. The sound of canned laughter from a TV program carried through the house.

A steady breeze had picked up, and it blew through the pines with a sound that reminded Seth of the ocean. The arc of the Milky Way spanned across the sky, and Seth had the sudden memory of his parents taking the family camping when he was a kid, and sitting around the campfire with his head tilted back, staring at the stars while his father pointed out constellations. His dad hadn't always been a jerk.

He found the bomber jacket under the bed and zipped it up against the falling temperature. He didn't dare use the flashlight until he was inside the garage. Making a quick assessment, he figured the most risk of being seen would be at the garage where a light shone over the door. That was an exposed position, one visible from any window on this side of the house or anyone driving into the compound. He set off at a trot, staying under trees until he got to the garage, then circled around the back, keeping to the shadows. At the corner, he glanced back at the house, and seeing no one, fished the key out of his pocket. In seconds he'd reached the door, unlocked it, and slipped inside.

The interior was black as pitch. He turned on the flashlight, casting its beam over the interior. There were no windows, so he wasn't worried about the light being seen from outside. There was an assortment of vehicles: a small tractor, a utility trailer, a couple snowmobiles, and an old pickup truck without its rear wheels supported by jack stands. There was a rollaway tool chest next to wire racks that held an assortment of tools that Seth envied.

He walked to the back where building supplies and lumber were leaned against a wall. A table saw was set up and sawdust littered the floor. He couldn't smell freshly cut wood, and guessed the saw hadn't been used for a few days.

Darkness kept him from speeding up his search, despite the fact that he could be discovered missing from his room at any moment or Dub could return to carry out Anthony's murder.

Seth pressed on, scanning with the beam of the flashlight, moving hurriedly through the space. Anthony was likely being held in some sort of cage, maybe framed with the lumber that had been cut by the table saw.

But there was nothing. No place a boy could be stashed. Seth swore under his breath as his frustration grew. He'd been certain that Anthony was being held in the garage. Standing at the back of the garage, he cast the beam of the flashlight around the interior once again. He paused, frowning as he followed the light. Something was off. He studied the room for a minute more before realization struck.

The dimensions of the inside of the garage didn't match the outside. He cast the light up and saw what had been invisible in the dark. The back wall wasn't an exterior wall. It didn't meet the roof the same way the other walls did, which meant that it was a false wall. Knowing he was on to something, he began searching for a door. Equipment and free-standing metal storage shelves lined the wall, some on wheels.

Now that he knew what he was looking for, he noticed marks on the concrete floor indicating where one set of racks had been repeatedly moved. Its shelves were lined with bundles of insulation, making them lightweight. He grabbed the rack and pulled, moving it easily to reveal a door framed into the wall, which had been hidden behind the insulation.

The door was locked, and Seth held his breath as he slipped the same key into the lock. The tumblers moved easily and he opened the door.

The space created behind the partial wall was perhaps fifteen feet deep and ran the width of the garage. The beam picked up more heavy-duty metal shelving, these loaded with an array of weapons. Serious weapons: carbines, sniper rifles, machine guns, plus communications equipment and tactical gear, all military issue.

Pushing back the urge to hurry to find Anthony, he did another careful scan. The various rifles were piled together on three different racks, in no order, and an open crate was piled with empty magazines. One set of racks held three forty-millimeter, shoulder-held grenade launchers. Another rack held materials that could be used for making bombs. Not surprising since RJ was responsible for at least two bombings. Seth whistled through his teeth when he saw bricks stacked on a rack, the wrappers clearly labeled C4 in block letters.

This was what Vivian wanted to sell to the *bratva*. Seth's team had learned that Freedom Defenders had been stealing from military bases in the Pacific Northwest. He thought they'd shut that down, but apparently they were still active. Anyone with access to this kind of weaponry could cause a hell of a lot of damage.

A rustling sound came from his left. Seth moved the flashlight farther along the wall, then came to an abrupt halt. The cage was about the size of a jail cell, maybe six by eight. A chemical toilet sat in a corner at one end, while a cot with a sleeping bag occupied the other end. Anthony sat on the cot with his back to the wall, his arms wrapped tightly around his upraised knees. His gaze held the same spark of defiance Seth had seen in the photos.

"Get out of here, you fucking pervert."

Shit. Seth shined the flashlight in his own face so Anthony could see him. "Anthony, I'm Seth Jameson, and I'm a US marshal."

The boy leapt off the bed. "What are you doing here? Your face is a mess. Did you come to get me out?"

"Yeah, I came to get you out." Seth shined the light over the enclosure. It was framed with two by fours with heavy gauge chicken wire stapled to the wood. The makeshift door was secured with a heavy-duty padlock.

"You have the key?" Anthony stood on the other side of the door.

"Ah, no."

"Then how you going to get me out?"

"I'm working on it."

"I got some of the wire lifted up."

Seth eyed him. "Yeah? Where?"

Anthony pointed to the corner of the structure next to the door. "See? I worked the wire back and forth until the staple lifted up, then I used that staple to work some others out. I got four out. I don't want them to see what I'm doing, so I push the staples back in the holes, but loose, you know? It doesn't look obvious that the wire is loose."

Anthony pulled back the wire and Seth examined the small opening.

"I thought if I could make the opening big enough, I could get out and get one of those machine guns over there and I'd break out of this place."

"Good idea, if you could find one with ammunition. The magazines I saw weren't loaded and I didn't see any ammo crates. Machine gun's not going to be any help without ammo." Anthony's shoulders slumped. Seth had to ask. "Has someone bothered you? Physically assaulted you?"

"You mean the pervert?"

"Yeah. Who's the pervert?"

"Dub. He keeps looking at me. He's a weirdo with all those tattoos on his face. He came in here the first night and I screamed my head off because I knew he was going to try something. Big Dog came in and made him leave, and told him he'd put a bullet in his head if he touched me. But Dub told me when he brought me food the next day he was coming back, and if I didn't let him do what he wanted, if I told Big Dog, Dub knows where my girlfriend lives and he'd take care of her. I don't think he meant *take care of her* in a good way."

"But he didn't come back."

"No."

Seth felt grim relief Anthony hadn't been forced to endure the additional trauma of sexual assault. "Listen up. I have to cut this lock. There are dozens of tools out there. I'm going back in the garage to see if I can find bolt cutters or something to cut it."

"You'll come back? Promise?" The boy was putting up a good front, but panic edged his plea.

"Yeah, I'm coming back."

There were no handy bolt cutters, but Seth found a cordless grinder, which, thankfully, still had a charge. At the cage again, he had Anthony step back.

"This will make a hellacious noise and kick out a bunch of sparks. If anyone's outside, they'll hear it."

"What do we do?"

"Pray like hell no one's outside."

Anthony moved back and Seth started the grinder. Ten seconds was all he needed. He didn't think the noise would carry into the house, but if someone was outside, they'd hear it. They were the longest ten seconds of his life. When the lock dropped to the floor, he threw down the grinder and pushed open the door, his gut urging him to get the hell out of there, fast. "Come on, kid. Give me your hand so we don't get separated."

He pulled Anthony to the door in the false wall. Seth didn't waste time wishing Dub had also stored ammunition so he could grab a weapon from the rack and even the odds a bit. He paused, listened, then stepped into the cavernous space. He kept the flashlight beam on the floor so they didn't trip and fall on their faces. They were making their way to the front when the outside door swung open and the lights flooded on. He pulled Anthony with him as he dove for cover behind the truck.

"Come on, Dub, leave the kid alone." Godzilla Pete's voice held a whine. "I'm flying high, I got a bag of Cheetos, I got a six-pack of beer. Let's go back to the house."

"Shut up, dumbshit. I heard something. We need to check it out."

"Stop calling me dumbshit. I hate when you call me names. That marshal was right. You're a bully."

"Goddam it, Pete. We got bigger problems than me calling you a dumbshit if that asshole marshal is in here. I wouldn't call you dumbshit if you didn't act like a dumbshit."

Crouched low, Seth glanced at Anthony, whose eyes were wide and scared. The voices were moving to the back of the garage. Seth had closed the door to the back, but that would only buy them seconds. Seth put a forefinger to his lips and jerked his head toward the now open outer door. His kept his voice barely above a whisper. "We're making a break for the door. Once we get out, we're running for the silver Civic parked under the tree. I snagged the keys." Anthony nodded his understanding. Voice low and urgent, Seth added, "If anything happens to me, you take off through the forest. There's another house a half mile up the river. Run as fast as you can, go there and ask for help. Got it?" Anthony nodded again. Seth took a careful look around, then, crouching low, moved past the utility trailer and the snowmobiles.

"God dammit, fucking son of a bitch." There was crashing that sounded like the door being slammed, then a clattering as metallic objects hit the concrete floor. "That asshole has the kid."

Seth was already streaking for the door, Anthony sticking to him like glue. A glance to the back showed Pete rampaging toward them like Godzilla through Tokyo, Dub right behind him. Seth took a split second to yank down a wire rack stacked with boxes, sending it crashing to the floor in hopes of slowing their pursuit. He and Anthony broke through the open doorway at the same time the crack of gunfire split the night. Bullets pierced the outer wall inches above their heads.

They raced to the Civic, visible from light streaming through the windows of the house. All Seth could think was he'd miscalculated and made a mistake that would cost both of them their lives. Keys in hand, he yanked open the door and grabbed Anthony, pushing him across the driver's seat as Seth fell in behind him. "Stay down!"

“Hold it right there,” Vivian’s sharp command was followed by another spate of gunfire. Windows on the Civic shattered and he felt a punch in the shoulder as he took precious seconds to find the ignition. He turned the key, and the engine came to life. He blinked furiously, trying to clear a sudden haze across his vision. Where was the gear selector?

“Holy shit, you’re shot.”

Anthony’s voice echoed in his brain as Seth fought to clear his head. If he could find the gear selector, he’d get them out of there but his brain seemed to have slowed down to a crawl. The driver’s door wrenched open and rough hands grabbed him. He was yanked out of the car and thrown to the ground. He heaved himself to his feet, squaring off with Dub, blinking desperately to clear his vision.

Dub was grinning, his inked face straight from a nightmare. His mouth was moving but Seth’s ears were ringing and he couldn’t make out the words. Pete came around the car and dropped Anthony in the dirt, shaking a bloody hand. Seth’s vision was narrowing, but not so much that he didn’t see RJ joining the circle, pearl-handled pistol in his grip. Eyes on his father, Seth braced himself for the kill shot, and never saw the sucker punch coming that dropped him into blackness.

***

“Don’t die, mister. Please, don’t die.” The words were whispered like a prayer.

Seth fought through what felt like layers of gauze wrapping his brain to reach consciousness, then wished he hadn’t. A burning hot poker was stabbing him in his left shoulder, every breath he took hurt like a son of a bitch, and he was lying on his back on top of that hot poker. He blinked open his eyes to darkness. Someone groaned, and it took several seconds before he realized the sound came from him.

“Hey, are you going to die?”

Since dying was a very real possibility, he thought it better not to answer. “That you, kid?”

“Yeah. You got shot.”

“Feels that way.” Seth forced himself to breathe despite the pain. There was a temptation to abandon the fight and simply float away to a place where he wouldn't hurt. He'd fucked up, but he still had a kid to save. He licked his lips and wished desperately for water.

"You hit?" Seth was surprised he could articulate anything approaching speech. His tongue felt twice its normal size and his body felt like he'd been put through an industrial meat grinder.

"I'm okay, I guess. I wish we'd gotten away."

"Me too. What happened?"

"You got shot, and they got us. Dub came up with his gun pointed right at you and pulled you out of the car. I tried to run like you said but Pete grabbed me. I bit him. Then the old man came out and Dub hit you and when you were on the ground he pointed his gun right at your head and I thought he was going to shoot you. The old man stopped him and said for them to put us back in the cage."

"Shit."

"Is the old man really your dad? Someone said that. I thought you said you were a marshal. My dad says marshals protect judges. I thought that's why you were here, because my dad's a judge."

"I am a marshal." Seth coughed and tasted blood in his mouth. He heaved in a labored breath against the fresh wave of pain that lanced through him. It was a minute before he could talk again. "The old man is Richard Jameson. He's my dad, and he's a fugitive." Another labored breath. "I came for you, but to arrest him, too."

"That sucks."

"Yeah."

A muffled sound reached them from outside that Seth thought might be a vehicle door being slammed shut.

Anthony dropped his tone. "We have to stay quiet."

"Why?"

"Cruella said she'd kill both of us if we made a sound, no matter what the old man said. I think someone is coming, someone they don't want knowing that we're here."

Fogginess was creeping around the edges of Seth's brain again. "Cruella?"

"Yeah. I don't know her name. She's Dub's mom."

"Why Cruella?"

"Don't you watch movies?" Anthony leaned forward to whisper. "*One Hundred and One Dalmatians*. She captured the puppies to kill them for their fur. She's evil."

"Got it. Dub's mom is Vivian, but I like Cruella better." Seth tried to work some spit into his mouth. "You got any water?"

There was a rustling sound. "Here. Can you lift your head?"

He could, barely. Anthony held the bottle while Seth gulped.

"Thanks. We're in the cage?"

"Yeah. You passed out and been asleep for hours. When the old guy wouldn't let them shoot you, they grabbed us and put us back in here. They didn't have a lock, though, 'cause you cut the other one, so they used some wire and twisted it. I can't reach it, but I worked more staples out. I got the flashlight from your pocket. I got your pocketknife, too. That's how I was able to get a bunch of staples out more easily. I think I can pull the wire back enough now that I can get out. I was working on that when you started making moany noises a minute ago."

"I don't make moany noises."

"Yeah, you do. That's why I thought you were dying. But then you woke up."

"Where's the flashlight?"

The light came on, illuminating Anthony's face. He had dark circles under his eyes and looked exhausted. The bruises on his face weren't as vivid as they'd been on the photo.

"I've been saving the battery. It's dark in here, but I think it's morning."

Seth rolled to his side and pushed himself to a sitting position, the pain threatening to take him back under. He closed his eyes, not opening them until he thought the world would stop spinning and stay in one place.

"You gotta stay lying down. I folded the pillowcase and bunched the sleeping bag behind your shoulder, kind of like a pressure bandage, to stop the bleeding." A glance showed the sleeping bag stained dark with blood. "You might bleed to death if you get up."

"You've got a lot of words, kid."

"Dad says words are my superpower. He says everyone has a superpower. You have to listen to yourself to figure out what yours is." The earnestness in his voice reminded Seth Anthony was young. Too young to be in this fucked-up mess.

"They put a big-ass tarp over the cage. They're trying to hide us."

"You're fifteen. You shouldn't be swearing." Seth found focusing on Anthony's voice helped to distract him from the pain radiating from his shoulder. That he could mostly move his left arm gave him hope that he wasn't too badly injured.

"Give me a break. I'm in high school. Besides, I use swear words in situationally appropriate ways."

"Your mom buy that?"

"Since I'm situationally appropriate, she doesn't know I swear. I'm not a dumbass like Pete."

"Bet your mom knows more than you think."

"You met my mom?"

"Yeah, and your dad. They're working with my team."

"Will your team rescue us? Do they know where we are?"

"I hope so," he said to both questions.

Metal rattled. Seth recognized it as one of the garage doors rolling up. With a click and a buzz, overhead lights blazed on, casting the cage beneath the tarp in a bluish light.

"They're coming back," Anthony whispered furiously. He clicked off the flashlight and shoved it in a pocket. "I bet they're coming for more guns. Before they put up the tarp, Dub and Pete took some of the guns from back here. They were arguing about which ones the *bratva* would want, whoever that is."

"Russian mobsters."

The highs and lows of people talking carried from the garage, far enough away that he couldn't understand their meaning.

Pitching his voice low, Seth spoke. "Right now they're distracted. That opening in the wire you made, is it big enough for me to get through?"

Anthony shrugged. "I don't know. Maybe if you weren't shot and almost dead. You're moving kind of slow. Oh." His eyes lit up. "I found something on the floor when we were hiding behind that truck." He dug in his pocket.

Seth stared at what Anthony held in his hand. "Kid, you may have just given us the break we need. Let's move, but quietly."

Suddenly, a clear voice spoke, only feet away.

"We require the ammunition. What is the use of weapons without ammunition?" The speaker must have been on the other side of the wall. Made of corrugated metal and with no insulation, the words were clear.

Clear enough for Seth to recognize the voice.
Alexei.

Chapter Eighteen

Alexei's Russian accent was exaggerated way past his normal speech. Seth frowned, fighting to block out the pain and keep his focus, to clear his head enough to think through the implications of Alexei's presence. Seth's team could have brought Alexei in and they were executing a plan to rescue him and Anthony. He hoped to god that was the case. The other possibility, one that Seth thought stretched credibility a bit too thin, was that Alexei was executing his undercover mission with the LAPD and had infiltrated the *bratva* and his appearance was a coincidence. What if Alexei had been playing Seth, had been playing his sister, and had, in fact, joined the Russian mob?

"Damn straight you want ammunition, and you'll get it. We're expecting another shipment and will be able to supply all the ammunition you could want, for any of the weapons we have. I can let you know as soon as it comes in." Dub spoke in a rush, sounding anxious and eager to please.

Moving carefully, Seth pulled himself to his feet, jaw clenched, a hand fisted into the wire cage to keep himself upright. He was making up his plan on the fly and prayed it would work. He pulled back the section of chicken wire Anthony had loosened, motioning him through.

Another Russian voice spoke, not a deep as Alexei's. Who the hell was that? Alexei responded, the volume of their exchange rising to a near shout. Seth's language lessons didn't help much.

"Doesn't he speak English?" Dub asked. "What's he saying?"

"My friend isn't impressed with what you've shown us so far. Your communication indicated more weapons than you have shown us. He thinks you've made us drive this distance for nothing." Alexei's words were clipped with impatience. "You haven't met our requirements. There is another seller who wishes to do business with us. You are closer so we came here, but you must have what we want to buy."

More was said in Russian by the unknown speaker.

"What did he say?" Dub demanded.

"He says he wants to see more."

Alexei was being diplomatic because what the other person had said was the Russian equivalent of *fuck you*.

"We've shown you only a portion of our inventory. We've got more, believe me." With FD's desperate need for cash, Dub's ingratiating tone made it clear they didn't want to lose their chance to build a business relationship with the *bratva*.

"We require automatic weapons, specifically the M4. Ammunition is available on black market. The grenade launcher you showed us is M203. We prefer M320. It is more accurate. The ammo is the 40mm grenade. We require the grenades."

"What the fuck, man? You trying to start a war?"

Dead silence followed that comment.

"Shut up, Dub," Vivian snapped.

"Sorry, sorry. It's a joke, a bad joke." Dub stuttered through his apology. "But no worries, man, we got a couple M320s, and I can see if I can get more. They're in the backroom. Pete and I will bring them out for you."

"We will go in backroom with you," Alexei stated flatly. "We wish to see all you have."

"Ah, it's better if we bring them out."

"Why don't you folks come outside and I'll bring you all coffee and something to eat." Vivian probably thought her tone sounded cajoling, but it was obvious she was steering the Russians away from the backroom.

"We do not come to drink coffee. We come to see weapons. We will go in backroom."

Relief flooded through Seth with a wave of dizziness. That was the voice he most wanted to hear, and it told him this *bratva* was with his team. Whoever the unknown Russian was must be working with the task force. This was good, but there was still a wild card, and that was RJ.

As quickly and quietly as possible, he moved into position. Back pressed against the wall, he closed his eyes for a brief moment. This might work if he could manage to stay conscious and not fall flat on his face.

***

Bella moved with the others through the door and took a moment to survey the storage room. Evidence of the Freedom Defenders' theft of military hardware was fully displayed on the racks in front of her. Besides weapons, body armor and communications equipment were haphazardly stored on various racks. A blue tarp in the far-right corner obscured a large, rectangular-shaped structure, which set her instincts humming. It could be hiding anything, but the top prospect was an enclosure designed for a kidnapped boy.

She breathed through her mouth and resisted the urge to lay a hand on her stomach. Her constant worry over Seth and Anthony had her in a persistent state of nausea-producing anxiety. At some point in the past week, she felt her objectivity as a US Marshal had been lost, and her personal and professional lives were on a collision course. She was probably developing an ulcer. The other possibility she couldn't ignore, but for now she had to push aside the personal in order to do her job.

That morning at first light, the local LEOs had sent up a drone, and with no one in sight, had been able to hover it low enough to get a visual on the white truck. It had dual rear tires, consistent with what RJ had been driving, and they'd gotten a shot of the license plate. Which led to verification it was registered to Richard Jameson.

Bella thought it reflected RJ's arrogance that despite being a fugitive, he hadn't used an alias or registered the vehicle to someone else. The team had taken the truck's presence as an indication that RJ was most likely at the compound. The image that had gutted her was Vivian's Civic with its windows blown out and bullet holes piercing the driver's side.

Bella had felt the floor drop from beneath her as she thought through the possibilities of how the car had come to be riddled with bullet holes. All those scenarios involved Seth being shot at. When she saw the images, it had been Linc's firm hold on her arm that had kept her upright. With a last look around the room, she pushed aside the turbulent emotions before they paralyzed her.

The bullet holes in Vivian's car had led to a sharp debate within the team as to whether evidence warranted immediately storming the compound. Ellie and Linc had overruled Bella and the decision was made to stay with the plan, which, if it worked, would get them inside the compound where they hoped to locate Seth and Anthony while minimizing the risk to all involved.

She returned her attention to Dub, who was shifting nervously from side to side, his gaze flitting between her and the two men she'd come in with. With the photo Seth had sent from the bar, she'd been able to identify Dub as Warren Robert Jacobs, age thirty-two, with an arrest record stretching back to his teenage years. He'd lived most of his life in the Reno area, and had served time for two convictions, one for misdemeanor assault, and the other for a third DUI conviction for which he'd been charged with a felony and had his driver's license revoked. There was currently a bench warrant for his arrest in Nevada for failure to appear.

"These are all the weapons you have?" Bella asked Dub.

"Like I said, you pay in cash and I'll get you whatever the hell you want. I got a guy on the inside who can get me anything I ask for."

Alexei took what she thought might be a grenade launcher from a shelf, turning it over in his hands, putting it to his shoulder. She felt like telling her brother to put the toy down and stop playing.

Frustration and disappointment intensified the queasiness in her stomach. She'd been sure Dub had balked at taking them into the backroom because that's where they were keeping Seth and Anthony hidden. But unless the two were under the tarp and unable to speak, she and the team were no closer to finding them.

Alexei returned the grenade launcher to the shelf. His military experience gave him all sorts of useful knowledge on weaponry he used to pepper Dub with questions. Bella used the cover of them talking to more carefully examine her surroundings.

The huge man they called Pete stood to one side, busily chewing on a fingernail with his silver-capped teeth, while Vivian Cochran watched from the doorway. The team's communication with FD had been with Vivian, who'd identified herself by her initials VC. Of those present, Bella thought Vivian the most unpredictable, and the biggest unknown. Like every other person in the room, she wore a gun holstered at her side.

Then there was the missing piece of the puzzle, Richard Jameson. They'd seen no sign of him since their arrival. The last thing they needed was RJ storming in, guns blazing. In all the years the Marshals had pursued him, he'd been hands-on in the Freedom Defenders organization, and she was surprised and worried about what his absence from the welcome party might mean.

Everything about the situation was wrong. Too many people in a small, enclosed space, with too many chances of getting caught in a crossfire.

If Anthony and Seth were under that tarp and somehow unable to communicate, they'd be in danger if there was any exchange of gunfire. In what she hoped was a casual move, she walked around the room, examining the weapons on the shelves, but also moving closer to where the edge of the tarp met the wall, looking for an opportunity to casually take a peek underneath.

A dark spot on the smooth concrete floor snagged her attention. She rubbed the tip of her boot over it and it left a dry, dark red smudge. Blood.

Holding her breath, she looked around. More spots were scattered on the floor near the blue tarp. Vivian stepped into the room to stand beside Dub. She too noticed the blood on the floor. Her gaze rose to lock on Bella's. Her hand moved to her side.

The half-open door swung closed. "Don't even think about drawing that gun."

Bella's heart catapulted into her throat as every person in the room turned toward the rough voice.

Seth stood behind the door, leaning back against the wall while holding a big military gun, his face pale and bruised, and his jaw clenched. The left side of his shirt was dark with dried blood, and he looked like he was staying upright through sheer force of will. Only Bella's training kept her from dropping to her knees.

"What the fuck?" Dub's hand hovered over the gun holstered at his waist. Gaze riveted on Seth, he said, "Don't worry, I'll take care of this guy."

"What's going on?" Bella moved forward, brow furrowed, trying to look the part of a buyer of illegal guns upset by the turn in events. "Who is this man?"

A sneer distorted the tattooed patterns on Dub's cheeks. He ignored her, instead speaking to Seth. "That gun's one of mine, asshole. There was a reason we moved any ammo stored back here. That magazine is empty. You're bluffing."

"Want me to test that theory?" The strain in Seth's voice worried her.

She spoke, exaggerating her accent, "What is this about? Perhaps we take our business elsewhere."

"This better not be a double cross," Alexei added.

"Don't worry, we'll take care of him," Vivian snapped. "Dub, you sure his rifle isn't loaded?"

"There was no ammo stored back here for any of the guns. The fucker's holding an M4 carbine, and like a dumbass, Pete used the last of the M-four ammo on target practice."

Seth aimed the muzzle to the ceiling, squeezed off a shot, the loud, sharp report echoing in the small room, and then he leveled the gun on Dub. That got their attention. With the Freedom Defenders all focused on Seth, Bella caught Alexei's gaze. He gave a slight nod, then moving like they'd practiced choreographing it, they drew their weapons. Alexei aimed at Pete, and Bella leveled her Glock on Vivian. Sasha did as previously instructed, and stayed out of the way.

"US Marshals," Bella identified herself. "You are all under arrest. Hands behind your heads and get down on your knees."

For one long moment, no one moved, then Pete dropped to his knees with a heavy grunt, his hands already laced behind his head. With quick efficiency, Alexei pulled zip cuffs from a pocket and restrained the big man.

"You fucking coward," Dub snarled at Pete. He pivoted and lunged toward Seth, who moved to the side, swinging the butt of the M4 and catching Dub square on the side of the head.

Dub crumpled to the floor while Bella, holding her aim steady, repeated, "On your knees, Vivian. I can assure you that my weapon is loaded, and it's aimed at your head." Indecision warred on Vivian's face. Nudging her to make the right choice, Bella said, "There's no way out of this. You're done. Put your hands behind your head and get down on your knees."

The fight seemed to seep out of Vivian, and she did as directed. Only when she and Dub were both cuffed did Bella turn back to Seth. He was gone. "Where'd he go? Where's Seth?"

"He left a minute ago."

The voice came from the corner of the room. The blue tarp had been pushed aside and Anthony Rebollar stood outside a cage made of twisted wire. Relief at seeing Anthony warred with fear for Seth. Bella crossed the room.

She couldn't help her smile as she examined the kid's pinched face. "Anthony, it's really good to see you. I'm US Marshal Bella Nikolaev." She extended her hand to shake, but Anthony launched himself at her, his arms going around her in a hug. She held him tight, savoring the moment. She dipped her head to whisper, "Your mom and dad will be so happy you're safe. Serena, too."

He stepped back, wiping his eyes on a grimy sleeve. "Thank you for coming for me. But you have to find Seth, he was shot and he's hurt bad. I thought he was going to die."

Bella nodded. "You stay here." She turned to her brother. "You and Sasha stay with the prisoners and keep Anthony safe. I'm going after Seth." She took a quick second to text Linc and Ellie. They were standing by with the rest of the task force, close enough to arrive in minutes. She wished the ambulance that was standing by could be brought in, but it was still too dangerous.

Drawing her weapon, she headed for the door.

***

Bella stepped into the cavernous garage, bright sunlight streaming through the rolled-up door. The side door was also open, and as she crossed the floor, she spotted what she'd missed before. More drops of dried blood spotted the floor. Worry was a greasy knot sitting heavily in her stomach. Dub and the others must have brought in Seth wounded, probably during the night.

Seth needed to get to a hospital, but she was certain he was going after RJ. As cool and rational as he could be, over the past weeks she'd learned that not revealing his emotions didn't mean he didn't feel them. They were locked down tight, but sometimes locks failed. She was afraid of what would happen when he confronted his father.

Above the door, the metal siding had holes pushed out from the inside. Someone had fired shots from inside the garage. Bella cautiously peered through the doorway to survey the scene.

A hot summer sun in a sky of deep blue warmed her skin, and she breathed in the earthy aroma of sunbaked grass. Sharp male voices drew her attention to the front of the house where the huge pine tree cast its shade. Weapon drawn, she trotted across the open area, using the big white truck for cover. The bullet-riddled Civic sat like a wounded warrior a few feet away. An older Suburban was parked beside it.

Crouching behind the truck, she heard a voice she identified as RJ's.

"You going to shoot your old man, boy?"

"Not sure yet. You going to pull the trigger on your son?"

Seth's speech was slow and deliberate. That more than anything had the greasy ball in her stomach swelling. Swallowing hard, she peered through the windows of the cab.

Seth's back was to her, his shirt darkened with blood. He had to be suffering from blood loss, and every minute he wasn't being cared for increased the chance of infection. Nothing mattered to her as much as getting him medical treatment.

As bad as Seth's condition was, the standoff in front of her was equally alarming. Seth stood with legs braced and his rifle aimed squarely at RJ's chest. RJ gripped a pistol pointed at Seth's heart. One twitch of a finger by either one of them could result in death.

The roar of an approaching vehicle eased Bella's fear a fraction. She dropped behind the front tire, her phone in her hand. Linc picked up at the first ring. "Seth and RJ are in front of the house, under the tree, weapons drawn. Park by the garage, prisoners are detained inside. Anthony is safe. I'm currently taking cover behind the white truck."

Bella raised her head to look through the side windows of the cab of the truck in time to see RJ slide his thumb and release the safety on his pistol, extending his arm like he was preparing to fire, the gun wavering slightly.

Bracing her arms on the hood of the truck, she took aim at RJ. "Richard Jameson, drop your weapon."

He ignored her, his gaze never wavering from his son. "Walk away, Seth. I don't want to shoot you, but I will if I have to. I haven't survived this long to give up without a fight."

Bella glanced over her shoulder when a big SUV pulled up the driveway, coming to a stop by the garage. Members of the task force exited the vehicle, most of them filing into the garage.

Linc and Ellie raced across the exposed space to join her, both wearing black polo shirts with the US Marshals star insignia.

"Got a plan?" Crouched next to her, Linc peered over the hood, Ellie on his other side.

"Not yet." They kept their voices barely above a whisper.

"Seth's not looking so good," Linc muttered. "He's not doing this alone."

"I'm with you on that," Ellie agreed.

"Then we'll all go," Bella said.

Together they stepped around the truck and moved to flank Seth, Linc on his left, Ellie on his right, Bella next to Ellie. All had their weapons drawn but pointed down. US Marshal protocols had been thrown out the window.

A layer of RJ's belligerence withered as he surveyed his adult children, united to confront him. He made no move to lower his gun.

"We're not going to shoot you." Seth sounded like he was speaking through clenched teeth. Bella didn't know how much longer his iron will could keep him from collapsing. "Richard Jameson, you're under arrest. We're taking you into custody to face justice for the crimes you have committed."

RJ's expression was grim, his face haggard. Despite that, it was jarring to realize how much Seth resembled his father.

"No way in hell you're arresting me. What I did, I did for our country, for what's right."

"It'll be up to a jury to decide if that's a credible defense. That's how it works, Dad." RJ flinched and Seth continued, enunciating each word carefully, his voice raw in a rare display of emotion. "We are a nation of laws. Individuals don't get to decide which laws they choose to follow. There are consequences for the ones you break, and it's time you faced those consequences."

Linc and Ellie stood with Seth in a unified wall, supporting each other as Bella knew they had since their father had abandoned them. She didn't discount her role but understood the importance in having the Jameson siblings confront their father together. Tension whipped between them and she wouldn't have been surprised to see sparks flying.

Then Seth crouched and laid his gun on the ground at his feet. Linc grabbed his arm when he swayed. After a slight hesitation, Linc and Ellie followed their brother's lead and set down their weapons. Putting her faith in Seth, Bella knelt to place her Glock in the dirt.

"If you shoot Seth, you'll have to shoot all of us," Linc said.

"Are you going to kill all three of your children?" Ellie asked. "Because that's your only way out. Would you do that to us? Would you do that to Mom?"

Something like panic flashed across RJ's face. "Let me go." Fear edged his voice. "You kids don't know what you're doing. Let me go," he repeated. "Let me go and walk away like nothing happened." RJ's gaze traveled over his children, his expression turning to regret and resignation.

"We're not letting you go. You're under arrest," Linc said.

"Put the gun down and put your hands behind your head," Ellie ordered.

The Jameson siblings were forcing their father to choose between their survival and his, and were counting on some remnant of love for his children to lead him to make the right choice. Bella didn't believe RJ had it in him to do that.

He blinked slowly, then nodded. He took a deep breath, released it, and bent his arm, arcing the gun toward his head.

"No!" Ellie lunged forward, but Linc beat her to him, taking their father down in a flying tackle. Linc's weight held him down and Ellie grabbed the hand holding the gun, forcing it into the dirt, and then disarming her father.

His children bringing Richard Jameson down and putting him under arrest would set them well on the way to the justice they were searching for.

"You should have let me do it. It would have been better for everyone." All RJ's vitality had leached out, and he looked like what he was, a defeated old man lying in the dirt.

"Shoot yourself in the head?" Linc spat out. "We're not letting you take the easy way out. Seth's right, you need to be held accountable for what you've done."

Linc rolled RJ over and searched him while Ellie pulled handcuffs from her back pocket and secured them around her father's wrists.

Seth coughed and swayed. Bella rushed to his side in time to catch him before he went down like a felled tree. She staggered under his weight, lowering herself until she sat with his head in her lap.

"Get that ambulance here now," Ellie snapped into her phone.

Bella leaned over, one hand fisted in Seth's hair, the other against his cheek, her face bent close to his. Tears blurred her vision. "Don't you dare die, Seth Jameson. I love you. You have to hang on for us." She murmured the words without thought, willing him to fight to stay alive.

He closed his eyes and she pressed her lips to his forehead, realizing every hope she had for the future was wrapped up with this man.

The wail of the ambulance echoed through the trees. Minutes later two big SUVs followed by an ambulance raced into the parking area, lights circling. Linc waved the EMTs over. The paramedics weren't able to rouse Seth.

She told them he'd been shot probably the night before. They worked swiftly and efficiently and in minutes had him on the gurney and were pushing him into the back of the ambulance.

Bella rushed forward. "I'm going with him." The paramedic nodded, and she climbed into the back of the ambulance, holding on tight to hope as the ambulance rocked and swayed on their way to the highway.

Chapter Nineteen

Bella shifted in the vinyl seat, trying to find a comfortable position. Exhausted as she was, she couldn't sleep sitting up. Ellie had brought her a thick cardigan, and she pulled it closer around her. Linc and Ellie had both wanted to stay with Seth, but work demanded their attention, so once they were confident he was through the worst of it, they'd left the hospital.

The team was still combing through the compound for evidence and processing the individuals they'd arrested. An hour before, she'd texted them an update on Seth, telling them he was resting and they should go back to the hotel and get some sleep.

Bella sighed. She could admit her restlessness was partly due to feeling overwhelmed, which she hated, and knowing major developments in her life were outside of her control.

She felt overwhelmed with love for Seth, with fear over his medical condition, and with the growing certainty she was pregnant. Becoming a mother would have a huge impact on her life, and she needed to prepare. But as important as all that was, the most urgent issue was Seth's recovery.

The lights had been dimmed for night. The nurses who came in and out of the room hardly made any noise with their soft-soled shoes. The antiseptic smell reminded Bella of the strong disinfectant used at the orphanage. It'd permeated her clothes. Funny how smells could evoke such strong memories.

The monitors attached to Seth by a myriad of wires and tubes hummed quietly.

She stood to see him better. His face was a pale shadow in the darkness. She'd listened with Linc and Ellie as the doctor had explained that Seth's blood loss was his most critical issue, and they'd treat the problem with fluids and medications. Linc had offered an artery if Seth needed blood. The doctor had said he'd keep that in mind, and the local blood bank would appreciate any donations.

Bella took the blanket from the chair and arranged it over Seth's legs. He was so strong, and had such a forceful personality, it frightened her to her core to see him lying in a hospital bed. She tucked the blanket around him, stopping when she glanced up and saw his eyes open, his dark gaze fixed on her.

She gripped his hand. "How are you feeling? Are you in pain?"

He tried to speak, cleared his throat, then tried again. "Not sure. Kind of floating."

"You will be for a while. They gave you some of what Markel called the double good juice after your surgery." She swallowed against the tightness in her throat.

Seth's thumb rubbed over the back of her hand. "Surgery?"

"Yes. To take out the bullet and repair the damage it caused. You're probably going to need some physical therapy. You also had a partially collapsed lung." Sitting in the ambulance, she'd watched the paramedics roll Seth on his side and cut away his shirt, revealing the ugly bullet wound under his shoulder blade that had scared her like nothing ever had.

"Anthony?"

"He's fine, and ecstatic to be back with his family. He wants to come see you in the morning."

Seth nodded and she thought he was struggling to stay awake. Eyes closed, he said, "Coming in as the *bratva* was genius," he mumbled. "Tell me how that happened."

"I talked it over with Alexei, and he called Sasha. Sasha got us onto the dark web where Vivian had advertised the stolen weapons. I'm hoping to convince him to leave the *bratva*." Seth's thumb had stopped rubbing over her hand and his breathing was deeper. She leaned over and pressed her lips to his forehead.

***

Seth woke to his sister and brother talking nearby in low voices. He looked for Bella but didn't see her.

"Hey, you're awake. Let's get some light in here." Ellie pulled open the curtains and had Seth blinking at the wash of sunlight. She moved to the side of the bed. “Hey, big brother.” Her words sounded light, but Seth could read his sister. She was worried about him.

Seth pressed the button to bring up the head of the bed. He had an IV in one arm being fed by a bag on a pole and his other arm hooked up to some other monitor. Tamping down on frustration over being virtually tied down, he growled, “When can I get out of here?”

Linc joined Ellie. “Not until you’re a hundred percent out of the woods. You lost a lot of blood, in addition to having a bullet go through your lung.”

“It went through a bit of your lung,” Ellie corrected. “The doctor said it could have been worse. He also said you need to increase your fluids. We talked to Mom and Arch. Once you’re released, they want you to recuperate at their house.”

Seth understood his mom enough to know she wouldn’t rest easy until she could see for herself that he was going to live. “I’ll talk to her.” Ellie held up a plastic cup with a straw and he drank the water gratefully. “Where’s Bella?”

The door opened, and his question was left unanswered. Anthony Rebollar came in, followed by his parents. A grin split Anthony’s face as he caught sight of Seth. Maria carried a pink bakery box, and Carlos an insulated bag in one hand and a stack of cups in the other.

“Hey, Seth, guess what? I was on the news.”

Ellie and Linc stepped back to give the family room around the bed.

Maria placed a hand on her son’s shoulder like she didn’t want to be too far away from him. Seth guessed it would be a while before she allowed Anthony out of her sight. “We brought coffee and pastries. Would you like coffee, Seth?”

“God, yes.”

She pulled a coffee dispenser from the bag and twisted off the spout. She poured the hot liquid into a cup and the rich aroma filled the room. He declined sugar or cream, and Maria topped the cup with a lid and handed it to him.

“Thank you.” Seth gratefully took the to-go cup from her. He eyed Anthony. “The news, huh? Did they make you look good?”

“Serena said I looked hot, so yeah they did. The reporter asked about you. I didn’t tell them your name or anything, but I told them you were a badass.”

“Anthony,” his mother exclaimed.

Seth felt the corner of his mouth turn up. Anthony's good nature was contagious. "This is situationally appropriate?"

Anthony gave his mom a sidelong look. "Maybe not." He reached into a pocket, then held out his hand with Seth's pocketknife in the palm. "Here's your knife back. It's good you had it."

"It's good you thought to use it to get out of that cage. That took brains, and that took courage. You did good, kid. Keep the knife, it's yours now."

Anthony's eyes lit up. "Really, I can keep it? That's awesome. Thanks." Anthony looked down, turning the knife over in his hand. When he spoke again, his tone was subdued. "I'm glad Dub and Cruella, and all them were arrested, but I'm sorry your dad was one of them."

"Yeah, me too." Seth motioned to Linc and Ellie. "These marshals are my sister and brother. You met Bella, she's on our team too. Richard Jameson is our father, but he made bad choices and broke the law. We did our job and arrested him before he caused any more harm."

"Like kidnapping me."

"Yes, like kidnapping you."

Anthony nodded, and Judge Rebollar spoke quietly. "We want to thank you," he nodded to include Ellie and Linc in his statement, "to thank all of you and the rest of your team for rescuing our son. We are in your debt."

Seth shook his head. "We may have helped, but I couldn't have done it without your son's help." He looked at Anthony. "You tell your parents about the stripper clip?"

"The bullets? I told them I found the bullets on the floor near that truck when we were trying to get away. I didn't know it was called a stripper clip."

"He found it in our failed escape attempt," Seth told Carlos and Maria. "There were three bullets still in the clip that I loaded into an M4 carbine. Luckily, I only needed to use one. Anthony picking up those bullets and prying loose the staples so we could get out of the cage were crucial to both of us getting out of there alive."

"It's good to know my son uses his head when it's important he do so." Carlos brought Anthony close to his side. "We don't mean to tire you, Marshal, but wanted to express our gratitude. If there is ever anything that I can do for you, do not hesitate to ask."

The door closed behind the Rebollar family, and Seth thought they took all the energy from the room with them. He suddenly felt exhausted.

Ellie smiled at Seth. “Nice gesture. Anthony is going to treasure that knife forever.”

“It’s one Arch gave me. Seemed appropriate.” He paused, then repeated, “Where’s Bella?”

“She was here until after midnight, then left first thing this morning.” Linc opened the lid on the bakery box, picking out a glazed donut.

Seth scowled. “What for?”

“Montrose called her back. That guy her and Alexei knew in Russia, the one she calls Sasha? He helped us convince Vivian and Dub they were part of the *bratva*.” That explained the third Russian speaker in the garage.

Linc held the open bakery box in front of Seth. He selected a maple bar and took a bite, chewing thoughtfully. “Okay, so?”

“Sasha wants out of the *bratva* and is willing to talk. Looks like the marshals could be setting up witness protection for him, at least for the short term.”

“Why does that mean Bella has to go back to LA?” Damn it, he had things he wanted to say to her.

“Couple reasons. RJ will be questioned in LA, and, reasonably, Montrose didn’t want RJ’s kids escorting him, so that fell to Bella. Since she knows Sasha, Montrose said they’re assigning her as part of his protection, at least for the time being.”

Linc’s words fell like lead weights.

“She’s being pulled from our team.” Seth knew it was more than that. Richard Jameson had been arrested and the Freedom Defenders dealt a devastating blow. The team had accomplished its goal and would be disbanded. He’d known the time would come, but that didn’t mean he had to like it. “Guess they’re breaking up the band,” he muttered.

Linc nodded. “Feels like. But I’ll be glad to stay close to home for a while. I miss my wife.”

“I’m missing Sam, too. But don’t worry, big brother. Our summer plans are coming together. Mikayla and I talked last night. We’ve decided to invite you guys to our cabin, so after you’re done climbing mountains and getting all stinky and mosquito bitten, you can join us at the cabin for an extra week."

"I'm in if Bella's there."

There was a moment of silence, then Linc said, "Well, finally, bro. I thought you'd never make a move."

"How the mighty have fallen." Ellie smirked. "I'm glad, Seth. But if Bella takes the assignment to provide witness protection for the Russian guy, she may not be able to come."

Seth frowned. They'd see about that.

"Isn't she coming to the family Fourth of July get-together?" Ellie asked. "Mom will be thrilled you two are finally together."

"Nothing's for sure. I need to talk to her."

Ellie gave him a peck on the cheek. "My money's on you, big brother."

"Thanks."

The need to see Bella was a bone-deep craving. If Seth could get out of the hospital, he'd have a chance to make the move he wanted, a move that would bind his future with Bella's.

He prayed to god that she wanted that future with him.

Chapter Twenty

Seth spotted a gap between two cars and pulled a U-turn, maneuvering into the tight fit. He stepped out of the vehicle into heat in the high eighties at only eight o'clock in the morning. He pulled at his shirt where sweat had it stuck to his back. His injured shoulder meant he'd forgone his preferred shoulder holster in favor of wearing his gun on his hip, a gun Linc had recovered from Vivian's house and made sure was returned to him.

He climbed the stairs to the second story, figuring being only partially winded was a good sign after having been shot all of three days before. He rapped on the door to 2D and was seriously pissed when it was opened by another Viking. He recognized him as being part of the *bratva* group at the Freedom Defender compound.

Sasha wasn't Thor-big like Alexei, but still had a look about him that said he'd seen trouble and could deal with it in whatever form it took.

"You're the marshal." His accent was thicker than Bella's or Alexei's.

"One of them. Seth Jameson. Bella here?"

The Viking gave him an assessing look, then stepped back. "Come in. I'm Sasha."

"Figured as much." Seth stepped into Bella's apartment to find Alexei sitting on the couch, an open laptop on the coffee table in front of him. He rose to his feet and grasped Seth's hand in a firm shake, running his gaze over him in an assessing look.

"You look like hell, man. Surprised they let you out of the hospital."

"I talked the doc into releasing me a little ahead of schedule." Seth did his own assessment. "Your face isn't as messed up as it was."

"I'm recovered. Your face is still messed up. You want coffee? It's Bella's freeze-dried shit, but better than nothing."

Seth banked his impatience. “Sure. Where is she?”

“Hey, did you hear I passed my background check and got an interview with the FBI?”

Seth ground his teeth. “Congratulations. Now where is she?”

“I’ll put the water on.”

Realizing Alexei would take whatever time he wanted, Seth followed him into the kitchen. Alexei filled the kettle with water and set the flame on the stove. He faced Seth, leaning back against the counter. The fucker was enjoying making Seth wait. Sasha took a seat at the table, arms crossed in front of him. He made a comment in Russian. Whatever Alexei said in response brought a scowl to the other man’s face.

Alexei raised a brow and locked his gaze on Seth. “Now we talk. My sister is the most important to me. I won’t let her be with a man who is not good.”

“She won’t thank you for interfering.”

“Too bad. You will treat Bella well.”

Since he also had a sister, Seth answered, “Yes, I’ll treat her well.”

“You will marry my sister?”

“Is she pregnant?”

A movement at the door caught his attention. In denim shorts that showed off long, toned legs and a bright yellow t-shirt, her hair a damp curling mass, Bella looked like a ray of sunshine. But hurt flashed across her face before shutters closed off her expression. *Shit.*

“I need to talk with Bella,” he told Alexei. “Alone.”

Not meeting his gaze, she turned to the other men. “He’s right. Seth and I need to talk. You two go.”

Sasha spoke in Russian, and Bella shook her head. Alexei took the opportunity to utter a low growl, “You hurt her, I’ll kick your ass.”

Seth nodded. “I won’t stop you.”

Alexei gave a curt nod, then motioned to Sasha. “Come on. There’s a good coffee shop not far from here where they sell beignets. That’s what I want this morning.”

Bella followed them to the door, shutting it behind them and turning the lock. She faced Seth and crossed her arms in front of her. “I’m guessing you want to know how the questioning of your father and the others went. I filed my preliminary report yesterday, but we're not done. Vivian and her son are using the same lawyer, and he's not letting them say anything. The defendant Peter Hoyer is seeking a plea deal. He has a lot of information that will be useful building a case against the others so I think the prosecutor will accept the plea."

Bella's attention was focused someplace over his right shoulder. When Seth stepped forward, she retreated into the kitchen.

"That's not why I'm here. I want to talk about you and me." The last twenty-four hours had seen one frustration piled on top of another.

Feeling well enough, he'd gotten the doctor to agree to release him from the hospital at midday on Friday. Linc and Ellie had been busy analyzing preliminary data from Vivian Cochran's laptop, and since Seth's phone was being considered evidence and he couldn't use it, he hadn't been able to call either of them or Bella.

When he'd finally tracked down his sister and got Bella's number—he didn't have it memorized—the call had gone straight to voicemail. He'd decided what he had to say to her should be said in person, but he'd needed to hear her voice and felt unsettled when he hadn't.

The kettle whistled and Bella turned off the burner. She opened the cupboard and reached for a mug, her hand shaking.

"Bella, look at me."

"It's better I don't. I…um…" She paused, taking a deep breath before pressing on. "I'm pregnant." She retrieved the carton with the packets of freeze-dried coffee, busily opening it. "I took a pregnancy test this morning, but I've been so nauseous lately, I already knew. We'll probably need a lawyer to, you know, work out a custody arrangement."

He let her words sink in and warmth fill him. He was going to be a father, a dad. He'd do a damned sight better job than RJ had done. Seth had kept his emotions locked away for so long it was hard to bare his soul. Harder than staring into the muzzle of a gun pointed at his head. But he was all in. He wanted a future with her and his child, and that meant he'd offer her his heart on a platter if that's what it took.

"Bella, look at me," he repeated.

She fumbled the carton and the packets spilled across the floor. She backed away from him, shaking her head, hands clenched at her side. "My brother is being protective, but I don't need you to marry me. Your obligation is to our child, not to me. I don't need you." The words were like an arrow to his heart. "You should go now. We've got months before we have to worry about the custody arrangements. I think it would be best for the baby if he or she stays with me for the first several months."

He grabbed her hands when she would have knelt to gather the packets. "You may not need me, but I need you." He used his thumb to open her fingers and pressed her palms flat against his chest. She tipped her face forward, but not before he saw her blinking back tears.

"Jesus, Bella. Don't cry." Taking a leap of faith, he said quietly, "Do you feel my heart beating? It beats for you. I'm in love with you."

She brought up her head and finally met his gaze. The storm of emotion in her eyes gave him hope he'd finally succeeded in breaking through the barriers they'd used to protect themselves.

She remained quiet, and he spoke again. "You said you loved me. You told me not to die and to hang on for us. I didn't die and I hung on. For us, Bella. For all three of us."

"I didn't think you heard me."

"I heard you. It gave me hope."

Suddenly she was in his arms. He pulled her to him, ignoring the dull pain from his injury, his eyes closed as he breathed her in like oxygen. Seth released a shaky breath as it sank in—what he wanted most in the world was within his grasp.

Holding her with one arm, he reached into his pocket and pulled out a small box. He watched her face as he thumbed open the lid. Her gaze was fixed on the diamond solitaire.

"Oh my god. It's beautiful."

"Will you marry me, Bella? Will you be mine forever?"

Her blue eyes were depthless when she lifted her head, her smile dazzling. She nodded her head vigorously. "Yes, Seth. I will marry you."

She held out her left hand steady as he slipped the ring on her finger. "It fits with a traditional Russian interlocking set. I thought maybe you'd like that, but we can change it if you want something different." He met her gaze. "What's important is that you said yes."

She threw her arms around him, her mouth against his neck as she spoke.

He cradled her head, brushing away her tears. "You want to say that again?"

"I love you. I love the ring, and I love you."

Every barrier between them was washed away as their lips met. He felt his heart finally breaking free of the chains that had held him back for so long and kept him from fully feeling. Her tongue tangled with his as the kiss deepened and turned hungry. He ran his hands over her hips then under her t-shirt.

"Mm," she hummed against his lips. "Are we going to get naked, Marshal Jameson?"

He pulled back enough to see her provocative grin. "You bet, Marshal Nikolaev. As often as we can."

He moved his hands from her back to her supple breasts, and she gasped when he brushed a thumb under the lacy edge of her bra to find her nipple already tight. Her fingers worked the buttons of his shirt, then eased it over his shoulders, letting it drop to the floor.

Her touch was feather light over the fading bruises on his ribs. "What happened here?"

He shrugged. "Not sure. I think it's a boot print. My guess is either Dub or Pete kicked me when I was unconscious."

"You were knocked unconscious when they hit you here." She brushed his hair back from his forehead.

"Yeah. Gave me a concussion. I need to take it easy for a few days, let my brain rest."

Nodding her head, she said, "I want to see your shoulder, turn around."

"All you can see is the bandage." She twirled her finger and he turned.

He felt her whisper-light touch as she traced the edge of the bandage and thought he could die a happy man if she just kept touching him.

"How's the pain?"

"Better. I'm not supposed to pick anything up or overexert myself for the next couple weeks, but all in all, I'm grateful it wasn't any worse." He turned to face her again.

"You have the most incredible body," she murmured as she ran her hands over his abs.

"If I wasn't shot in the shoulder, I'd lift you up onto the counter so I don't need to bend down to kiss you."

"If you Jameson boys weren't so tall you wouldn't have to bend down." Bella boosted herself onto the counter. He moved between her legs, cupping her face as he kissed her, rubbing his growing erection against the hot center of her. She splayed her hands over his chest, making a sound in her throat that he could only describe as purring.

Even with his lips busily moving over her neck, he fought for restraint, trying to slow down. She wasn't helping because she unbuttoned the fly of his Levi's and slipped her hand inside. He nearly lost his mind when she closed her fingers around his erection, which had been growing more insistent from the moment she'd walked into the living room. She stroked him with strong and silky movements that felt like heaven, and nearly undid him.

He caught her mouth in a fierce kiss and grabbed her hand before she sent him over the edge. "I want you in bed."

She scooted off the counter and took his hand to lead him out of the kitchen. By the time they got to her bedroom he was so hard and ready it took every ounce of control he possessed not to rip off their clothes and let madness guide him as he plunged in.

Their first time together he'd felt like a stallion racing to the finish line. This time he wanted to savor her, to make it a promise of what was to come.

He nudged her to sit on the edge of the bed, moving back when she would have reached again for the open fly of his jeans. "We're doing this my way, and my way is getting you naked first." He tugged her shirt over her head. Bending over her, he murmured, "There's no rush. Let's take it slow and easy so we don't miss any steps."

He knelt in front of her, unsnapping her shorts, and she stood so he could draw them down her legs. The tiny little scrap she wore for underwear followed. She sat and he reached behind her to unclip her bra and groaned in appreciation as her breasts spilled free.

Her breath hitched when he pressed kisses to her breasts, to her hip bone, to the dark triangle of hair.

"We won't miss steps," she breathed.

"No, we won't, because this time I'm taking care."

He began to show her exactly what he meant, and pulled down the bedcovers to lay her against the pillows. Mindful of his injury, he braced himself with his right arm to brush the hair back from her face, then used the tip of his finger to trace her lips.

"Have I told you how incredibly beautiful you are? How every time I see you, I catch my breath?" She stared at him as if mesmerized, slowly shaking her head. He kissed her because he couldn't help himself, then murmured, "See? That's a step I missed, because you are so beautiful. Do you remember when we were first introduced?" He spoke quietly. "You were the rookie, the new team member, and I was your boss. You were so off limits." He kissed her temple, under her ear, moving over her collarbone to the swell of her breast, taking in the scent of her with each breath. "I couldn't stop thinking about you, couldn't stop wanting you." Then his gaze snared hers. "Did you think of me, Bella? Did you wonder then how it might be between us?"

***

Bella felt like her mind was moving slowly, mired down by the overwhelming onslaught of sensations Seth was raining down on her. Every place he touched responded with a surge of heat that spread across her body, igniting fires, arcing from one kiss or caress to the next until she thought she would combust and go up in flames.

"I did. I wondered how it would be between us."

"You know what was driving me insane? That we couldn't be within ten feet of one another without generating sparks." He nuzzled between her breasts, his tongue laving the tender skin and setting it tingling. He continued to speak in that low, rumbly voice, which set her close to orgasm. "Every time we argued, all I could think was it was foreplay. If we ever were together, our minds would be blown. Then we were together and it happened, you blew my mind."

She caught his face in her hands and waited until his gaze met hers. "I fell in love with you so hard and so fast, it scared me. Especially when you acted so irritated with me half the time. You treated me like I was a big pain in the ass, and I was so confused I didn't know how to act." She pressed a kiss to his lips. "I've been in love with you all that time. It's always been you."

He turned his head and kissed her palm. "I fought it hard, trying to do what I thought was right. But no more. You're mine."

She said the words back to him. "And you are mine."

His hands stroked across her hips, the backs of her thighs, smooth and sensual, until finally, finally he had her releasing a pent-up sigh when he reached the sensitive folds of her labia.

He kissed her long and deep, using his fingers to build her response, working her to a heightened state of arousal. He pushed off the bed to shuck his jeans, then paused, gaze locked on hers in the dim light coming through the curtained windows.

"I have a condom, but there's that horse and barn door situation again. I was tested before I met you and am disease free."

She frowned at his phrasing. "I am as well."

He returned to the bed, whispering in her ear, "I haven't been with anyone since I met you."

She closed her eyes. "God, Seth, what took us so long? I couldn't be with anyone else either. The only person I wanted to be with was you."

She felt him shaking his head, and instead of speaking, he returned his attention to building her up to the point where she was shaking.

He wouldn't let her touch him, instead focusing on bringing her ever closer to the brink of release. She felt she would lose her mind and was panting his name when he finally, finally pushed into her, thrusting forward, filling her. He held still for a long moment as they both savored the feeling.

Wanting more, she put her hands on his buttocks and tilted her hips to bring him in deeper. With a throaty groan he began moving in long, hard strokes. The sensation of finally being fully together, mentally and physically, intensified her arousal.

Together they found a rhythm that built in intensity, growing, swelling to a final crest. She came with a keening cry, and he thrust twice more before following her over the edge of oblivion.

Panting, he collapsed over her, his face in the crook of her neck until his breathing evened out. He rolled, pulling her into his right side.

"Is your shoulder sore?"

"It's fine." He stroked her side, long sweeps of his hand from her shoulders to her rear. He stilled for a moment, and her mind flitted to the last time they had been like this and how her heart had been soaring before crashing with those fateful words, *That should never have happened.*

"Seth?" She hated the quaver in her voice. She propped herself on an elbow to see his face.

He reached up and ran his thumb between her brows. "Do you know you get a V here when you're worried? What are you worried about?"

She shook her head. "Nothing."

"It's not nothing if it worries you." He paused, then his own brows furrowed. "Are you thinking about the last time we were together?"

"It doesn't matter."

"It does matter. I hurt you, and I'm sorry." He lifted his head from the pillow to kiss her. "It might take time for you to completely trust me, but know this, Bella, I'm committed. I want you. I want our baby." He took her hand, lacing their fingers together, rubbing his thumb over her engagement ring.

She let the last of the walls she'd carefully erected around her heart fall away, and pulled his words around her like a security blanket.

"I trust you, Seth, and I love you."

Epilogue

Seth relaxed with Bella's head tilted on his shoulder, their fingers laced together as they sat on a cushioned wicker loveseat on his parents' deck. They'd eaten until they were stuffed, and then eaten even more when Arch had proclaimed the homemade ice cream was done, so they'd polished off the Fourth of July barbecue with fresh berries and ice cream. Then Seth had asked for everyone's attention, and he and Bella had announced their engagement. They endured some ribbing with a lot of *what took you so long?* and *we knew you two were hot for each other* comments. Alexei had slapped Seth on his non-injured shoulder in congratulations. Margaret had kissed both him and Bella, tears shining in her eyes, while Arch had engulfed them all in a group hug.

"This will be so exciting." Margaret had taken Bella's hand to examine the ring. "We'll need to get your mother on a conference call so we can start planning this wedding."

"I already have an officiant."

Bella had looked at Seth with raised brows.

"Carlos Rebollar said he'd be happy to do the honors."

Bella's smile told him he'd made the right move by asking the judge. "There's more, Mom."

Her brows lowered. Margaret had been vocally displeased her eldest son had been shot, especially after Linc had been shot the previous year. "Tell me."

He'd glanced at Bella, and at her nod, shared the rest of their news. "We're pregnant. Only a few weeks along, and we're pretty damned pleased about it. You and Arch are going to be grandparents."

Margaret's hands went to her mouth and tears trailed down her cheeks. There were more hugs and kisses, then she put her hands on either side of her son's face and looked into his eyes. "You're going to be such a good daddy."

Her reassurance and confidence settled something in him that he hadn't realized needed settling. He glanced from her to Arch. "Thanks, Mom. I had a good example."

Word spread and there were more congratulations. Now with the long twilight fading in the west, everyone had found a spot to watch the fireworks.

Linc and Mikayla were on another loveseat, while Ellie and Sam lay on a blanket spread on the grass. Some of the younger crowd were floating on inflatable loungers and inner tubes in the pool.

The first stars were showing themselves when across the valley the sky exploded with sprays of red, white, and blue light.

Bella nestled closer.

"You doing okay?" he asked in a quiet voice.

"Better than okay."

"How's the nausea?"

"Not so bad today." She rubbed her thumb over the back of his hand. "Don't worry so much."

"Not going to happen. You're the center of my world, and I intend to worry accordingly."

Volley after volley of mortars echoed off the hills and exploded into wild plumes of light.

"Independence Day is my favorite holiday," Bella murmured.

He pressed a kiss to the top of her head. "Why is it your favorite?"

She gave a slight shrug. "Even with its problems, America stands for something good. I will always be grateful to my American parents and to this country for taking a chance on a couple of orphans from Russia. I would never have met you in Russia."

He tightened his grip on her hand, and for the first time in his life, he believed some things were fated to be.

TURN THE PAGE TO SEE HOW IT ALL BEGAN:
HIDDEN BETRAYAL

HIDDEN BETRAYAL

Gun gripped tight, back to the wall, Linc breathed slowly to settle himself. Shit. A leak. There had to be a leak within the Marshals Service. No other explanation fit. Bullets still slamming into the not-so-safe safe house were evidence enough. The witness he'd dragged out was cowering next to him. Adrenaline surging, Linc pulled out his cell and yelled, "We're under fire. Get me backup." He shoved the phone back in his pocket.

Odds are, by the time help arrived they'd all be dead.

"What the fuck, man?" Rounds fired and his witness had lost the gangster swagger. "You marshals are supposed to protect my ass." Joey "the Mouse" Medrano huddled beside him in the shadowed hallway. Blood dripped from a cut over Joey's eye, adding a scarlet bloom to the teardrop etched onto his right cheek. Linc wiped the blood from his own forehead. Shots through the front windows had sent shattered glass flying.

"You're alive, aren't you?"

"That's the fuckin' cartel out there. Fuckin' trying to kill me, man." His voice, irritatingly high pitched—hence "the mouse"—quavered. Linc suspected the tattoos covering every available skin surface, including Joey's eyelids, were more an attempt to appear badass than proof.

"Don't know what happened, but we'll get you out of this." Linc listened intently. Where the hell was his partner? "Donny!"

Outside, tires squealed and a door slammed.

"They're fuckin' coming for me. You gotta fuckin' protect me."

He didn't have time to marvel at Joey's ability to use "fuck" at least once in every sentence. Linc yelled for his partner again. "Donny, you hit?"

"I'm fine." Donny's voice came from the other side of the wall in the kitchen. He sounded odd, like he had to force the words out.

He spoke again, clearer this time. "I think we can get him out the back, through the gate. Take him out through the alley."

"I ain't goin' through the fuckin' alley. They'll know you'll fuckin' go that way."

"Shut up. Let me think." Footsteps rushing the front door decided for him. Grabbing Joey by the collar, Linc pulled the other man with him into the kitchen. And came to a skidding stop. "Shit, Donny. Lower your weapon before you shoot me."

His partner didn't lower his weapon. "Sorry, Linc."

The front door crashed against the wall.

"What the—"

Even as Linc raised his gun, a muzzle flashed with a sharp cracking sound. The instantaneous punch to his chest sent Linc reeling. A second flash and the world went dark.

***

"Wake up, Lincoln. Wake up, baby."

The warm caress on his forehead soothed, almost enough to lull him back into the gray.

"Oh no you don't. Stay with me this time."

"Mom?" He must have actually spoken, because the hand against his skin stilled. He blinked open his eyes to see his mother's face crumble. Shit.

"Good job, you made Mom cry."

His gaze traveled around the hospital room before resting on the tall woman standing on the other side of the bed. Despite the jibe, his sister's lowered brows over serious blue eyes and clenched jaw screamed worried. Couldn't mistake that. He would have tried for a snide comment but his throat felt like he'd swallowed rocks.

"Water."

His mother dabbed her eyes with a tissue and dipped her face to kiss his forehead before reaching for a plastic cup with a straw. "You bet, sweetie."

He swallowed the icy water with relief. His gaze sought out his sister's. "What happened?"

"Your double-crossing, snake-in-the-grass, backstabbing partner is what happened."

"Ellie, not now. Your brother needs to rest." Margaret Bollinger's voice held the same tone that had kept a teenaged Linc from straying too far out of line.

"Did he get Joey?" They needed the pathetic bastard to testify against the crime boss of the Zecena cartel. And the trial started in less than two months. But more than that, it had been Linc's job, his sworn duty, to protect the witness.

The hospital door swung open before Ellie could answer. Two men entered, completing the family. Linc's brother, Seth, and their stepfather, retired Chief Deputy US Marshal Archer Bollinger. Like Ellie, Seth wore his Marshals' badge hanging from a chain around his neck. His brother's face might have been carved from granite. Seth didn't do feelings. Arch Bollinger didn't give much more away, other than a decided air of tension. Seeing that Linc was awake, Arch crossed the room to put an arm around Mom's shoulders. "Glad you've decided to stay with the living, Lincoln."

"What the hell happened?" Linc's voice cracked like an old man's.

"What do you remember?" Seth's slate-gray eyes narrowed.

Wishing for a dose of his brother's cool focus, Linc tried to shake his head to clear the lingering fuzziness, but even that small motion resulted in a throbbing that made him wince. He found the button to raise the head of the bed so he was sort of sitting up, clenching his jaw at the pain in his chest that accompanied the movement. He rasped out the words. "Enough to know Donny shot me. I want to know what happened to my witness."

"Medrano's dead." Seth's clipped words fell like bricks.

"Shit. God damn, son of a bitch." He held Seth's gaze. "I lost a witness."

"This isn't on you, Linc." Anger whipped through his sister's voice. "Donny Bertola owns this one."

"I'm sworn to protect my witness. I told the little shit I'd get him out of there alive." The Marshals Service had never lost a witness who'd followed the rules. That made him the first. The weight of his failure settled over him like an iron blanket. "He's dead. That's on me."

Ellie looked ready to argue the point, but Seth cut in. "Chief Deputy Montrose said he'd be in tomorrow morning to take your statement. You up for it?"

"I will be." He'd been awake for a few measly minutes and Linc felt like he'd run a full marathon. Exhaustion with an added layer of abject failure dragged at him. His mother held up the straw and he took another sip of water, and then directed a question to his brother. "What happened with Donny?"

"He's on the run. We've got his laptop, phone records, bank records. The usual. Only thing we know for sure is they got to him."

A tiny nurse in polka dot scrubs and a cap of pewter hair whisked into the room. "Sorry, folks, it's time for the shift change. You all will need to step out." She assessed Linc with a shrewd gaze. "And it's time for Mr. Jameson's meds. You're welcome to come back in forty minutes or so."

Margaret kissed him again, squeezing his hand like she couldn't stop touching him. Linc was grateful when Arch gently urged her out the door. Ellie took his face in her hands and kissed his cheek. "You scared me."

"I scared myself."

"Don't do it again." She left, and Seth moved closer to the side of the bed.

"You're not going to kiss me too, are you?"

"You wish." Seth paused, then continued, voice deeper than usual. "We're tracking Donny, Linc. We'll get him."

ABOUT THE AUTHOR

USA TODAY Bestselling Author, Diane Benefiel has been an avid reader all her life. She enjoys a wide range of genres, from westerns to fantasy to mysteries, but romance is her favorite. She writes what she loves best to read—emotional, heart-gripping romantic suspense novels. In her stories, she puts the heroes and heroines in all sorts of predicaments that they have to work together to overcome. Her novel, ***Solitary Man*** was a National Readers' Choice Award winner.

A native Southern Californian, Diane enjoys nothing better than summer. For a high school history teacher, summer means a break from students, and time immersed in her current writing project. With both kids grown and gone, she enjoys her leisure time camping, especially in the Sierras, and gardening, both with her husband.

Diane loves hearing from her readers.

Website: dianebenefiel.com

Twitter: twitter.com/dianebenefiel

Instagram: diane_benefiel

Pinterest: diane_benefiel

Facebook: facebook.com/DianeBenefielRomance

BookBub: bookbub.com/authors/diane-benefiel

Goodreads: goodreads.com/author/show/8075321.Diane_Benefiel

Newsletter: https://landing.mailerlite.com/webforms/landing/n1i2u8

Sign up for Diane's newsletter for sneak peeks, and inside info on her next series.

www.BOROUGHSPUBLISHINGGROUP.com

If you enjoyed this book, please write a review. Our authors appreciate the feedback, and it helps future readers find books they love. We welcome your comments and invite you to send them to info@boroughspublishinggroup.com. Follow us on Facebook, Twitter and Instagram, and be sure to sign up for our newsletter for surprises and new releases from your favorite authors.

Are you an aspiring writer? Check out www.boroughspublishinggroup.com/submit and see if we can help you make your dreams come true.

www.ingramcontent.com/pod-product-compliance
Lightning Source LLC
La Vergne TN
LVHW010058110826
845155LV00028B/390

* 9 7 8 1 9 5 3 8 1 0 3 3 5 *